The Carter Boys:

A Carter Boys Novel

The Carter Boys:

A Carter Boys Novel

Desirée Granger

www.urbanbooks.net

Urban Books, LLC
300 Farmingdale Road, NY-Route 109
Farmingdale, NY 11735

The Carter Boys: A Carter Boys Novel

ISBN 13: 978-1-62286-649-6
ISBN 10: 1-62286-649-5

First Mass Market Printing April 2018
First Trade Paperback Printing January 2018
Printed in the United States of America

10 9 8 7 6 5 4 3 2 1

*This is a work of fiction. Any references or similarities
to actual events, real people, living or dead, or to real
locales are intended to give the novel a sense of reality.
Any similarity in other names, characters, places, and
incidents is entirely coincidental.*

Distributed by Kensington Publishing Corp.
Submit orders to:
Customer Service
400 Hahn Road
Westminster, MD 21157-4627
Phone: 1-800-733-3000
Fax: 1-800-659-2436

The Carter Boys:

A Carter Boys Novel

by

Desirée Granger

Red Light Special

Jade: The Alpha Female

"I can't believe y'all got me out here with y'all asses," I mumbled as we crossed the dark street from the campus yard to the backwood neighborhoods of Atlanta. It was dark. Had to be around eleven o'clock on a Friday night. We were so far off the yard that we couldn't even hear the university marching band anymore. Fuck was they still practicing for anyway?

Cars were lined up against the streets, niggas chilling on their respective porches, with girls walking around looking like they were trying to fuck something. Shit, look at us. I guess I really couldn't talk.

"Girl, shut up and come on," Tia pressed as she tugged at her dress to keep it down.

Fuck, why I gotta start this story off in the middle of a ho mission, yo? That's that bullshit, but whatever. Let's get this shit popping.

So, at this very moment, Tia, myself, a bitch named, Porscha, whom I'd just met, and my other roommate, Jordyn, got a text message from some niggas. Cool, right? Nah, nigga. Not at all. I, apparently, didn't see the big deal in it, but they were flipping the fuck out because it was some fraternity niggas specifically asking for them. Yeah, okay. I didn't know who they were, and I didn't care either way. I knew right off the bat it was a booty call, but some girls go to it. I prefer the nigga come to me. So, Jordyn and I tagged along just to make sure everything was everything. Even though we weren't for this whole "let's fuck the cool niggas on the yard," we still came.

"Aye, where y'all walking to? Looking fine as hell!" some older man yelled out as he stepped off his yard, shirtless, pot belly busting as he rubbed his head.

"Eww, let's keep it moving," Porscha said to us as we turned down a block.

Looking down at my phone, I saw I was missing at least three shows on TV, a smoke session with my niggas, and some time buying clothes off the Internet, all because we were chasing dick right now.

"Why these niggas couldn't pick us up?" I questioned.

Tia sighed. "Because they didn't want to make it obvious that they were coming on the yard to scoop us up. Jade, come on. You can sit outside if you don't feel comfortable. You too, Jordyn. I already know you're not down with this."

"I don't feel uncomfortable. I'm just tired of walking. Where do these bum dudes stay at? Like, fo' real?" I snapped as I crossed my arms over my chest. I was not even trying to complain; I just didn't understand why they couldn't get a car and get us.

Jordyn started, "Well, do you know anything about these guys? What if they're carrying diseases and you plan on having sex with them? Do they even have condoms? These kind of—"

"Hush, girl. You killing the mood. I'on even know why yo' nerdy-ass even stepped foot out the room," Porscha snapped as she dragged her hand down to pat that stiff-ass weave.

I bit my lower lip to keep from saying something out the way. I could have, because I didn't like this Porscha bitch, but Jordyn did have a tendency to overanalyze shit like a mothafucka. It could be annoying at times.

We cut the corner, stepping onto another yard just to cross over into the next like it was nothing. I wasn't trying to fuck up my shoes with this grass, but it was too much going on in the streets tonight. Glancing at Jordyn, who constantly looked around checking her surroundings, I smirked. Yeah, her ass should have stayed in the room.

I could hear the ambulance sirens as we stepped up to a two-story house that was painted all red with white Greek letters bordered up to the side. Shit was the straight hood, but they somehow made the Greek houses look decent enough. It was a couple of cars pulled in the dirt driveway, and you could hear music blasting from inside. Immediately, I prepared myself for the fuckery of the night. I hated Greeks. They ruined just about everything on campus, and nobody could see that because they were too busy worshipping them. Ugh.

Let me introduce myself to y'all before I even continue. My real name is Aria, but I prefer my middle name, Jade. I'm Brooklyn born and bred, straight from the concrete jungle. Maybe a little too rough, too brash for these niggas down here. Definitely not a girly-girl type, but I ain't overly manly either; I'm smack down the middle. Can rock high heels and a thot dress, or rock a pair of Tims and be chill. I moved down here for school with my sister. I'm a junior, just turned twenty-one. I'm a dark brown complexion with short, thick, honey-blond locs that hover a little over my shoulders and constantly stay in my face; piercing on my eyebrow, two piercings on my tongue, and both arms are completely covered in tattoos. I have my nipples pierced, and thought about getting my clit pierced. Still thinking on it, really.

Anyway, I'm cute. Not going to lie. Matter of fact, I'm fine as hell. Too bomb for these country niggas down here. Chestnut brown eyes, quick tongue, slim thickums is what they call me—one of those skinny girls with the ass. That's me. I pride myself on being different from the rest. I don't like to dress like the basic females, and don't care to do these basic things they do. Although, unfortunately, I was on a ho mission with my roommates that night. That's about as basic as it gets. Whatever, though.

While Tia and Porscha wore short dresses with their weaves swinging and their asses and titties out, me, I kept it chill. I wore some boyfriend jeans that had more holes in it than I could count, a Yankees baseball cap turned backward, and my giant square earrings hanging low, a red flannel shirt tied around my waist, with a long-sleeve cropped shirt and Tims. Locs were loose and hanging down in front of my face. Fuck what you think. I thought I looked bomb, nigga.

"You think it's other girls in there?" Porscha asked, looking back at Tia as she pulled her dress down so her chest could pop out more. Jordyn was straggling behind, still checking her surroundings. I rolled my eyes. "I don't care what you think, Jade. We already know you not trying to fucking be here."

"As long as y'all know," I retorted as we walked up to the porch. Red cups were spread throughout the yard as the door swung open. Soon as the smell of weed hit my nose, I smiled, body reacting to that feel-good floating in the air. Shit, I guess it wouldn't be a bad night after all.

"Aaaye, what up, beautiful ladies?" the tall guy said with his arms out as he walked down the wooden steps toward us.

I immediately tried to hold in laughter at this pretty boy walking like it was a runway show. He was shirtless, showing off his defined, light brown pecs, abs, and V-cut disappearing into his basketball shorts. Nigga had a serious happy trail going on. Clean-shaved face with bright, hazel eyes was the first thing that stood out after his naked frame. He had plump lips with a charismatic smile, and low-cut hair that was neatly shaped up, looking like he bathed in roses and baby powder. I'm still trying to figure out what fashion show was he walking for because the nigga kept looking off into the distance, licking his lips like a camera was behind us, sudden wind blowing in his direction as he held his chin up with that "I'm fine and I know it" smile.

Hmmmph. Nigga was gay. *Nobody is that fucking pretty, yo*, I thought to myself with a snort of the nose, stifling my own laughter. I needed to be high. Only way to accept what the hell I was seeing. Hope y'all reading this will laugh at this fuckin' shit.

"Heeeeeey, Kodak," Tia and Porscha sang in unison as he reached his arms out to hug them both. I bet this nigga didn't even remember their fucking names.

"Damn, you smell good. What are you wearing?" Tia pressed as his hazel eyes fell on me curiously. I just smirked. I couldn't take this seriously. I hoped there was someone else in there that wasn't looking like a Ken doll from *Vibe* magazine.

"Polo baby, what's up?" He was looking at me with a chuck of his chin in my direction. "You look like you not trying to be here," he said to me as the front door opened again with more dudes peering out.

"I'm not," I replied without looking at him, tone dull and dry as can be. I felt him step closer to me, still smiling like the sun was out and it was raining gumdrops around him.

"Uhh, don't mind Jade. She was going to wait outside anyway with the other girl," Porscha started, but Kodak shook his head, already tucking in that lower lip as he looked at me in a sexual manner.

"Nah, she should come in. Hopefully we can change her mind," he said, looking back at Jordyn, who nervously tugged at her hands, looking through her thick glasses. "She can stay out here, though." He laughed to himself as my mouth dropped. Already didn't like the nigga, just off that statement alone. "Aye, baby girl, what's yo' name?"

"Who? Me?" Jordyn fumbled over her words, pointing at herself as she pushed her glasses up. He nodded, wrapping his arms around Porscha and Tia, pulling them close to his body. "I'm Jordyn with a Y."

"Jordyn with a Y, do me a favor, beautiful, and wait out here. It will only be a minute. I can bring you something to—"

"So, you won't let my roommate in the fucking house, nigga?" I snapped, hands on my hips as his hazel eyes grew wide at me, almost like he didn't think I would say something.

"Nah, she can go inside, but I can see she's already uncomfortable. What we got going on in there ain't for her. She can wait out here."

"I'll be fine, Jade." Jordyn waved me off, sitting down on the steps. "I have a really good book on my phone and homework that I need to catch up on, plus a test, and—"

"A'ight." I cut her off. Shit. Jordyn would go on forever if you let her. "I'll be right back out anyway since I'm not trying to be here either."

"Ahh, come on," Kodak started as my eyes shifted to the pretty boy again. "We doing something special for the ladies. Yo' friends didn't tell you about the red light special?"

"The what, nigga?" I choked, trying not to laugh. Fuck was a red light special? A group of men living in a house together talking about red light special, strobe lights and shit going as they danced about?

"We always invite a select group of ladies to a private night with us. You know, show them our appreciation for their loyalty," he said as we all started toward the front door.

I looked at Tia and Porscha like, *Bitch*!

"What the fuck y'all got me doing?" I whispered harshly.

"Just go with it. Don't ruin this for us," Tia snapped as we walked in the house.

Moment you walked in, it was steps leading upstairs and downstairs. Walls were bright red with their letters and picture frames all over the place. I could hear noise coming from one of the rooms downstairs, like somebody was getting it in. Not with these gay niggas. It was definitely not for Jordyn. She wouldn't last a minute in this house without having a panic attack with her nerdy self.

So, we walked upstairs where the kitchen and living room was, with most of the niggas chilling. I immediately plopped down next to a big dude holding a blunt, and I smiled sweetly at him. He started laughing as he passed it to me, and we took turns taking a pull on it. No introduction needed for that. Weed brings any and everybody together.

"Aye, so y'all rocking with us this whole weekend?" one of them asked as I watched Kodak cop a seat on a chair in the dining room, eyes staying on me. So, I stared back.

Shit. Blink for blink, my dude. We can both be creepy together.

"If you want us to," Tia answered.

"I'm leaving in a few minutes," I stated, moving my locs out of my face.

"Ahh, you gotta stay for the red light special, baby. Why you trying to leave so soon?" dude asked.

"She scared," Kodak let out with a shake of his head. Nigga was trying to bait me to talk to him. I peeped it, and you know what? I took it.

He wanted my attention? I was going to let him have it.

"Why they call you Kodak?" I asked, blowing smoke out as big dude took my arm, trying to look at my tattoos.

"Because every time you're with me, I make sure it's the best moment of your life. Kodak moment," he said with all the seriousness in his voice.

Pin-drop silence. . . .

You could literally hear a fucking pin drop and a random awkward-ass cough that usually came out of nowhere. I looked around, making sure everyone heard what the fuck I just heard before falling out laughing. He couldn't be serious. How could he even say that with a straight face? Like that shit was cool?

"Really, nigga?" I laughed before taking my hat off, shaking my dreads loose. "Only a moment?" Dude was a straight lame.

"Ahh, she slick trying you, bruh," my smoking buddy said as the boys started ragging on him. I slipped both tongue rings out before slipping it back in, eyes never leaving his.

"I mean, that's cool," Kodak started with a shrug like he was cool as shit. "She can say what she wants, but only a few girls get to know what that actually truly means, bruh.

Know what I'm saying?" He laughed as he slapped hands with his brothers.

I stood up with an eye roll. Kodak thought he was big shit just because he was fine as fuck with hazel eyes. Nah, I would shut that shit down in a heartbeat.

"She not ready for it, bruh," another said.

"Nigga, I can handle both of y'all," Tia challenged, eyes clearly on Kodak only.

Yet his eyes remained on me. *Okay*, I thought, nodding quietly to myself.

"Nigga, let's go," I pressed, eyes on Kodak. His face lit up, somewhat confused by my challenge. "Unless I'm not one of those girls that can know what your nickname really means?"

"Damn," I heard one of his frat brothers mumble as all eyes were on me. I smiled, turning on the sex appeal as I licked my lips before playfully sticking out my piercings. Like I said, these niggas down here wouldn't know what to do with me.

Kodak stood up, cheesing, before passing his drink to somebody else. "Aye, y'all mothafuckas have a good-ass night," Kodak started with a laugh as he placed his hand on my lower back to guide me down the steps. "I'm in for the night. Nobody come knocking on my shit!"

"Aye, I got next after you!" someone yelled.

I quickly turned around. Before I could even say anything, Kodak cut in.

"Nah, not with this one you don't. Fuck them other girls," he yelled as we walked down the second set of stairs. I could hear a consistent knocking noise and what sounded like a girl moaning every other beat. Damn. Whoever was fucking her was getting it in.

"So, this what y'all do?" I questioned as I waited for him to step inside the bathroom for a second. Looking him over once again, I smiled. Even caught a peek of the dick print through the basketball shorts. I knew that shit was thick; I just didn't know if it was long or not. He thought he was so cute with his muscular body. I watched him check himself in the mirror, dragging a hand down over his head just as he glanced at me with those bright eyes. I smirked, and in response to that? He blew me an air kiss.

"Nigga, chill." I laughed slowly. "I'm not into all of that, yo."

It was four rooms total down there, and at least two of them seemed occupied. We stood in the small hallway as I peeped one guy stepping out of a room where the girl had been screaming out, and then another guy stepping out, both sweating like crazy as they eyed me greedily. What the fuck was going on?

"Nah, usually we throw parties, but tonight a few girls hit us up on some other shit, so you know." Kodak shrugged as he grabbed a few condoms. "A little pre-party before tomorrow's party."

"What party tomorrow?" I asked, not once hearing anything about it on the yard.

"The Pretty Nasty party at the Clubroom. You should stop by, and come look for me when you do," he said, licking his lips.

I rolled my eyes. *Not in ya wildest dreams, nigga.*

"Aye, Trent," one of the sweaty dudes called out to Kodak. "Who is she?"

"Don't worry about it, nigga," Kodak, or Trent or whatever, snapped back. "She's with me. It's two other bitches upstairs."

The front door opened as a few more girls walked in, loud as hell. *So, girls just come up here, middle of the night, to fuck?* I looked back at Trent, who was just watching me, smiling.

"You scared?" he questioned, cutting the light off in the bathroom.

"Son, chill on that. Nobody is scared. I'm just realizing this is a ho house, and I'm about to play right into that shit," I said with a laugh. Either way. If he sucked, I could brag to his brothers he was whack. If it was good dick, then I mean . . . I just got good dick. Didn't happen often, so it was a win-win situation for me.

I followed him to the room on the far left as he closed the door behind him. It was pitch black in there. Smelled like cinnamon and weed. All I needed was a bed. Soon as I found that bed, I could take control because I wasn't into niggas dominating. I kicked my Tims off and untied my flannel shirt.

"You want the lights on or off, baby?" he asked, his breathing already starting to sound labored.

I could barely see him since there were no windows in the room, but I stripped down completely and felt around for his chest.

"What was your na—?"

I immediately went in for that neck as I pressed my body against his, fingers gripping lightly at his sides.

"Shit," he mumbled, dropping the condoms.

Damn, he smelled good. Whatever lotion he put on his body made me want to lick it off. With my nails digging lightly in his skin, I gently bit down on his neck, hearing him groan in response. I felt his arms grip my body tight. That dick was pressing so hard against me that I just went on ahead and slipped his basketball shorts off, hands sliding down into the material to pull down along with the boxer briefs. I could feel his hand trying to come in between my legs, but I stopped him. I didn't need all of that.

Instead, I pinned his hands back, pushing him against the wall as I proceeded to work his chest with my mouth. I found at least three hot spots on him already, but enough of that. I needed to get ready to go soon. The moment I let go of his arms, he aggressively picked me up so quick that I let out a shriek.

"You good?" he breathed, walking me to the bed as his mouth started working on my neck.

"I want to be on top," I demanded, pushing his mouth away.

"Nah, I'm doing it," he stated, laying me back on the bed. I tried to squirm from underneath him as he spread my legs, but Trent kept me pinned to the bed. "Lay yo' wild ass down."

"I don't like when niggas take control," I let out, moving from underneath his body, trying to push him back. I could hear a sarcastic-ass laugh escape from his mouth, like he couldn't believe I even had the nerve to question his abilities.

"So, we really about to sit here and fight over who's fucking who? I'm the one with the dick. Let me—"

"You don't know what to do, or how I like it," I retorted, trying to sit up. I hated being on the bottom. I felt like I had no control, no say-so whatsoever. "Trent, I'm not about to let you waste my ti—" He dove in between my legs, letting that wet mouth slowly close down on me before slipping his tongue inside of me. "I—I . . . Shit! I—damn." Like, I couldn't say shit but moan in response. I gripped his head, pressing his face all in it as I lifted my hips. His thick, slick tongue separated the folds, lapping up the honey he created for himself. Massaging my being like . . . Shit, I can't even finish this sentence.

"Got yo' ass to shut the fuck up," he bragged before he continued, eating it up like it was fucking melted ice cream. "And you shaved, damn," he mumbled, dragging that tongue down. Wrapping his arms around each thigh to bring me closer only made me go even crazier.

"Trent," I breathed, feeling that tongue flicker. "Trent!" I screamed out, trying to sit up to look at him before falling back down. I couldn't see a thing. It was dark as fuck in that room, and I was getting master head from some nigga I thought was gay.

"Shit, you taste good," he mumbled, gliding a tongue on my inner thigh before proceeding to slurp up what he had caused. What he created. "You haven't even told me yo' name." I could barely focus on the nigga's constant chatter, but I managed to whisper my name to him. "You like that, Jade?" he asked, slipping his sleek tongue inside me.

"Shut the fuck up and do what you do, nigga," I snapped softly, gripping his ears as I pressed my hips deeper into his face. I could feel him smile, which in turn made me smile before moaning. Damn, dude, I'm talking tip of his nose was rubbing the fuck out of me. Deep in it.

"I want the dick," I breathed, feeling him shake his head.

"You not ready yet," he replied before pulling me closer to his mouth once again, this time adding finger work. The moment I felt that flicker of the tip of his tongue again, I nearly cried, letting my body release all that shit on his mouth. I was weak. I'm not going to even lie to you. He was in my top five right now, based off of head alone.

"Chill, nigga," I said in a shaky voice, feeling him continue to ride my orgasm out with that mouth. I felt him sit up, placing his complete body between my legs as he gripped the back of my left thigh, pushing it toward my chest.

"You ready?" he asked, tip of his dick teasing the entrance. "I don't think you ready for this, baby."

"Nigga, hurry the fuck up," I snapped, still trying to keep my body from shaking.

"What's my name?" he asked, slipping the tip in before pulling out.

I groaned, wishing I had a pillow to throw at him. "I don't fucking know. Hurry up with all this pretty shit, nigga, and give it to me," I snapped angrily. I couldn't see him, but I saw those bright-ass teeth, cheesing like fuck.

"Nah, you gotta be nicer than that. What's my name?" Trent asked again with a groan, pushing the tip in before pulling out. I could tell he was testing himself because his breathing became labored every time he went in. "What they call me?"

"Yooo," I let out slowly with a laugh. "I swear if you don't—"

"What they call me?" he asked, pushing his tip in once again. "Shit, you wet as hell, girl."

I took that chance to lift my hips up, sliding my own self on his dick, body gliding on his length, coating his muscle with my own until—

"Ahhh, shit!" Trent spat with a jerk of his body, yanking himself out of me so fast. "Fuck!"

I sat up, confused, empty, and body left feeling cold, wondering what the fuck had just happened. *I know this nigga didn't just—*

"Aye, hold up, I wasn't expecting that."

"What just happened?" I questioned, feeling a slow smile creep on my face. I quickly got off the bed to look for the light switch. I could feel warm gooey shit on my thighs. I just wasn't sure if it was mine or his. Finding the light switch, I quickly cut it on only to see it was a red light. Of course. I looked down, seeing white shit all on my thigh, as he sat on the bed, head dropped in shame, holding himself. Sucking my teeth, I stared at him in disbelief. A slow smile stretched across my face.

"Really?" I laughed. "Nigga, you bust a nut and only got one stroke in? Like, you really just did that? Did I miss the Kodak moment? Was that it?" I laughed even harder.

"Aye, we gotta start that over. I gotta redeem myself because that shit has never happened before."

"Nah, son, I'm good on you, nigga." I laughed, slipping my clothes on. Trent tried getting off the bed to come to me, but I backed up.

"Aye, for real. We gotta start ov—"

"I'm good, son," I said. "You was too busy trying to show off and ended up looking stupid." I swung open the door, seeing all his brothers were in the hallway, popping in and out of rooms.

"Ahh, shit, Trent gave it to her good! She probably couldn't even handle it, nigga. I bet you she's gonna go crazy like the rest of the bitches," one of the boys said, laughing.

"She wasn't ready," another said as Trent stayed his sorry ass in the room, unable to come out.

I went straight upstairs, looking for Tia, since the girl getting it in the room next door was another random ho.

"Tia!" I called out, seeing she was sitting on the couch naked, smoking. I couldn't even believe I participated in this shit. I let my ego get the best of me. "I'm about to leave. Nigga busted a nut on the first stroke, so I'm going back to the room," I told her as his brothers damn near fell out laughing.

"Hold up! I got you, baby. Let me make that up to you," another called out as I walked back down the steps, ignoring all of their sorry asses.

Waste of my fucking night. Unbelievable.

"All of y'all are whack as fuck. I'm out," I said, opening the door and seeing Jordyn still sitting on the steps like a lame. I hated that I even let her ass sit out there by herself for that long. I knew Tia didn't fuck with her like that, and she didn't have a lot of friends, but she was cool in my book. So, when she turned around, looking at me through those thick-ass glasses, I smiled, putting my hat back on.

"You ready?" I pressed, jumping from the steps.

"What happened? Did they—"

"Nigga is lame as fuck, that's what happened," I said, cutting her off. "Let's go."

Fuck-ass nigga. If this was what those Atlanta boys be on, I didn't want no part of it. Real talk.

Trent, the Pretty Boy

"Bruh! What the fuck happened, my nigga?" Cory yelled out as I walked out the room with a shake of my head. I couldn't believe that shit just happened my damn self.

"You heard what she said. Bitch said he nutted early. Ahhh, nigga, you whack as fuck, bruh. Made us all look bad," Armond cracked as everyone laughed.

I couldn't go down like that. I just invited a girl to my room in the frat house, trying to show her the moves—you know, put it down, take my time—but she was something else. I couldn't explain it, but it was different. It was like messing with a wildfire and all I came prepared with was a small glass of water.

So, you know, ya boy was trying to put it down on her. She had sexy chocolate skin, and I don't usually fuck with dark-skin girls. Yet this girl, though . . . Moment she stepped up on the porch with her homegirls, I couldn't take my eyes off her. Not even close to my type. Dark meat, I never fuck with. No offense to those reading this. I only fuck light-skin girls. They're just naturally pretty and look good standing next to me, but this girl walked up, hat on backward, blond dreads, dark skin with tattoos all over her arms, tongue piercings I still could feel on my neck when she kissed me. I wasn't sure how to come at her. Shit. That thick New York accent was what did it, though. She was a little rough for my type, but the moment I had her in the room, I don't know . . . something just happened. I felt like . . . fuck! I guess my dick was saying the same shit, like, *We wasn't ready for that, my nigga.*

"Bruh! You know she's going to tell the whole yard about that, right?" Cortez said as I walked up the short steps to get to the second floor where the living room was, keeping quiet as I quickly thought of a way to rebuke what had just happened. I couldn't have this fuck up my reputation.

"Nah, man, that's not what happened. I don't even know if I want to even really say what happened because it's not right, but . . ." I shrugged, sitting on the couch next to her other homegirl. Forgot her name, but she was already dressed for the occasion, just panties and socks, smoking a blunt on the couch.

"So, what the fuck happened then for her to storm out like that?" Cortez asked as I dropped my head in shame.

"She had a smell, my nigga," I said as her friend gasped with a smile. "I let her know I couldn't do nothing with her, so she walked out mad as fuck, talking about I came too quick."

"Ohhh!" all the bruhs said in unison as I nodded like it was unfortunate.

"Not only that," I let out, hand in the air to silence everyone. "Nigga, she had bumps and sores and shit. I mean, that shit was nasty, bruh. I couldn't do nothing with her. She smelled like straight raw fish, nigga."

"Worrrd?" Cortez let out as I nodded, lying like hell. I couldn't let my reputation go down because I came too quickly. She was already ragging on me the moment she laid eyes on me. I couldn't let that happen again.

"Shit was diseased. Probably had AIDS or something. Shit, I don't know. I ain't never seen nothing like it. It was all over the place: big, small, sore-looking bumps, with white shit all on it."

"Ehhhh," everyone listening let out in unison.

"What was her name?" one of the girls in the kitchen asked, pulling out her phone. "I wanna see what she looks like."

"Jade. Her Facebook name is Jade Brooklyn Banger," her friend said as I smiled at her. Bitches ain't shit. They will do anything and say anything to look good for the moment. I hope y'all reading this catch on to that shit about yo' own friends.

"Is this her?" one of the girls asked as everyone crowded around to see her Facebook profile. "With dreads? Oh my God, she looks like a bum. I bet you she don't wash down there. She looks like she don't. I'on know why you messing with her, Kodak."

"I'on know either." I shrugged as all three girls in the kitchen picked Jade apart based on her pictures and what I said.

Did I feel bad? Nah. She should have let me redeem myself.

"Oooooh, I hate getting bitches like that," Armond agreed as her friend giggled.

"I can believe it. She always had an odor. Smelled that around the dorm," her friend said with her nose turned up as I smiled, licking my lips at her. She wasn't nearly as interesting to look at as Jade, but she would do for the night.

"So, you wanna help me forget about yo' homegirl, beautiful?" I pressed, sliding my hand on her thigh, trying to find that spot, that button. Every female got a button that once you press it, she's all yours.

"You should have came to me first, nigga," she retorted with a roll of her eyes before standing up, taking my hand.

My mind kept flashing back to Jade, mouth still able to taste her juices. Usually I was quick to get rid of it, but I wanted it to linger in my mouth a little longer. Yeah, you reading this thinking this nigga a straight freak. I'm about that nasty shit; fuck what you heard.

The girl took me to the master bedroom, where her friend was getting fucked, and laid down on the bed, pulling me on top of her. I'm looking at my brother Kendrick like, *We switching, bruh?* We already knew the deal. Everybody shared a bitch in this house. If a girl knew she was coming over, she knew she was gonna get fucked by at least six of us, sometimes more.

So, while I'm sitting here trying to get my dick wet with this chick, I can introduce myself. The ladies of Atlanta and the schoolyards of the representing HBCUs in the city know me as Kodak. Niggas on the streets know me as Trent. Mama calls me Trenton. Born and raised in Atlanta, I'm straight country nigga all the way at the age of twenty-three. Am I a pretty boy? I mean, shit, I look good. I don't step out the house, out my bathroom, unless I look, smell, and feel good. If that makes me a pretty boy because I'm into myself, then yeah, I guess so. Don't let that shit fool you, though. I have seven brothers. All we did was fight growing up, so fuck with me if you want to.

"Oooh, Trent!" the girl hollered as I scrunched up my face, looking down at her body, pumping in and out, thinking about the dark-skin girl with the tattoos.

"Trent. Damn, baby, you feel good," the girl moaned.

Wonder how she felt me when I hadn't felt a wall yet. I rolled my eyes, just trying to hurry up and bust a nut already.

So, back to me since we on my story. Overall, I'm college educated. Graduating this year in December with a degree in criminal justice. Of course, I represent my fraternity proudly and catch bitches with my hazel eyes. Never had a problem getting a girl. Relationships aren't my thing, but I could see myself settling down in a few years, having a family, beautiful wife who stays at home to raise the kids. No problem with that, but right now? Nah.

I was looking down at this naked, sweating body, titties bouncing as she moaned repeatedly and obnoxiously, licking her lips at me as she tried to put on a sexy face for me. *Fuck, bruh, bust a nut and get the fuck out this room.* Bitch was dryer than a desert, and just as wide.

"Oooh, Trent! I'm cumming! Ahh!" she yelled as I pumped faster, with her grabbing on to her friend's hand who laid next to her, getting it in. She started screaming to the point where I could feel my dick starting to go soft. *Hell, nah. Hurry the fuck up, bitch.* Ain't nothing worse than having to force yourself to cum. But as soon as she did, I hopped up, slipping my dick back in my shorts, and walked out the room, letting Kendrick fuck with them both.

I was done for the night.

Jordyn:

The Undercover Freak

"Do we have to keep going?" my friend Rita whined as she collapsed her head and arm on the wooden table, being oh so dramatic. We were in the library at nine a.m. on a Saturday morning, working on homework. Papers, essays, math—so much I had to do, so little time. I pushed my glasses up as I began typing fiercely on my Mac, line after line, doing a sixteen-page paper on the history of Egypt. It didn't have to be so long, but there was so much to talk about when it came to Egypt that it was only right that I do it justice. Right? I mean, come on.

"Jordyn, can we at least break? It's so early. I can't even believe I let you drag me out the bed for this bullshit," Rita complained once more. "Nobody is in this library but us. I wanted to get ready to go to this Pretty Nasty party tonight. You need to come out too. Get out of these damn books."

"No, thanks," I said, pushing my glasses up as I continued to type my thoughts on the ancient history of the pyramids, and—I have to stop myself or I'll keep running my mouth about things no one really seems to find interesting besides me. So, I guess I'll start out by introducing myself.

My name is Jordyn with a Y. Obviously. Don't know why I was being dubbed the nerd in this book. Clearly, I have a 4.0 GPA. In school on a full academic scholarship, I play several instruments, speak three different languages fluently, and I prefer to be alone—unless I'm surrounded by people who like to have intelligent conversations like me. How am I a damn nerd? It doesn't make sense. Because I'm smart? I'm not going to waste time analyzing why I'm even partaking in this book. Just something to get my thoughts out, I guess.

"When's the last time you even went to a party? When is the last time you got you some? Huh? Every girl needs a man every now and then to get them right in life," Rita stated.

I rolled my eyes, continuing to type my paper with speed. She smacked her teeth with an eye roll as she pushed her weave back. Rita was that kind of friend that encourages you to have fun, not even thinking about the consequences later.

Will get you in some shit and make you have to think on your feet on how to get out of it, if you can. I can't do that. I overthink, analyze, become nervous when things aren't going as planned. I have to know what's happening, how, who, what, when, and where at all times. I need to predict the outcome so I can make a formal decision on whether I will do it. But, she was the only true friend that I had and the only one who knew just about everything about me. I could always count on her to have a wild night, but going out to a party that night? I didn't have time, nor did I care to go.

"Are you listening, Jo?" Rita asked, using my nickname as I looked at her through my glasses. "When is the last time you got you some?"

"It's been over a year," I mumbled.

"Can we do it like the old times? Go out, find some random-ass niggas, one night stand them mothafuckas, and bounce before they wake up? What happened to my heartless girl that used to be like, fuck it. Let's just do it," she pressed as I struggled to keep from smiling.

"That was with much-needed alcohol, Rita." I smirked, thinking back.

I'm sure y'all reading this assumed I was a virgin. The whole "nerd loses her virginity to a guy then falls in love" story. Nope. I've had sex before and actually enjoyed it. Love? It isn't logically possible to fall in love because it doesn't exist. Proven fact. Love is just—

"Jo, are you listening?" Rita quipped, snapping her fingers in my face as I looked at her, blinking quickly to focus on her. "Can we do that one last time? I'll join your little cheesy online book club, and I'll show up to these homework sessions every time. Just one night? That's all I'm asking."

"I don't have anything to wear, don't even own a dress or a pair of heels," I argued while typing up my paper. "Besides, if me having to go out to find random dick is as hard as it was last time, I'm not interested. You know, they say—"

"Nah-uh," Rita started, cutting me off while texting on her phone. Everyone always cuts me off. "I know a few guys going out tonight. Have you heard of the Carter Boys?"

"Not likely," I replied, flipping through the pages of my book.

"Well, I'm in good with a few of the brothers, and they are performing at the Pretty Nasty party at the Clubroom. I'll just hit my friend up, say a homegirl of mine wants to chill for the night with the Carter Boys. Wassup?" she said out loud while texting. "I'm trying to get Jodie's fine ass alone, girl. Wait until you see him. All of them are fine as fuck, but Jodie is the one with that voice."

I glanced at her before returning to my studies.

Okay, so back to me. I was born and raised in Detroit, moved down here on my own for college, and decided to pursue a degree in music. Did I make any friends down here? Hardly. I grew up with no friends, and now that I was grown, I just didn't see the need to have so many. I didn't see the need for relationships and social activities they tried to force on us on this yard. I had one goal, and one goal only: to take over this world, become a successful solo violinist, and travel. As far as how I look? Well, Atlanta is a city full of superficial, fake video-vixen women walking around with fake asses, fake hair, and fake breasts, makeup caked on their faces, and string from the tracks hanging in their weave. I, on the other hand, embrace natural looks. No such thing as being ugly; just different, unique. So, my mom is half white and half black. My dad is Mexican. Don't know how they even came about, but I'm a good dose of all three races.

"Are you going to come out tonight before I send this text message? Getting these boys all hype for nothing?" Rita asked, interrupting my thoughts.

"I'll go," I said, waving her off. "But whether I have sex with a complete stranger is still up in the air, Rita."

"Whatever, bitch. I know how yo' freak ass get," she retorted with a laugh.

Anyway, I wear glasses because contacts, for some reason, do not want to stay in my eye. The thought of constantly having to stick my finger in my eye isn't appealing. I have a brown cinnamon complexion with jet black, thick, wild curly hair that I usually keep in a ball, with black, thick eyebrows to match, and dark gray eyes I got from my mom. I work out regularly to keep my slim frame, and overall, I'm just your average girl. Not the definition of pretty, I guess, but at least I can speak basic English, unlike some of the people here. Allergic to peanuts, I don't smoke, I have occasional panic attacks or anxiety attacks, and despise the concept of society wanting us to fall to the idea of a basic way of life: born, grow, fall in love, get married and have kids, then die. It's all unrealistic and complete bullshit.

After leaving the library and Rita going to her own room to rack her brain on what she was going to wear, I stood outside for a minute on the steps of the library, watching the marching band march by. I almost forgot there was a football game that day. I never went to those either. I tugged at my sweat pants before unzipping the matching hoodie to let some air in. Early

September and it was still hot like midsummer in Atlanta.

"Aye, excuse me," a guy said, startling me. I turned to look at him, a tall, lanky guy with short baby dreads sticking out and a duffle bag strapped to his body. "What are your plans for the night, Miss?"

"Excuse me?" I started, looking confused as the band continued to march toward the stadium with a huge crowd following behind, recording with their phones.

"What are your plans tonight? Saturday night, I know you and yo' homegirls looking for something to get into, right?"

"I don't think—"

"You should come check us out tonight. Pretty Nasty party." He handed me a promo flyer with a damn-near-naked girl standing in front of a flashy car with a candy cane–like stick in one hand representing one fraternity, and a purple-and-gold dog collar in the other representing the other fraternity. *Club Room, 21+, ladies free before midnight.*

I looked up at him with a bewildered look. "I'm not going to—"

"Aye! Excuse me, sexy shawty!" he called out to another girl, completely walking away from me.

I started to walk off, still looking at the flyer, scanning for details, before bumping right into this tall, large body of a man who was linked up with a girl. It nearly knocked most of my books out of my hand and caused my glasses to drop from my face.

"I'm so sorry," I started, but the girl smacked her teeth in annoyance as she gripped her guy's arm tighter.

"Watch where the fuck you walking, like, damn!" the girl snapped as her boyfriend laughed.

"Bae, chill," he said, wrapping his arm around her neck before kissing her on the side of the face.

"I'm saying, fuck you got glasses for if you not looking where you going?" she continued as they walked off, leaving me to scrape up my papers and books from the concrete.

Welcome to my life, I guess. Hope you find it as interesting as I do. Also hope you understand sarcasm, because that last statement . . .

Whatever. Forget it.

Worldstar Fight

Jade

"But I'm not understanding why the fuck this nigga is running his mouth about me, though!" I screamed as I sat at my desk in my box-sized room, looking on Facebook. It was a Saturday night, and I was supposed to get ready to hit up my friend's house for a smoke session, but boy, did my day turn around fast. This nigga, this gay, pretty-boy mothafucka Trent told everyone in that house that I had herpes, that I smelled like fish, and that . . . Ooooh! Don't even know how crazy I can get. He don't even fucking know!

"I mean, you know how guys get," Tia said as she laid on my bed, texting on her phone. She had just gotten back from the frat house, claiming to have had a wonderful night with no complaints. According to her, Trent—or Kodak, whatever the fuck this nigga name is—told everyone in that house he couldn't have sex with me. That's why I supposedly stormed out like I was mad. Nigga came all on my leg without even getting a full stroke, son! Like, who lies on their dick like that? Insecure bitches do that! Oooh! Let me calm the fuck down.

"Look at this shit. Who the fuck are these people?" Somebody took a fucking picture off my page and had it posted everywhere, saying: BITCHES BE LIKE, U AINT GOTTA WEAR A CONDOM WITH ME. Then, the picture next to my face was clearly a disease-ridden don't-even-know-what-the-fuck-to-call-it. It had bumps and sores all over it, looking like they were ready to burst. The picture was spreading like wildfire on Facebook and Instagram. Like, someone deliberately took the time out to take a bunch of pictures off my page and Photoshop them to make memes. Who has the time to do bullshit like that?

"Don't even worry about it, Jade. I'm sure it will pass." Tia waved it off as I scrolled down, seeing my face and that caption again on another profile. Reading the comments talking about, "I know this girl. She's in my class," I felt my face burn in embarrassment and my eyes water up in rage. These comments were just as bad as the pictures, if not worse. I even saw Trent commenting on a few of them:

AYE, CAN'T LET THEM DARK-SKIN BITCHES FOOL U. THEY BE HAVING THE WORST STANK-ASS PUSSY OUT OF ALL OF THEM.

NAH, BRUH, NOT THE ONES I FUCK WITH. U JUST HAPPENED TO GET THAT BITCH. I AIN'T NEVER SEEN NOTHIN' LIKE THAT.

Y'ALL NEED TO STOP. WHAT IF THIS GIRL IS SITTING HERE LOOKIN AT THIS SHIT? Y'ALL STRAIGHT EMBARRASSED THIS BITCH! LMAO

SHE DID THAT SHIT TO HERSELF.

OMG I KNOW THAT GIRL! SHE IS A FUCKING BITCH! LIKE, OMG I'M GLAD THIS IS OUT. ALWAYS TALKS DOWN TO PPL.

The list kept going on and on, and that was just one picture floating around. I slammed the laptop shut as I buried my face in my hands, screaming to myself to keep from crying. I had just moved to this damn city, and already I was experiencing fucking shit.

"Is Jordyn here?" I asked her, wiping my face.

"Probably not. You know she's probably out with her imaginary friends," Tia joked snidely. "Ugh, I want to exchange her ass for Porscha. I can't bring no niggas over here with Jordyn scaring them off. You remember that last time? I brought someone over and she ran her mouth the whole time about the reproductive system.

Like, bitch, who the fuck does that shit?" She laughed, playing with gum as she stretched it out of her mouth before taking it back in.

"You sitting here talking about Jordyn while I got this bitch running his mouth about me. You really think I give a fuck about you wanting to change roommates because she's lame, nigga?" I snapped.

"You gon' have to get over it anyway because he's gonna be at that party tonight," Tia said, smacking on her gum hard. "He probably ain't even thinking about you like that. This Facebook shit is something some bitches put together. Besides, dem Carter Boys are going to be there. You know I love me some Jodie with his fine ass. He can sing to me any day."

I turned all the way around and stared hard at my roommate. I couldn't consider her a friend just yet, but two things stuck out. One, Trent was going to get a beat down at a party I had suddenly decided to go to. Two, why the fuck was she being so calm about that shit? She laid there on her back, legs in the air, with her wavy weave braided down underneath a scarf, popping on her gum like she was cute.

"What time does the party start?" I pressed, standing up.

"Girls free before midnight. Who you riding with? Porscha's car is full," Tia said, suddenly sitting up as she watched me dig in my dresser for an outfit.

I had to look extra fly that night. I don't even normally say "fly," but this was a special occasion. I was about to beat this nigga's ass, and I wanted to look cute while doing it.

"I'll find a way. Get out my room so I can get dressed. It's going on ten o'clock, so go." I rushed as she got up to open the door.

Jordyn was just coming out of her room across from mine. She waved, looking like a straight dork in sweats and a long T-shirt with hot-ass socks on.

"Come here, Jordyn!" I called out, and she walked in my room. "Close the door and lock it."

"What's wrong? Were you crying?" she asked, scanning my face hard as she closed the door behind her and then sat on the bed. I liked how our apartment was set up. The moment you walked in, the kitchen and small dining room area was right there. Down the far left side was Tia's room and our bathroom. On the right side, Jordyn's room and my room were directly across from each other, with the living room in the middle. It was perfect because Jordyn kept to herself most of the time and was quiet. Tia stayed walking in somebody's room without so much as a knock and a "wassup." It had to be a southern thing or something, because Jordyn and I were from up north. We didn't play that shit.

"Look, are you staying here tonight?" I asked, already knowing the answer. I just needed her car.

"No, I'm thinking about going out to this stupid party." She sighed, looking down at her hands.

My mouth dropped before smiling as she pushed her glasses up. "Wait, hold up, nigga. You what? You? Going to the party?" I laughed. She almost made me forget about beating that nigga's ass. "So, are you getting dressed right now or no? What's up? Can I get your car if you don't go?"

"Um, I can drop you off," she suggested. No girl was going to let another girl borrow her car. Hell, if I was her, I wouldn't let me borrow her car. I barely knew how to drive, didn't even have a license, but this was an emergency.

"That's cool. I'm getting ready now."

"Okay, just so you know, I'm not going to pick you up, so you need to—"

"A'ight, bet," I said, cutting her off. She dropped her head and walked out of my room, closing the door. She talked too fucking much.

Let me just say this about Atlanta parties: they do know how to turn up. There is definitely nothing like parties down in the A. We constantly blast their music up north, and niggas treat Atlanta like it's the city to be, but you don't really experience it until you actually get there and see it for yourself. So, you know I had to look bomb for the night. I wore a royal blue body con two-piece set with a cute high-waist skirt and cropped top that was see-through, showing off my pierced nipples. My honey locs were wild and all over the place, and to beat the cold, I wore a thin leather jacket that had the silver buckles jingling all over the place, with matching black heels. Blunt in the pocket of my jacket, lighter in the other, and I was good to go.

"Are you ready?" Jordyn asked as she stood by the door in sweats and a hoodie with a scarf on.

"So, you not stepping out?" I asked as we opened the door.

"Maybe another night, but not tonight." She shrugged.

Tia was already gone with Porscha, probably sucking a nigga's dick. I bet both of them helped spread that shit about me having AIDS or herpes and whatever else was out there about me. I knew they didn't defend me like one could expect them to. Oooh, the more I thought about it, the madder I became. I just needed to chill out for a minute, not stress myself out that night. So, on the way to the club, the ride was silent, at least on my end.

Jordyn kept going on about something she saw on fucking TV the other night, but I tuned out as I scanned Facebook, seeing who else was posting about me and talking shit. I wanted to remember everyone's faces so when I saw them, I could make my move. Wouldn't be no fucking talking on my end. I wanted to clear all this confusion up by the time I made it back to my bed. One thing I hated was being embarrassed, and this nigga right here managed to go beyond that, so I was going to shut all this shit down and set everything straight. Nigga could talk all that shit if he wanted to.

"Is this it?" Jordyn asked as she pulled up to a parking lot. Why did all the hood clubs in Atlanta have to be in a shopping plaza? Didn't make sense. Everyone was outside, though, hanging around in the parking lot, talking, laughing it up, and smoking. The line looked long as fuck, but I was going to find my way in, one way or another. The valet niggas were in their high-yellow vests, directing traffic as we followed the line of cars before pulling into a designated parking spot. Looking around and seeing girls with the fake asses and long blond weaves walking in their six-inch heels and caked-up makeup, I smiled. Atlanta broads knew they was basic as fuck.

"I'm kind of glad I decided not to go," Jordyn mumbled to herself as she looked around.

"It's not as bad as it looks." I laughed, breaking my neck to see if there were any signs of his fraternity in the parking lot. I was looking for red-and-white niggas with bowties. They stayed wearing bowties like it was fashion forward. Fuck outta here.

"I just want a peaceful night. Making me some hot chocolate, a small dinner, and—"

I opened the door, knowing she was about to start going on and on once again. "Text me when you make it back home, Jo."

"Okay, I guess," she managed to say as I closed the door.

I checked myself once again before walking around the small two-door Civic. I'd be damned if I was gonna wait in line. I had to know somebody. Anybody. Pulling my phone out of my small wristlet, I scanned through my contacts, texting a few party promoters to see who was working this party.

"Aye, sexy! Damn, shawty in the blue! You look fine as hell, guhl! Come here!" someone yelled out. I smirked, keeping my stride.

"Damn, she look good with them locs, bruh," another guy said as I continued to make my way to the main entrance of the club.

Shit, it looked like everyone stepped out the hood in their finest. Girls were lined up with weaves the color of the rainbow, colored eyelashes, heels and dresses. Studs were out there macking on the girls.

"Aye! What it do, shawty!" One whistled as I turned to see a group of niggas surrounded by a bunch of cars. The one who was calling me out grabbed his dick, blowing an air kiss at me. "Come here! I like a bitch with tattoos!"

"Nigga, get the fuck outta here, yo," I snapped back just as my phone rang. *About damn time.*

"Hello?"

"Yeah, where you at, mama?" Eric answered.

I smiled, walking quickly up to the front of the line, already hearing the girls smack their teeth in annoyance and talk shit.

"I'm outside, right out in the front," I said. He hung up, and I waited. Eric was a nigga that liked appearances. He liked to look good and liked the bitches on his arm to look good, and he knew I would do just that. So, when I saw his short, chunky frame walk out the packed building, I smiled, making my way past the security guard, who said nothing.

"Nah-uh! How come she get to go in?" I heard a girl yell. "That ain't even right! I been standing out here for at least an hour. Y'all supposed to let bitches in fo' free."

"I know that's right!"

"You good, baby?" Eric asked, looking me over with a smile. "You look good as fuck."

"I know I do, nigga." I laughed, pushing my locs out of my face. "But no, I got a bone to pick with a gay mothafucka who spreading that shit about me on the Internet."

"Yeah, I saw that shit." He laughed as we entered through the double doors.

The club was huge! Only one level, but damn was it packed full of people, with a small stage in the front. The bar was wrapped all the way around, with seats and booths lined up, red lighting on one side and purple lighting on the other.

"Aye, I'll be right back. Go enjoy yourself. Don't even worry about that nigga," he told me.

"You right!" I replied over the music, watching him work the crowd. I kept walking, maneuvering through the thick crowd as I took off my jacket. Eyes lingered on me from both girls and boys.

"Aye, damn, come here, girl," someone said, grabbing my arm as I turned around. Tall, brown skin, decent face: I could chill with that for a minute, until I found who I was looking for. "You want a drink, shawty?"

"What you think?" I asked, head to the side, as he smirked.

"Come on," he said, putting his hand on my lower back.

I let him lead the way, feeling hands grab up on my ass as the DJ started to get shit turned up.

"Aye! All my sexy ladies in the house! Who repping for that Pretty tonight? Who came here to see the pretty boys tonight?" he yelled on the mic as girls hollered out, drinks in the air. "I know we got some girls that came here to see them Nasty boys too! Drinks in the air if you here for them Nasty dogs!" Girls screamed out at the same time the fraternity started barking like dogs. I could see most of them up front, closer to VIP and the DJ booth, so I hoped Trent was there. I prayed he was there that night. I would let him enjoy his night a little longer. "We about to get it in! ATL, turn up! Let's go! Greek takeover!"

The song switched to Trey Songz's "Touching Loving" featuring Nicki Minaj. Ahh, shit! This was my jam. I took the drink I was babysitting for a minute as I took dude out to the dance floor to show him a li'l something. Just because I'm on the small side don't mean yo' girl don't know how to twerk.

"Aye! Aye! Get 'emmm!" someone hyped as a girl and I stood side by side, dancing on these niggas who I guess were friends, because they were slapping hands like they won a million bucks together. She bent low, so I went even lower, dress completely up, no panties on whatsoever as he gripped my hips. Nigga's dick was poking so hard he might as well have came all on himself. I flipped my locs back as the song switched to "Anaconda." Shit, I guess I was just getting started.

"Yo, let me get in! I got this!" someone hollered out as they jumped behind me, throwing it back at me. *This nigga here! LMAO!* I was enjoying my time, though. Music was right, crowd was straight, my mood was on one, and the drinks were bomb. I felt good. *Trent who? Nigga I don't know.*

"Nah-uh! Y'all ain't ready. I got her!" a girl in heels called out as she whipped her weave off her shoulders, trying to come in between me and dude. Yeah, they be doing that shit down here too, girls twerking on girls. Niggas loved it, and I didn't mind as long as that's all it was.

"Bruh, she killing it with the dreads, though! What's yo' name, shawty?" another guy asked over the music as the song switched.

Suddenly, I felt like we were surrounded by niggas all trying to get a piece of me. I couldn't blame them. I was the only bitch in this club who had blond dreads, tattoos, and boot-buckled heels. I looked completely different from these weave-wearing, plastic-looking broads.

"Aye, yo, B! Lemme get a hit, son!" I called out to dude smoking a black.

He smiled.

"And she from up north, too. Damn, I love a chick with that accent," another said. "What part of New York you from?"

"Why the fuck I gotta be from New York? It's other states up there too, son," I joked, taking a pull on the black. "From Brooklyn, B. Born and raised."

"You like girls?" the girl I was dancing with asked as she looked me over slowly.

"Nah, but my sister do. You can get at her," I told her, thinking about DJ, who was probably still at basketball practice on the yard. Biggest ho I knew.

"We gonna keep this party going! What y'all know about this right here?" the DJ called out as the song transitioned into "Numb" by

August Alsina. I nearly screamed! I loved this damn song. I had niggas giving me drinks left and right while trying to stay up under me, and the DJ was doing me right by playing all the songs. Shit! I might just have to deal with Trent another damn day because all I was focused on was having a good time, not even worried that I didn't have a ride home.

I guess I spoke too soon, though, because something told me to look up in the direction of the bar, and sure enough, there he was: Trent, Kodak Moment, AKA gayest mothafucka in the world right now, staring back at me before walking off with a chick underneath him.

Fuck that.

"Ayo, hold my drink and jacket," I said to whoever was beside me as I started to walk toward his direction, following his every move through the thick, sweaty crowd. The closer I got to the front, the more I started recognizing people from school. I guess they knew it was me, too, because the girls started whispering amongst themselves while pointing, looking at me like I disgusted them.

Bitch! Speak the fuck up! I hate that shit. If you talking mad shit, say it to my face. Don't be chill about it.

When I came to a stopping point, seeing Trent leaned up against one of the booths, his whole fraternity was present, all wearing some type of red. Trent had on a red button-up Polo shirt with a bowtie, straight leg jeans, and red Jordans with a fresh cut. His hazel eyes were surrounded by a reddish tint from his high. A girl was leaning in front of him as she eyed me like she dared me to say something to him.

"Ain't you the girl from last night?" one of the boys asked, slowly smiling while looking at Trent. "Oh, shit! You are!"

My eyes stayed on Trent, who just lazily smiled at me, blowing a small air kiss my way.

Be chill, Jade. Be easy, nigga. Let me at least let him say his last words before I fuck up his night.

"Ayeee! We not trying to have no issues over here, girl. Take that shit somewhere else. You can't even be over here. This is strictly VIP," another said, trying to grab my arm.

"Nah-uh, nigga, don't touch her. She may have crabs," a girl joked.

I kept quiet, staring at Trent. He knew, just like I knew the real story, and the reason I was there. That's why his ass wasn't saying nothing. Yet.

"So, you not trying to tell these mothafuckas the truth, nigga?" I started, stepping closer to him as I crossed my arms over my chest, back hunched over, feeling like I was back home on the sidewalk, about to bust a bitch straight in her mouth. Trent was no different.

"I did tell the truth." He laughed with a shrug. "I couldn't fuck with you like that because of what you got going on."

"Oh, word?" I let out, head tilted to the side.

"Aye, she standing like a straight nigga right now, like you about to fight or something. Fuck is the problem, shawty?" another asked as I turned my attention to the next gay-ass brother.

"My problem is all of y'all running y'all mouth about me on Facebook because of what this nigga said. He didn't tell y'all he ate me the fuck out like a champ then turned around and bust a nut on my leg after one stroke. This gay-ass nigga lied to y'all, making me look stupid in the process. So, I'm going to give you one last chance to get yo' story straight or it's gonna be a problem," I threatened as the girls became silent. Niggas was still talking, but the girls stayed hush-hush. They better be glad my sister wasn't there because her hands were much meaner than mine.

"Oh, so I'm gay because I ain't fuck with you?" He laughed.

"Nah, nigga, you gay because you act like a straight bitch. Let that shit be known, son!" I snapped, clapping my hands together. "You Atlanta niggas be on that shit straight up, so correct the fucking story, tell everyone the fucking truth or I'ma correct ya life, nigga. Simple! Let everybody know yo' dick is weak."

His mouth slightly dropped as his eyes widened, like he couldn't even believe I said that.

"Aye, it's looking a li'l tense over here. I'm about to throw y'all something to stroll to. Give the ladies a li'l something!" the DJ yelled out on the mic as the song transitioned into Miguel's "Vixen." The girls screamed in excitement as the boys, including Trent, started to smoothly stroll around us, with him leading the line. He dipped low, eyes never leaving mine, blowing small air kisses my way before winking.

"Tell the truth!" I yelled, feeling myself about to reach my breaking point.

"I did! I don't fuck with dark bitches anyway, and you just proved why I don't. Clean between ya legs, bitch," he said as everyone laughed.

My heart was racing, watching him seduce the girls to the beat of the song, all of them moving in precise unison, like clockwork. I grabbed a full glass of whatever and went straight to the front of the stroll, disrupting everyone.

"Trent!" I called out, wanting him to look at me.

He turned around, smiling just as I jerked the glass in his face, liquid hitting him hard. In that small second of him being shocked, I took that moment to deck him straight in the face, hitting him near the left eye just as someone grabbed me, pulling me back.

"Whoa! Whoa! Hold up!" someone yelled as I started kicking high in the air, not caring who I hit. I just wanted to get out of whoever's grip so I could get to Trent, who was now on the same level I was.

"You fucking hit me!" Trent screamed, wiping his face from the drink. "Nah! Let me go! Let me go! She wanna fight a nigga? I'ma fight her like a nigga. Move!" he let out as they grabbed hold of him.

"We need security!" someone called out. "Security!"

I squirmed out of one of his brother's grips as I ran up on Trent, hitting him again, slapping him as hard as I could just as he grabbed hold of my arm.

"Let her go!"

"Bruh! You can't—"

When I say this nigga got loose and grabbed me . . . he gripped my small frame tight before jerking me back to the ground. I fell so hard my left ankle went *POP!* Trying to fight in fucking heels, run, and kick wasn't the move, and I swear my whole left leg became numb.

Everyone started crowding around, niggas stepping on me, trying to back Trent up, who was being held back by six niggas now. Some girl took that chance to kick me while I was down, but another girl saw that and snapped, causing another fight to break out.

"Take him outside! Take him out!"

"Tell that bitch to come here!" Trent yelled as I struggled to get him, fighting through the pain.

I wasn't done yet, nowhere near done. I took my shoes off, leaving the heels there, and went after the crowd pushing Trent out. I was limping like a mothafucka, but I managed to grab drinks out of random hands, throwing them in his direction, soaking everybody.

"Somebody get her! Someone get her crazy ass!" someone yelled. Everyone was too busy trying to record with their phones, to be the first to post to Worldstar Hip-hop.

"Aye! S-stop! Stop! Stop!" one of his brothers screamed at me, grabbing me to keep me away from Trent, who was still talking shit, even from the entrance.

"Get them out the club! Both of them!" the DJ yelled. Music was at a complete standstill as I was carried out on this dude's shoulder, no shoes, dress hiked up to my stomach, exposing everything.

"Put me down!" I screamed. I knew everyone outside waiting in line was looking, like, "What the fuck just happened?" but they, too, had their camera phones up.

"Aye, come at me again!" Trent yelled from across the parking lot. "Bring yo' ugly monkey-looking ass over here, bruh! Come at me again!"

"You talking mad shit, my nigga, but you all the way over there!" I snapped in response, trying to get to where he was.

"Aye, be cool. We not trying to have y'all fight," the guy said to me, but all I saw was Trent.

"Nah, let me go. I'm not about to hit her. I just wanna talk to her," he said, sounding like he was lying as hell.

I watched him walk over to me, shirt coming off, hazel eyes staring hard at me in anger, with a small cut on the side of his head where I had thrown a glass at him. Yeah, I'm a crazy bitch.

"Don't hold her back, Armond. Let her go. She ain't gonna do shit. I got this."

"Bruh, just—"

"Say what the fuck you gotta say, nigga!" I snapped, trying to move past Armond's strong ass. "You still wanna talk shit about this?" I lifted my leg up, exposing myself to him and anyone watching, not caring. "Do this look like I have fucking herpes or AIDS? Do y'all see any bumps? No! My shit is clean! You see any, Armond?"

"I mean," he started, sounding nervous as he glanced but quickly looked away. "Nah, but you know how it is. Probably just started as a joke."

"A joke? My picture is everywhere on the fucking Internet because of this joke! You started this shit, and I can't never take it back!" I cried, looking at Trent, who didn't show one ounce of emotion in his pretty face. "Tell everyone the fucking truth, nigga!"

"Fuck you," was all he said.

I worked my mouth up quick, gathering up as much spit as I could before hacking it in his direction, barely missing his mouth, then immediately regretting it.

Nah, I take that back. No I didn't.

"Ohhh, shit," Armond said slowly as Trent closed his eyes, fist balled up tight like he was fighting against himself to keep from reacting. "Bruh, go. Go get in the car. I got her. Just go before you do something stupid."

"Gay mothafucka deserves it," I stated in a low voice, eyes never leaving his face as he wiped off my glob of spit, looking at me.

"You know what?" Trent started in a calm voice as he nodded his head. "Even if I did lie, take that shit as a compliment. I nutted early because I wasn't expecting you to feel the way you did. Yeah, I said that shit about you, but I have nothing to do with how that shit got on the Internet. Ask yo' homegirls about that. And as far as embarrassing you? Look around you," he said, pointing at all the phones held up in our direction. Security even had their phones out, recording. Nobody was trying to get in the club; they were staring at us.

"You embarrassed yo' fucking self by how you acted tonight. Look at you! No fucking clothes on, half-ass naked, drunk, throwing shit, and spitting on people. I'm not gonna hit you, and I apologize for putting my hands on you, because my mama taught me better than that. I keep classy-ass women in my presence, and you ain't nowhere near that. All I gotta say." He walked off as he reached in his pockets for his keys.

Armond stood there, still holding my arm as if he was afraid to let me go because I might do something stupid. Then he eventually followed

Trent to the car as the rest of the brothers piled out of the club. I stood there, dress looking like a T-shirt, ankle throbbing, and tears coming down my face. I had lost my cell phone, jacket, heels, and my fucking pride.

Shit! Where the fuck is Jordyn when I need her?

When Controlled Met Chaos

Jordyn

"Oh my God, this is so crazy," I said to myself, watching the Travel Channel. I had the apartment to myself for the first time this semester, and I was loving it. My roommate Jade wasn't going to be back for a while, and Tia was probably spending the night with some guy after the party, so I kicked back in my boy shorts and T-shirt with my curly hair loose, falling to my mid back. I wore long socks with my feet propped up underneath me, eating a bowl of cereal as I watched Andrew Zimmern eat a cow's brain. How insane is that? I was young and living in one of the wildest cities in the south. I guess I could have found something better to do with my time besides sit there on the couch watching TV, but this was what made me happy. I loved to be alone with my thoughts—no one to interrupt me, no one to look at me funny when I spoke, and no one to judge me. I liked quiet and silence. Best sound there is. Plus? I had a bottle of Absolut with gummy bears in at the bottom, so really? I was having a blast all by my ol' damn self.

Looking back at the kitchen, I thought about what I truly wanted to eat. Rita was probably pissed I bailed on her, but I know she was probably having the time of her life right now with whoever she was sleeping around with. Least she was getting some. Letting out a huge sigh, I got up and threw on a jacket, slipping my glasses on my face. I had a strange feeling Jade was going to call me up and tell me to get her, make all kinds of threats if I didn't, and then not offer any gas money. So, to avoid all of that, I decided to just go put some gas in and grab something to eat for the next day while I was at it. Tia was going to come in drunk and high, eating all the food in the fridge which was mine, and I just wanted to avoid another pointless argument. Grabbing the keys, I stepped out of the clean apartment and headed toward my two-door Civic.

"Fuck!" I let out, looking down at myself before rolling my eyes. "Of course I would walk out with just my underwear. Very smart, Jordyn, really," I said, tugging my shorts down. I was already to the car, so I just got inside, feeling the cool air surround me, and turned the car on.

"Where did I put my hair tie?" I said to myself, looking around in the seats. I hated my hair down. It was so annoying, all over the place and constantly in the way, yet I never wanted to cut it. If I ever straightened it out, I know it was probably touching my ass. Had to be. In its natural curly state, it was mid back.

I pulled out of the parking space, turning on the radio, and just started for my favorite gas station. Am I the only one that has a favorite gas station? Go to the same one all the time? Maybe it's just me.

"Thanks for tuning in to the people's station, V103. We out tonight, Clubroom Fourteen. We wilding out! Pretty Nasty party! All my ladies looking sexy tonight. Who you came here to see, baby girl?"

"Heeey! Whet ssuuup! You already know I came here to see August Alsina sexy ass!" the girl hollered on the radio. "And I heard them Carter Boys gon' be here."

"You already know we only bring out the hottest artists," the DJ yelled out.

"Can I give a shout out?"

"Go 'head, baby."

"I wanna g'on 'head and give a shout out to my baby daddy. Mell, nigga, you be holding me down at my worst of times. I love you!"

"Damn, no shout out to yo' kid?" the DJ said as I laughed. Ignorant. These people down here were so stupid it was unbelievable.

"A'ight, come here, sexy. Who you came here to see, baby girl?" the DJ asked another girl.

"I came here to see dem Carter Boys! I know one of them personally. I'm the girlfriend of Jodie. Let nan one of these bitches try me tonight over my nigga. So, you already know I—"

"Maaan, sit yo' lying ass down," the DJ said, cutting her off as the music changed.

I shook my head, pulling up to the well-lit gas station.

Who the hell were the Carter Boys? Didn't make sense, I guess, because I didn't listen to rap music nowadays. I liked the old stuff, but this stuff they were putting out now? I couldn't get with it.

Pulling up to the tank, I cut the car off and got out, counting my money, lips moving silently in count as my head stayed down. I was walking toward the store, not even paying attention to what was in front of me. The sudden sound of an engine nearly caused me to stop dead in my tracks, almost getting run over.

"Oooooooo weeee! Shawty, move out the way! Move out the way wit'cho sexy ass!" someone called out as I stopped in mid stride to let these

trucks abruptly pull up. One of the guys was hanging out the driver's side, tongue sticking out at me.

"Pull up, bruh!" another said in the truck
behind him as I watched these . . . group of guys
literally disturb the peace, music blasting, sitting
in all black trucks and rims, looking like they
were the party. The one who stuck his tongue
out at me hopped out of his truck and headed
straight toward me, pulling his jeans up.

"Aye, what up? What's yo' name, baby? Damn,
you got a nice body," he said as my eyes grew
wide at his bluntness. He was tall, dark brown
complexion, with a body that looked like a map
because he had so many tattoos. Too many to
count, all on his neck, hands, even on his face.
The edges of his hair were lined up and tapered
on the sides. He had thick dreads that were
pulled into a messy, crooked bun on top of his
head, dark brown low-lid eyes like he was high
off something, and dark brown lips. You could
tell he smoked a lot, with his naturally high-like
face. He was shirtless, decorated in chains and
fancy watches, with straight leg jeans that might
as well be skinny, sagging so low his ass sat literally sat on top of the waist of the jeans, showing
off his pinstripe Polo boxers.

He was gross, to say the least. Too all over the
place for me: too noisy, and too much. Definition

of an Atlanta boy. I just kept walking, with him no doubt following behind me.

"She trying to play hard to get like she don't know who I am. Everybody know me, nigga." He laughed.

I glanced back at him with a confused face before turning back around. Who the fuck did the guy think he was, and why would he think I should know him?

"Bruh, this nigga is a fool!" another said.

"I bet I get that pussy by the end of the night, though," he challenged.

Our eyes locked, and he blew a kiss at me while grabbing his dick.

Oh, no, sir. Not in your wildest dreams.

I pushed open the glass door and kept walking straight to the back to grab some drinks.

"Aye! Shawty, you not gonna tell me yo' name? Why fuck around like this with the games? Let me get yo' number and we can go ahead and do what we gotta do."

"I don't talk to strange men," was all I said, looking at the drinks, nodding quietly to myself with the mental decision I just made: *It's official. I'm drinking myself to sleep.*

"I don't talk to nerdy-looking bitches, either, but here we are," he said as he stood next to me in front of the drinks.

I glanced at him as he bluntly looked at my ass, licking his lips. I knew I should have put some pants on. I tugged at my shorts, backing away from this Lil Wayne wannabe.

"So, what's up?" he pressed as the bell chimed. The rest of his little crew walked back to where we were, just grabbing drinks, not even thinking about the cost, what kind, or whatever. They just took them.

"Nigga still trying to get with her, bruh. I've seen better-looking girls than her," another said as I looked at him, eyes squinting at the ignorant statement before turning my head. Whatever. I didn't have time to even dumb myself down to their level. Instead, I grabbed a thing of Arizona and headed to the front, grabbing some chips and Skittles.

"I mean, I'm saying, she playing hard to get like she don't know me. Everybody in the A know who the fuck we are," the guy continued, following me to the register. "She know she wants this dick, so why she—"

"Excuse me?" I said, turning around, having enough of whatever this crap was. "First of all, I don't know who you are, and the way you're acting, and speaking toward me? Honestly, I don't care to know who you are. God!" I flipped. "I hate this fucking city. Nobody knows how to talk right. Everyone is so . . ." I turned back around as

I started rambling to myself, "self-centered and ignorant. *Aye, shawty? Aye, shawty? Bitch this, bitch that. Pussy, pussy, pussy*," I said, mocking in a deep voice. "Ugh. Can't wait until I get my degree and leave this place. Move to New York like I wanted to in the first place. I should have—"

"*Hola*, Jordyn," Marco said as he slipped behind the register to take my money. I smiled. Only time I'd seen a Mexican man run a gas station in my life was there. It gave me a chance to use my Spanish. That's why this was my favorite gas station.

"*Hola*, Marco," I said, letting my accent come out as we spoke briefly in Spanish, completely forgetting about the guys standing behind me, who were probably too dumbfounded to speak. Pushing my glasses up, I grabbed my bag and walked out, ready to pump the gas and go back to the room. I was done for the night.

"Aye! Hold up!" I heard the guy call out.

I rolled my eyes, walking to my car.

"Hold up! Come here!"

I turned around after slipping my bag in the car and proceeded to pump the gas. He walked over to me, legs wide apart, diamond chains moving about as he stepped over the concrete divide to stand in front of me, smiling. His heavy-looking eyes were slightly red, and I realized he had *ATL* in small letters underneath his left eye, with two nicks on the right eyebrow. There were rings on just about every finger. He was decked out in jewelry. I was sure he stole it or it was fake. Had to be.

"My bad about that in the store, shawty," he said, looking my body over slowly.

I pushed my glasses up again as I continued to stare at the small screen, watching the numbers go up ever so slowly, like the pump purposely slowed down just so I was forced to have a conversation with this guy. "I'm used to girls coming at me, so it's been a minute that I had to work a little to get a name from a girl, you know what I mean?" He laughed.

I didn't. Not once did I even glance at him.

"So, look." Clearing his throat, he pulled out his phone. "Why don't you give me yo' number and we can—"

"I don't own a cell phone," I said, cutting him off.

"What you mean you don't own a cell phone?" he asked, looking confused. "Everybody gotta have a phone."

"Well, I'm not everybody," I replied. "I have a house phone, but no cell phone."

"So, let me get the house phone then," he pressed, stepping closer to me as I scooted back on the car, moving away from him. I stayed quiet, watching the numbers go. Why the fuck was this thing taking so long?

"Come on, shawty," he said slowly while dropping his head in shame. "I apologize for how I came at you, a'ight? My name is Elijah." He put his hand to his chest as I looked at him.

"Jordyn with a Y," I mumbled, tapping the pump to keep the gasoline from dripping before placing it back in the slot.

"A'ight. So, Jordyn with a Y, why don't you have a cell phone?"

"Because I don't need it. I don't talk to anyone, and I like to be alone. Cell phones are just a way to keep people from actually doing shit for themselves and a way for the government to keep a track of you. So, no cell phone for me," I said, walking to the other side of the car.

"No Facebook, no Instagram, nothing?" he questioned.

"Nope," I answered, opening the door.

Elijah quickly came over to the driver's side, holding the door open as he leaned in the car. My mouth dropped at this fool and his brashness.

"So, make an exception for me then. Let me get your house number. I'm not gonna let you go until you do."

"Bruh, come on! We already late as fuck for this club!" one of the guys yelled as Elijah and I stared at each other.

I pushed my glasses up before letting out a frustrated groan. I didn't even have the guts to give him a fake number. I reached in the glove department for a paper and pen.

"Oh, shit!" Elijah said excitedly. "I was ready to do some reckless shit to get this number, baby," he joked and I smiled. "And she smiles. You actually smile."

"Course I smile," I retorted softly, handing him the piece of paper.

"What color are your eyes?" he asked as his friends came walking over.

"Gray, sometimes hazel," I said, starting the car.

"Bruh, come on! We gotta go!"

"I'm calling you tonight!" he let out, letting go of the door. "Better answer that phone, Jordyn with a Y!"

I just waved before backing out. What a damn night.

The moment I got back to my place, I grabbed the pink cordless phone out of my room and immediately dialed Rita's number. I wasn't lying when I said I didn't have a phone. Never owned a cell phone in my life, no matter how hard my parents tried to get me one. I didn't know how to work it, and I didn't want to get caught up in its technology grasp.

"Hello?" she answered loudly. The sound of loud music in the background almost overpowered her voice, but I could tell she was trying to move out of the way.

"Can you hear me?"

"Yeah, girl. Wassup? I told yo' ass you should have come out here! I think yo' roommate about to get into a fight with someone, and I just seen August Alsina! Girl, he is too fine! I'm waiting on the Carter Boys to come out so I can see Jodie fine ass."

"Don't care. Look, I got a question," I said, thinking about the gas station incident. "Who is Elijah?"

"Who?" she yelled.

"Some guy named Elijah. I just met him at a gas station, and he was acting like I was supposed to know who he was."

"I ain't never heard of him, and you know I know everybody. Was he cute?" she asked as I rolled my eyes.

"He's your type, not mine."

"Ooooh! Did you get his number for me?"

"He has the house phone."

"Well, when he calls, start talking me up, girl. I gotta go. I'll talk to you when I get to your room."

"Okay," I said as we hung up. I doubted if Elijah would call me anyway, so I shouldn't even have been the least bit worried.

The Carter Boys

Tia: The Jump Off

"Ahh, this is my jam!" I hollered out, arms raised to the ceiling as I watched one of my favorite rap groups, dem Carter Boys, perform my song, "She Ready." It was the middle of the night at the Clubroom. Drinks were being passed out in red cups, some niggas was going around spraying drinks in girls' mouths using an old Windex bottle, and the food from the bar was on point. This was it. This was what college life should really be about, surrounded by yo' best bitches, drinks, clubs, sex, and good times.

So, whessuup? Y'all finally reached my part of the story, and just so you know, a bitch gets down. If I want to fuck, I will fuck. If I feel like fighting a ho, best believe I will fight a ho. No problems telling you I can be your best friend one minute and then turn around and talk shit about you the second you leave. I am that bitch and proud of it. Let's keep it one hundred. You reading about me, so you're going to know about me.

My name is Tiana, twenty-two years old, born and raised in Atlanta, Zone 6, Ellenwood Beeetch! What it do? I'm five foot five with a light caramel complexion and pretty, slanted dark brown eyes. Got a long, honey-blond weave, twenty-four inches to be exact, with a side swoop; dimples on each cheek, small waist, big booty, thick thighs, and dressed to impress. Stay popping on some gum, stay up to date on the latest shit including niggas, parties, shoes, and gossip.

I was responsible for Jade's Internet shit. I was the one who create the meme that got spread throughout Facebook. Yeah, it was me and a few other chicks that were at the house that night. Whatever. I didn't like Jade. She walked around like she was the shit just because she was from New York. Every nigga was sweating her like she was something new to look at.

Nah, boo.

"Girl, we got to find a way to get with them later on," Porscha told me as we looked up at the stage watching dem Carter Boys perform.

So, let me fill y'all in on what was going on and what was about to happen, because I was quick to put myself into situations I knew would benefit me in the long run. We were at the Clubroom for the Pretty Nasty party, right? Niggas was there, girls were there, the fraternities was doing their thing with the strolls around the place. Girls were in and out of VIP like it was nothing. Been there, done that. They brought out dem Carter Boys to come perform a few songs and serenade a few girls. Now, they been around for a minute, touring colleges and doing homecomings, but it was just now that they were starting to appear on TV with their music videos, traveling to different places to perform around the country.

My main focus was Jodie Carter, the lead nigga in the group who can sing. If Trey Songz was a straight hood nigga? He would be Jodie.

"Where my twin at?" Jodie said into the mic, looking around as he stepped down from the stage. "Where Trent go?"

"Nigga got kicked out!" someone said as girls started to surround Jodie, who was walking in my direction. Damn, he was fine, and he knew it. Tall, dark, sexy brown with those tattoos and sleepy bedroom eyes. Teardrop tattoos underneath his right eye only made my body respond even more. I loved me a thug nigga, especially one in a gang, and I knew all of four of them were affiliated. Red flags stayed hanging in the back pockets. Rarely would you catch them wearing blue.

"Ayo, fellas in the building! I know this y'all party, but uh . . ." He called out into the mic as he looked back at his brothers with a huge grin, laughing. "I'm taking a few ladies with me back to the crib. Who trying to roll with the Carter Boys?" Jodie asked as every girl in the building started screaming.

Fuck that, I grabbed Porscha's hand and started to make my move. "Jahiem, you grabbing a couple of bad bitches with you tonight, bruh?"

"Hell, yeah," Jahiem answered into the mic as girls nearly tore at each other to get to the four of them. All of them were fine, don't get me wrong. All fine as fuck dread heads with different styles, but there was only one Jodie. He was the one that was going to make the most money, the one I wanted to fuck with.

"Where are we going?" Porscha said as we stepped outside the club, heading straight to the side of the building where four black trucks were parked, posted up. "How you even know this is their ride?"

"Because I watched them pull up in it, girl. We going to his house, and when I tell you I'm fucking Jodie's brains out? I'm going to make sure he remembers my name, okay?" I declared as she laughed, waving me off. "I will be that nigga's main girl by the end of the night."

"This nigga grabbing bitches off the dance floor. What makes you think he's going to take us with him?" she questioned as I flipped my hair off my shoulders.

I glanced over, seeing the crowd move. The boys were making their way over to the trucks now as the music cut off. I quickly slid my panties off from underneath my body con dress and tossed them in the parking lot. Didn't need them. I knew what I wanted, and I wasn't going to stop until I got it.

"You straight crazy." Porscha laughed with a shake of her head just as I heard Jodie's voice.

"Bruh, we about to get it in tonight! You feel me? I'm talking I want all three of you bitches in the bed with me," Jodie said as the girls giggled.

I recognized two of them from the yard as the boys all came around the car to see Porscha and I standing there, smiling. I flipped my hair back, licking my lips as I eyed Jodie.

"Oh, shit. You got girls waiting by the car," Anthony Carter said with a laugh. "Prepared hoes, nigga. You might as well take them too."

"Nah, he can't have them all," Jahiem argued, letting go of his girl. I recognized her from psychology class. Girls were trying to get it in tonight.

"What's ya name, baby?" Jodie asked, pulling his jeans up as he eyed me, completely ignoring Porscha.

"Tia." I smiled. "Trying to see what's up with this little after party you trying to have."

"Oh, yeah?" He smirked, looking back at his brothers. "I mean, I got a car full, baby. You may have to ride with my brothers until I can get to you."

"She can ride me," Jahiem joked as they laughed. I didn't.

"Only thing I'm riding is Jodie," I said, making it very clear I didn't need the backup rappers interfering.

"Nah, that's not how we work," Jahiem started, trying to get an attitude. "You fuck one, you fucking them all, baby. So, if you ain't down with that—"

"Nigga, you wasting everybody's time," I started, cutting him off, eyes never leaving Jodie.

"Shit, she not playing no games, bruh. Let her ride with me," Jodie said, opening the car door. "Yo' friend gotta bounce, though."

"What!" Porscha gasped as I quickly went over to the other side, making sure I sat in the passenger's seat, not once looking back at Porscha.

If it was the other way around, she would have done the exact same to me, and she has. Soon as Jodie got in and started to drive, I could feel myself getting excited. I had to bring out all the stops to impress him. All my tricks, all the sexy moans. A nigga love it when you moan for them. Even if the sex is bad, you fake it till you make it, boo.

So, I listened to the girls in the back try to talk to Jodie, trying to impress him, but I stayed silent. No need to do all of that. I'd let the sex speak for itself.

"Why you so quiet, baby?" Jodie asked, merging onto the highway as he looked at me leaning back in the seat. Nigga was a straight thug the way he was leaning with one hand on the steering wheel, dreads pulled back. Fine as fuck.

"Because I want to let my body speak for itself when I get you in that bed," I said, and he smiled, licking his lips.

"Oh, for real?" He laughed. "You talking a lot of shit, shawty."

"That's because I can back it up."

"How you know Trent?" one of the girls asked. I rolled my eyes.

"That's my brother, baby girl," he said, rolling his window down as he sped up to get beside his brother in the next lane over. "Nigga, fuck wrong with you? You driving like a little ol' bitch!" he yelled out the window, laughing as the girl in the passenger's seat stuck out her tongue. Jahiem flipped him the bird before speeding off, weaving in and out of lanes with Jodie trying to follow him.

"Yo' real brother, or play-play?" another girl asked, and I rolled my eyes again. Bitch sounded so stupid.

"Nah, that's my real blood brother. I'm a triplet. Me, Trent, and my sister, we all the same age, born same day. My sister is the oldest, then me by a minute, and Trent came out late as fuck. Probably like two minutes after me."

"Whaat? Oh my God!" The girls screamed as I thought about how I had fucked Trent. Shit, I would keep that to myself.

"Since y'all ladies looking good as fuck and taking the time out of yo' busy lives to come fuck with a real nigga like me, I'll let y'all know my first name," he said, sticking out his tongue. Damn, I felt myself get wet just off that alone. You could tell he was a freak, and now looking at him, I could see he had the exact same mannerisms as Trent. They didn't look nothing alike, but Jodie was a pretty boy too. "Jodie is my middle name. First name is Elijah."

"Oh my God, that's so sexy. I like Elijah," one of them said as he looked at me, blowing me a kiss. Yeah, Trent all the way, hands down.

When we got to his house over on the east side, we all stepped out, with me hiking my dress up to show a peek of the cheeks sitting right. We were rolling deep as fuck: four boys, about ten girls. Somehow, I had to get Jodie by myself, alone, and with me for the rest of the night. I wasn't about sharing, and damn sure not about fucking a bitch to look cute in front of niggas. Keep that gay shit at a distance. I don't play that.

"Yo, Ontrell! We got drinks?" Jahiem yelled out as he came up behind me, smacking my ass hard. I quickly turned around. He kept walking, laughing like the shit was funny.

"Nigga, that's okay, because that's as close as you're going to get to this ass!" I yelled, following them in the house.

"You still think you fucking with my younger brother?" Jahiem laughed, dreads moving about.

Now, don't get me wrong. Nothing wrong with how Jahiem looked—tall, caramel complexion, with locs and dark brown, low-set eyes like Elijah; big, beefy body, with the tattoos all over him. Red bandana stayed hanging out his back pocket. He was cute, but he had no future, no promise, nothing. I wanted the one who was most popular, able to make the most money, so I could fucking quit school and live up under him for the rest of my life, spending a nigga's money, okay?

"Let's get these girls some drinks in their hand." Elijah started passing out bottles.

I looked around the huge house and smiled. Niggas were living straight. I could hear music coming from the basement down below, and I spotted the huge flat screen that took up the whole wall in the living room. They had a dining room fully decorated for show, and another for eating near the huge kitchen. It was nice in there—brand new furniture, bottles that had yet to be opened decorated the countertops, money stacked up on the table we were sitting at, with duffle bags full of money on the floor. Yeah, I had to make sure I was on my A game that night. Definitely wouldn't drink too much because I was focused. I saw who I wanted, the life I wanted, and the way to get it.

"Aye, turn that music up. Let's see who trying to dance for some money," Jahiem said, and Anthony turned up the sound system, blasting one of their strip club anthems.

Jahiem eyed me with a stack full in his hand. "Bitch with the biggest attitude better twerk the best or you out the house."

I smirked as I lifted up my dress, revealing the lack of panties, and started twerking for my life.

"Ohhhh, shit! Oh, you definitely getting fucked tonight!" Elijah laughed, tossing bills at me.

I decided to throw it in Jahiem's face, letting him get a taste of what his brother was going to get. Bending over, I revealed how I was completely shaved, bump free, smooth skin, smell free, and tight all around. The other girls tried to compete, but all eyes were on me as I dropped it like it was hot before bringing it back up.

"Aye! Aye! Yo, Jahiem mad, bruh! Look at him!" Ontrell laughed as I glanced at Jahiem's sour face. Yeah, nigga was salty as fuck, but his eyes were roaming hard. I didn't let him touch me, but he was always welcomed to look. Always.

For that next hour, we all spent it drinking, dancing, and just playing new music that had yet to be released, before Elijah stripped down to his boxers, taking my hand as he led me upstairs.

"Y'all mothafuckas good night," he said as I smirked at the jealous bitches who were left with the rejects of the Carters. "I'm about to get it in."

"Aye, I got next!" Ontrell called out with two girls on his lap, kissing his ear.

"Nah, no you don't," I answered, and Elijah laughed with a shrug.

"She only want me, bruh," he said as we walked down the long hallway to the master bedroom.

He cut the lights on, revealing the huge California king-sized bed, the flat screen on the wall, and a wooden dresser. There were two huge windows with blinds closed tightly shut, and a door that led to his own private bathroom. I turned around to smile at him as he closed the door, dreads moving about. His dick was already hard for me, so I just stripped down out of my dress and took off my bra, standing before him as he rubbed his chin, looking me over.

"You really not playing no games," he said in a low voice. "Come here. Back all that shit up you was talking in the car, shawty."

"Gladly." I smiled, cutting the lights off. It was pitch black in there, exactly how I wanted it. All I wanted him to focus on was the feeling.

I started kissing his neck, pressing my body up against his while sliding my hand inside his boxers. Oooh, shit, the nigga was big. Exactly how I pictured it.

"Hold up, baby," he breathed. "Let me get a condom."

"You don't need it with me. I'm on birth control," I lied, feeling him smile against my skin before gently biting my shoulder then replacing it with a smooth, wet kiss.

Hmmm . . . sensual nigga. Just like his voice.

"Nah, I'm wrapping my shit up, baby, just to be on the safe side. Hold up. Go lay on the bed for me and wait," he demanded as he stepped out the door.

I quickly checked myself, smelling underneath my arms, sticking my fingers in between my legs to smell. I wanted to make sure all was good. No mistakes needed to happen tonight. Everything had to be perfect. So, I lay back on the bed, legs wide, wondering if I should play it freaky or sexy. My mind was racing with so many ideas. I decided to go with sexy. Too many hoes had probably been in that bed doing the most, trying to be freaky as hell, doing shit they probably would never do with anyone else. Nah, not me. I lay back on the bed as the door crept open before closing again.

"You ready?" I asked.

"Hell, yeah," he said, making me smile.

The moment I felt him get on the bed, I did a quick move, pushing him back down as I straddled him.

"Shit, you got it, baby." He laughed as I started to kiss his neck softly, feeling his hands slide down my back to grip my ass.

Damn, this nigga's body felt good on mine. We were perfect together, and I wanted him to see that. I let my tongue drag down his chest, kissing each nipple, hearing him groan in response as he gripped my ass hard. Hot spot for sure. I worked my way over to the other one, circling it before clamping down hard on it, politely pulling at it with my teeth.

"Fuck, baby, chill," he breathed in a shaky voice.

I continued to kiss his stomach before dipping my tongue in his belly button. Nails lightly clawed down his thickly tatted skin as I sucked, dipped, and pulled at the belly button. Another hot spot. Nigga nearly bucked me off of him.

"You like that?" I asked, mouth against his body like it was my life support to feed.

"Hell yeah, baby. Do it again," he whispered, grabbing my head.

I dipped my tongue in his belly button again, feeling his hips stiffen up. Got this nigga ready. I slid back as I pulled out his—Damn! Nigga got even harder. Nigga was huge. That belly button lick must have done it. Didn't matter. Watch a bitch like me work. Take notes, readers. This? This is how you get a man and keep a man like Elijah Jodie Carter.

With my mouth making its way between his legs, my fingers smoothed down the prickly hairs as I trailed his length, pre-cum dripping from the head. I took the entire muscle into my mouth, careful to keep my teeth from rubbing as I went in on his dick, lips moving, tongue moving, and head moving at different strokes like a pro.

"Ssssssssssst! Ahhh, shit!" he hollered out, grabbing my head with both hands as he pushed himself farther into me. "Faawk!" He groaned, head going back as he bent his knees. Nigga was acting like a straight bitch as he came in my mouth hard. I took it in, though, swallowing every bit as I continued. "Please . . . Please . . ." he begged in a shaky voice. "Chill out, shawty. Shit!" he mumbled in a shaky voice. "Damn, you got head game like a mothafucka."

I slid up as I flipped my hair off my shoulders, licking my lips as I proceeded to straddle him, aiming myself on top of him. The second nut was always the hardest to bust. I smiled, looking down at him as I slid down slowly on him, gripped the headboard, and started twerking, making my hips pop on beat. I could barely make out his face, but I could see he was smiling hard as hell, loving every minute of it.

Suddenly, without warning, he grabbed me by the waist and damn near flipped me back on the bed, with my head hanging off the edge, and slid right into me without missing a beat. Dreads grazing my face as I cried out. Damn, I wasn't expecting that. I gripped his locs, with my legs wrapped around him to bring him closer.

"Baby," I moaned, feeling my legs shake violently against his body. "Wait, baby. I don't want to cum yet. Please wait," I begged softly, feeling him lift my right leg up, holding it in place.

He leaned in, kissing my neck as he slowed down, pressing up against my body. I gripped his back, closing my eyes, enjoying his lips on me as he sucked on my collarbone. Our bodies were just rocking up and down as one, breathing together.

"You feel perfect in me," I breathed, and I wasn't lying. Wasn't faking it like I normally did. This nigga really did feel like my perfect match.

"I do?" he said, smiling against my skin as he lifted my chin up to gently bite underneath my jaw.

I let out a moan, feeling those lips caress my skin. He was a lover for sure. His singing voice matched the way he had sex: rough when he wanted to be, but could slow it down and make love to your body like it was nothing.

"You like me being in you, baby?"

"Mm-hmm," I moaned, feeling him pull out.

He backed up and took my right leg, kissing my ankle. Oh, shit! Nigga was about to start over from the beginning. When I tell y'all he damn near kissed every inch of my body—calves, knees, thighs—before spreading me wide to taste me like I was his last meal? Let me just say I came before he even got a chance to eat. No dick, no tongue, nothing; I had an orgasm just being in the bed with him period. That's how good I had it. I couldn't wait until I told everybody about Elijah.

By the time we slowed down, I was on top, with him sitting up against the headboard, arms wrapped around me as we kissed, bodies interlocked, slowly riding him just because I could.

"You had a good time, baby?" he asked as I moved his dreads back, smiling as he kissed my shoulder. I nodded. "Who's the best you ever had?"

"You are." I smiled, feeling him pull me closer to his body.

"Nah, baby, what's my name? What they call me?"

"Jodie," I moaned, running my fingers through his locs.

"Nah-uh. What's my name, baby? You know it," he continued.

I smirked. "Elijah, baby."

"Nope," he said with a small laugh. "Wrong Carter."

I felt my body go numb as I froze, hearing him laugh to himself as he let go of me. Heart beating wildly, I tried looking at him, but the room was pitch black. All I saw was an outline of a face with dreads. They all had fucking dreads, though. Quickly, I got up, nearly falling off the bed. I slid my hand along the wall and flipped on the light switch. My heart dropped, seeing Jahiem laying on his side, naked and laughing.

"Ahh, shit," he said. "I can't even talk shit about yo' ho ass because you might just be the best head I ever had, baby. Real shit. Sucked my dick like a true champion."

"Bruh, you done? I need the room!" Elijah yelled out from outside.

I opened the door, seeing he was standing there with two girls who smirked at me, like, *Bitch, you so dumb.*

"Aye! E, you missed out," Jahiem said as my eyes watered up.

I couldn't . . . I didn't even know what to say.

"Bitch speechless." Elijah laughed, moving past me to get in the room. "Nigga, get the fuck on so I can get my bitches right for the night."

All I kept thinking about was, *I let this nigga cum twice in me.*

Jahiem tossed me my dress as he walked out of the room, slipping on his basketball shorts.

"Why would you do that?" I yelled at the both of them, feeling a tear slide down as I quickly wiped my face. I felt so disgusting and so fucking stupid. I'm not even trying to mention violated, but that's how I felt.

"I mean, shit," Elijah said with a shrug, hand on the door. "That's how us Carter Boys do it. Ain't that right, bruh?" He slapped hands with Jahiem as they laughed.

Elijah tossed me a look with another shrug of his shoulders. "I only fuck with bisexual hoes, shawty. Sorry." He closed the door in my face.

I looked at Jahiem in disgust as he smirked, slapping my ass.

"You are welcomed back any time, baby. Remember that. Here." He tossed me a fifty-dollar bill, letting it cascade to the floor. "Go call you a cab and get the fuck on. Next time you want to disrespect one brother for another, remember this night."

"Nigga, fuck you," I spat out hatefully as Jahiem laughed, shaking his head.

"You got a special spot in my bed for when you want another go." He grabbed his dick before turning away, laughing. "You thought I wasn't about to hit. Ha!"

Sundays

Trent

"Shit," I mumbled as I rolled on my back, almost falling off the bed. I opened my eyes, looking around to see two girls laying in the bed next to me, naked, and taking up most of the space. I smirked before grabbing my phone to check the time. It was going on eleven o'clock in the morning. Sunday. Party was wild as fuck last night. I was having a good time until a bitch punched me in my shit. I touched my eye, still feeling tender as I slowly sat up, careful not to wake the girls.

Checking my Instagram, I saw snippets of the fight on my timeline before logging on to Facebook. So, these mothafuckas really put it out there. The whole video of the fight between me and that Jade girl was on the Internet. I clicked on it and watched a little bit of it, seeing she was half-ass naked, throwing drinks in my direction. Only showed me briefly before going back to her, because she pretty much had on nothing. No panties, nothing. Squinting my eyes, I could tell she was crying the entire time. Her eyes were watery as she yelled at me before I watched myself push her down to the floor. Fuck! I wasn't trying to be that dude. I hated that I even got to that point of anger. I never put my hands on a woman in a violent way like that. Am I wrong for saying she deserved that shit, though, and was lucky I didn't beat her ass? Hell nah, I'm not wrong, but I did want to fix this shit before it got worse.

So, after kicking the girls out my room, I showered up, got dressed, and met up with my brothers at the local park just a few blocks down from the yard. Every Sunday, I played basketball with these niggas. I wasn't about that street life and hustle this, hustle that. I'd hustle for my fucking degree and to become the most successful lawyer out there, but it didn't mean I couldn't vibe with niggas from the hood, because that's where I grew up. You feel me? They were my blood, my family. So, if my demeanor changes while you reading, it's because I'm getting to my true self.

"What up, pretty boy! I heard about yo' crazy ass," Jahiem said as he passed me the ball.

I just laughed with a shake of my head, taking off my shirt. It was hot as fuck, with the sun blazing on an early Sunday afternoon, the backdrop of the city behind us as cars drove by, blasting music. We was straight in the middle of the hood.

"Who was the girl? It happened before we got there, because we were looking for you, but they said you got kicked out," Ant said.

I set my stuff down on the wooden bench before bouncing the ball, taking a shot. "Shit was crazy, bruh," I let out with a shake of my head. "She just came at me. I know I fucked up by saying what I said, but I wasn't expecting her to hit me in the face. That shit still hurt."

"Man, yo' bitch ass could never take a hit!" Jahiem laughed as a black Yukon truck pulled up. At the moment, it was Jahiem, Anthony who we called Ant, and Shiloh who we called Shy, sitting on the bench, chilling. Then there was Ontrell, who goes both ways, and the youngest at twenty-one. We knew he was gay ever since we were little, and I personally didn't give a fuck. He wasn't over the top with that shit like most of those mothafuckas, and he still fucked around with girls. Had a boyfriend and everything, but stayed cheating on that nigga like it was nothing. Then there was Talin, who was the only other brother who went to school with me, and now Elijah, my wild-ass twin brother, who just pulled up. We were actually triplets, but our sister was always late to come here, because she usually went to church with our grandma. All of us together didn't share the same mamas, but we all kept close and practically grew up together. Only other brother that shared our mama with me, Elijah, and Olivia was Shiloh. Talin and Jahiem had their own mama, and Ontrell and Ant shared a mama. Confusing as fuck, right? Pops was a fucking rolling stone back in the day. All of us together make up the Carters. All of us were born hood as fuck, but Talin, myself, and Olivia made it out that shit by going to school. The rest were in and out of jail like it was nothing, but now Elijah, Jahiem, Ontrell, and Ant were becoming big in the local music scene, so I hoped this kept them out of the pen for good.

"Look at this mothafucka right here." Jahiem laughed as Elijah stepped out the truck, trying to flex. "Bruh, ain't no bitches out here. Who you trying to impress with yo' ugly ass, boy?"

"What up, Jodie Carter!" Talin joked, calling Elijah by his stage name.

"Nigga, shut up!" E laughed, stepping onto the blacktop as he smirked at me. "What up, wife beater? Heard you got yo' ass beat by a bitch last night."

"Fuck outta here, nigga," I said, slapping hands as I hugged my brother.

All we were missing was our sister. Since we didn't see much of each other during the week, we made sure we used Sunday afternoons to catch up and stay close as a family.

"Aye, Ant, how you deal with yo' baby mama being pregnant? Toni getting a li'l too crazy for me," Talin complained as I watched my sister's red Volkswagen beetle pull up. She and I favored each other with the hazel eyes, but she had the dark complexion of Elijah. Nobody believed we were triplets, but that's cool. Didn't have to prove shit to nobody. Just know when our birthday hit, watch how we turn up.

"Shit, just tune that shit out, Talin. She can't help it sometimes. You just now starting out, and I know Toni probably been snapping on yo' ass since y'all were little, so just stick it out."

"Ayo, Livie!" E called out, being dramatic as usual.

She stepped out of the car in her church dress and heels, taking her hat off and waving. She was the definition of a good girl. You can tell Grandma raised her, kept her away from us boys so she could still grow into a young lady. Hear my grandma tell it, growing up we were always told to protect her at all costs. She was the only female and considered the baby even though Ontrell was the youngest. That's why she almost never brought a boyfriend around, and if she did, he was gone by the next day. We didn't play that shit.

"I want to know what happened last night, Trent," she called out as she walked onto the blacktop, heels clicking before sitting down next to Shiloh, linking arms with him. I dropped my head, knowing I wasn't going to escape this shit.

"How did all of that shit start? I heard she just came up to you and started going crazy on you," E put in.

"I would have straight hit that bitch in the face if it was me," Shiloh chimed in.

"Really, Shiloh?" Olivia retorted, pushing him as he smiled.

"Aye, just because a bitch can hit a male don't mean a nigga should sit there and take it. You did what you had to do. I saw the video. She looked crazy as hell."

"That's not what you should have done at all," Olivia countered, looking hard at me through her shades.

"I probably would have—"

"Can y'all let me tell the fucking story?" I snapped, taking the ball from Ant's hand as I started taking free throws. When it became silent, I started the story from the beginning.

Y'all know what the fuck happened, so I'm not repeating it, but I told them everything, including the truth.

"Ahhh, you lied with yo' pussy ass! No wonder she was ready to beat yo' ass, nigga. Damn!" E laughed, nearly falling out on the ground, dreads moving about.

"I didn't think she was going to react like that," I argued, playing one on one with Talin, trying to take the ball from him.

"So, now what are you going to do? You need to apologize," Olivia demanded.

"I already did. She spit in my face. You didn't see that in the video?"

"Who is she?"

"I want to meet her. I ain't seen the video. She look good?" Ant asked as I blocked a shot from Talin, who laughed.

"I got the video up right now," Olivia said as they all crowded around the bench. I could hear Jade yelling at me like a nigga talking to another nigga.

"Oh, shit," E said, watching the video with a huge grin. "She straight handled you, bruh. You'on even know how to react. Look at his face!"

"Ohhh!" they all let out in unison as I kept shooting the ball in the net by my damn self on the court.

"She's fine as hell, though," Ant said, taking the ball as he started to bounce it.

Olivia shook her head in shame as she put the phone down.

"She's straight. She's from up north," I said, snatching the ball back, dribbling in between my legs, moving with a quickness.

"You know how to shut girls like her up? Give her the D, bruh. That's all girls want at the end of the day," Talin said. "It works for my girl every time. When she start going off at the mouth, fill that shit up. Dick calms hoes down; I'm telling you."

"He ain't lying." Jahiem agreed with Ant, putting in his two cents as we played a two-on-two, but Elijah somehow managed to disrupt that shit.

"Oh, them bitches rough as fuck up there," E said, snatching the ball from me.

"Nigga, move!" I snapped, pushing him. Wasn't even part of the fucking game, but I watched him take the shot, barely making it.

"Aye, don't take yo' anger out on me because you got hit by a girl," he cracked, hitting me hard in the chest before taking off like a bitch, laughing. I hate—and love—my brothers. I swear I do.

"Oh, bruh, tell 'em about last night. So, this fool went out to the gas station, met this chick who was walking around in her fucking panties, bruh. Swear to God on my mama," Ant started as E laughed.

"Aye, she got a fat ass, though. I couldn't ignore that shit, but I went up to her like, I know you gon' let me hit, shawty," E said, acting it out. "I'm thinking she knew who I was. She was staring so hard at me, I just knew. Bitch had no clue."

"Oh, yeah, I remember her. You ever called her?" Shiloh asked, lighting up his blunt.

"Nah, I'ma call her tonight. See what she getting into. I'm just trying to smash. That ass was too perfect to ignore. Don't even have a cell phone. Bitch said she only got a house phone."

"You know she lying," I told him blatantly. Who didn't have a phone these days?

"I know. All I'm trying to do is hit it and move on. She making me work for it, but I'll chase it for a minute until I get bored. Oh, shit, then we switched up on one of them hoes last night. She wasn't trying to fuck with none of these niggas but me, so I let Jahiem hit it without her knowing."

"Bruh, what?" I said, confused, as Olivia's mouth dropped. Jahiem was just cheesing like a kid in the candy store.

"We switched up on her ass. I wasn't about to do it, but she cut the lights off, and I was like, I wonder can we pull this off. Yo, she fucked that nigga thinking it was me," E said.

"Damn right! Said I was the best she ever had," Jahiem boasted with a laugh.

"That's rape!" Olivia cried out.

"Hell nah, she came in there willingly, wanting to fuck," Jahiem argued. "Don't say I raped a bitch, because she wasn't trying to stop it."

"What did she say when she found out it was you?" Shiloh asked as Ontrell laughed with a shake of his head.

"I mean, what can she say? At the end of the night, I got the pussy, so that's all that matters. Ho gave award-worthy head, too," he said. We laughed—all but Olivia, who turned to look back at me.

"Trent, you have to go seriously apologize to that girl. I'm sure she's hating waking up to seeing these videos and pictures of her," Olivia continued.

"You seeing anyone, Livie?" Jahiem asked, and she rolled her eyes.

"If I was, I wouldn't tell you guys until I was already married. Last time I let you guys meet my boyfriend, he never called me back. So, no."

"I mean, that nigga was a punk anyway. You can do better than that," I said, taking a shot at the net.

"I trust you guys will stay out of my business like I do yours?" was all she said as I smiled. We all knew what that meant. She knew more stuff about all of us—the cheating, the baby mama drama, watching the kids when someone wanted to go fuck someone—and for the most part, she kept her mouth closed. She even covered for me a couple of times on the yard. Without warning, we all went over to her, sweaty bodies and all, and hugged her as she screamed, "Oh my God! I can't stand y'all! Get off me!" She laughed.

"We love you, Livie!" I cooed, kissing the side of her face as she tried squirming out from underneath us.

Shiloh just chilled. He was like that, but the rest of us were over the top as we attacked her, tickling her, making her laugh before letting her go.

"I can't stand none of y'all," she mumbled.

"Aye, you know you my favorite sister, right?" E said as she laughed.

"I'm your only sister, dumbass," she retorted.

Shiloh put his arm around her and kissed her cheek before letting go. Like I said, the nigga was simply chill, but even he appreciated all that she did for us, because without her, we would have been looking like the dogs we truly were to these girls in Atlanta. Shit, I guess I could go find this Jade chick and attempt to apologize again. I just didn't know how she was going to take it now that the videos were up.

Jade

"I don't even fucking know, son." I laughed, passing the blunt back to my homeboy, Chris. It was a late Sunday night, and I was sure by now everyone had seen or heard what happened at the party the night before. I had copped a ride back with a girl I knew from school and went to bed icing my ankle. Now I was sitting out here in the middle of the yard, watching everyone walk the campus at night. Class was starting back up the next day, and I was ready for this weekend to be over. I hadn't expected it to turn out the way that it did. I was all over the Internet. People were coming up to me in the café, asking me what happened, was I okay, and saying they can't believe he pushed me. I wanted to tell them don't make me out to be the fucking victim. I murked that nigga straight in the face. Hadn't seen or heard from him since, and I was glad. But, what he told me that night stuck with me hard, and I ended up regretting my actions completely, knowing I could have handled it better.

"Has DJ seen the video?" Chris asked, taking a pull on the blunt.

"Yeah, we talked about it. She wasn't happy about it, and she told me she wished that nigga would have tried that shit while she was there. You know she ain't scared of nobody," I told him, watching the marching band walk to the field in their practice uniforms.

"Hell, no. These cats down here, boy, I swear," Chris said, shaking his head. "They wouldn't last a day up north, especially in Jersey."

"Nigga, especially in New York! Fuck you mean, son?" I laughed, playfully shoving him.

We fell into an easy silence, just people watching. Everyone was out tonight—girls cliquing up, niggas posted on the steps of their dorm watching the clique of females. A couple of guys behind us were tossing a ball back and forth. We sat on the brick circle that held the statue of the first president and founder of this college. I kept it casual, you know, wearing jeans, red Chucks, and a cropped red sweater with my blond locs up in a ponytail, a few hanging in the front and back. My eyebrow piercing was a matching red, along with the two on my tongue. Ankle still hurt like shit, but I was a trooper.

"Here," Chris said, passing me the blunt.

I took a pull on it, watching a couple of broads walk by thinking they were cute. Fuck they dress up for in the middle of the night on a college campus? I didn't get it. Heels and purses to class? Save that for outside the yard at a club or something. Some of these girls here did the most, for the least bit of attention from dick. Didn't make sense.

"Aye, bruh!" someone said, coming up to Chris, slapping hands with him while smiling hard at me. "I heard about you."

"What did you hear?" I smirked.

"You whooped a nigga's ass," Chris came in, and I laughed.

"I wish I did," I mumbled, blowing smoke out. "Put all that stuff out on the Internet about me—fuck is wrong with you? Think I won't say nothing?"

"Nah, that's not it," I heard a voice say as I turned around quick, almost literally falling back to see Trent walking with a few of his fraternity brothers. Shit, he was fine, no denying that: gray pants with black dress shoes, wine-colored button-down shirt balancing out his light complexion, clean-cut hair, with his toned body trying to peek through his shirt. Damn. Nigga had the nerve to wear frames like he suddenly needed glasses, but damn if he wasn't fine with those light eyes.

"Oh, shit," Chris coughed, trying to contain his laughter.

They walked up over to us, looking like they had just got off a nine-to-five job. Armond smirked at me, but I didn't smile back, not even a hint of happiness in my face.

"Can you give me a minute with her?" Trent asked Chris, who looked at me, wanting to know my answer.

"Go. I'll meet you back in the room," I told Chris, and we hugged.

Looking back at Trent, I watched his eyes squint, lingering on Chris before looking at me. Fuck kind of look was that? Gay. Had to be.

"So, what's good? You can't tell yo' boys to leave, or you can't talk to me without backup?" I pressed as he rolled his eyes, looking at his brothers.

"Y'all go. Meet y'all back at the house," he said as they walked off, giving each other dap.

"Don't hurt 'im too bad, Jade!" Armond called out, and I smiled. "Nigga got a thing for you!"

"Bruh, shut the fuck up!" Trent snapped, and my smile dropped. "Look," he said, looking at me as our eyes locked, "I came to the room, but they said you were out on the yard."

"Okay?" I said with an attitude. "You found me. So what?"

"I'm trying to get to that if you let me finish."

"Nigga, I really don't have shit to say to you. You see this?" I lifted my leg up to show him how bruised and swollen my ankle was. "You did that shit, B. Not me."

"You tried fighting me in heels," he pointed out. "You did that shit to yo'self. Come to me on some grown-up shit."

"Oh, after you went around lying on yo' dick like a li'l-ass boy?" I snapped, watching a couple of guys walk slowly by, all in our conversation. Even Trent turned around like, *fuck y'all staring at?*

"Ain't that the girl with the bumps?"

"Nah, it ain't the girl," Trent said, cutting him off as he turned fully around. "Nigga, get the fuck on." They quickly kept walking as Trent turned to look at me, sighing. "I'm trying to tell you I'm sorry, but holding a conversation with you is impossible."

I stayed quiet, waiting. He stared at me through the frames, and I stared back, fumbling with my tongue rings.

Fuck it.

"Nigga, speak! I'm quiet and I'm listening. Say what you gotta say," I snapped suddenly.

"See, this is why I can't do this shit." He backed up with a shake of his head.

"You sound like a straight-up female just then," I said, laughing hard. "Oh my God, yo. I don't even know how I let you attempt to fuck me, but you give some bomb-ass head, though. I'll give you that."

The face he made looked like I'd struck a chord in him.

"You know what? Let's settle this shit once and for all. All this started with sex; let's end it with sex," he stated.

My eyes grew wide. "Huh?" I let out, head cocked back.

"Talking all this shit to each other when really you mad because of what I said, and I'm mad because you wouldn't let me redeem myself. Let's end this shit now, and we don't ever have to speak to each other again. One time. One night. You and me. Let's go. I will tear that ass up and shut you the fuck up for good."

I nearly choked on my own spit as I looked at him, trying to catch my breath without being dramatic about it. He was serious. No smile, no nothing. Dead-ass serious.

"What happened to 'I don't fuck dark-skin girls'?" I reminded him, mocking his annoying, soft-ass voice.

"You'll be my first and last," was all he said. "You in or out? I'm not playing no games, and

I'm not trying to have this conversation last longer than it has to, because I really don't even like being around you like that."

I continued to stare at him, feeling myself already getting wet. Shit, if he came early again, he already knew it was a wrap. His pride, manhood, his everything would be over. Might as well drop out of school, because I would never, ever let him live it down. I stood up, straight making sure I was close to him so he could hear me.

"Nigga, if this thing here"—I looked down at his dick, seeing he was already hard—"bust one nut before I get my first, then it's a wrap. No head, all I want is dick."

"Bet," was all he said as he started walking.

I followed him, trying to cover up my limp. No sense in looking weak, because I was about to throw every move, every trick in the book at this pretty boy. He wasn't going to last five minutes with me.

"We going to yo' place?" he asked me.

"Yeah," I said, following him to the parking lot where his car was. Drove a nice white Chevy Cavalier. I wish y'all reading this could feel how intense this was, because nigga was not playing no games. Shit, neither was I. I came ready to ball, nigga.

"Aye, don't fuck up my floors with yo' dirty-ass shoes," he said as I looked at my Chucks, seeing they had a few grass cuts on them.

"How about drive the fucking car, pretty boy?" I retorted, slamming the door. He looked at me like he was ready to try something. "Fuck you staring at?"

"Why you slamming my door like that?"

"Boy, just drive! Damn! You about to get fucked and you trying to argue with me, like, really?"

"Take them piercings out yo' mouth. I don't wanna feel that shit on me. And take 'em out yo' nipples, too," he said, backing out as my mouth dropped. Dude had some nerve.

"How about you focus on not spitting yo' kids out ahead of time?" I came back sarcastically before thinking.

Let me just end the chatter now, I thought.

"No, how about shut the fuck up talking to me altogether? We don't gotta speak. Just do what you gotta do to prove a point and then bounce, nigga."

"Say no more," he said, speeding out of the parking lot. Literally we could have walked to my building, because we made it in less than thirty seconds. He found a parking spot, and we both got out, me slamming the door even harder just to piss him off.

He looked back at me, eyes wide. "I said don't do that shit!"

"Well, I did it," I said, rolling my neck and eyes as I kept walking. "With yo' plastic glasses–wearing ass." I shook my short locs loose as we walked inside the building.

"You so fucking childish, I swear," he mumbled as we hit that corner to go on the stairway. "Don't even know you like that, but you childish as fuck. Don't even act like a grown woman. Don't even dress like one."

"Whatever, gay mothafucka," I snapped. I hated that. I hated that he continued to say that, knocking at my lack of womanhood. *Well, nigga, if you would have acted right in the first place, you would have never saw this side of me.*

"I'll be that," was all he said as we made it to my floor. "Who's in the room right now?"

"Nigga, how would I know? Didn't you just leave—"

"Shut up," he said, cutting me off with his hand up. My mouth dropped. "It was just a simple fucking question; not trying to hear that mouth."

"Son, regardless of us fucking? You not gonna talk to me any kind of way!" I snapped, digging in my back pocket for my room key as we came to my door. "Let's get that shit straight right now." I opened the door, seeing Tia, Porscha, and another girl in the living room, staring at me as Jordyn walked out of the kitchen with a spoon hanging in her mouth, eyes wide at us. I know we had to be loud as hell in the hallway.

"Heeey, Kodak!" the girls all cooed, getting up as he walked in behind me, setting his stuff down.

"Girl, you ain't tell me you knew Trent like that," the unknown girl whispered to Tia.

"What up, ladies?" He smiled then turned to me without warning and picked me up with one arm wrapped around my waist, taking me to my room. I dropped my keys, wrapping my legs around him as we walked in. He closed the door with his foot. *Shit. Okay, nigga.*

No words were needed. Our eyes locked, and he immediately went for my mouth, kissing me hard while placing me back on the bed. Only light we had was from my laptop's screen saver and small lava lamp. We were breathing heavy as we quickly took off our clothes, him reaching to pull my shirt off. I smacked his hand away.

"Nigga, you got mad buttons on yo' shirt. Worry about that," I snapped, glancing at the floor near the door. I spotted feet hanging around. Bitches was at the door trying to listen. Kicking my shoes off, I was stripped down first in just a bra and panties as I sat up, kissing him once more, pressing myself against him. Shit, maybe I did want some head after all. Couldn't rely on the weak dick to get me through. The kiss was real as shit, though. I mean, I gripped his ears trying to deepen it, feeling his hands pull my body closer to him, snapping my bra off, mouth never leaving mine. It was almost like we were at war: who can kiss harder, who couldn't handle who? It was a control thing. He wanted to control because he felt like he was the man; I wanted control because I just felt like my way was the only way.

"Fuck," he let out in a low groan, slipping his hand down my panties, separating his two fingers as he slid them back up. "You wet as shit right now."

"Nigga, shut up talking," I snapped against his mouth, feeling his hand grip my ass, smacking it hard in response. I needed to be on top. I had to be.

"Lay down," he commanded, putting his fingers in his mouth, same fingers that was just in me. Nigga wanted to eat badly, though. He was one of those that couldn't help it. He had to do it.

I laid back as he slipped my panties off, and without further notice, dived in. I let out the loudest moan, one leg high up in the air before clamping down on his neck to keep him in place.

Nigga had a cow tongue. I swear that shit was thick as fuck and wet for no reason at all. My body was already trembling because he was moving with a quickness with that mouth. I just started repeating his name, over and over, begging. Eye twitching, toes curling, mouth dry; I was done.

He came up quick right before I was about to cum and spread my legs wide, placing himself in between me. Dick was standing hard at attention, long, thick, and proud. I wasn't ready. Fuck no, I wasn't ready.

"Trent, wait."

He slid in me, pulling out completely before diving right back in as I cried out. I wrapped my legs tight around him to keep him in me. I couldn't handle that pull out, slide and glide, stroke and rub, pull out all the way, snatching his warmth from inside of me before sliding right back in. I was barely keeping it together.

"Shit," he mumbled, hands coming to my neck as he gripped it firmly enough to apply just enough pressure while stroking faster. "Who's fucking you right now?" he breathed. I couldn't do shit but moan in response. "Who giving you this dick right now, Jade?"

"You are," I cried, trying to grip my bed sheets.

"Louder so everybody can hear you," he demanded, moving faster, turning himself at an angle. "I want everybody to know." He pushed deeper. "Who's fucking you?"

"You are!"

"My name isn't 'you are.' What the fuck is my name?" he let out, pushing even deeper.

My eyes closed and I felt his hands grip the backs of my thighs to push them back and spread them wide so he could have better access. "Fuck is my name, Jade?" Skin was slapping and clapping in rhythm, pound for pound, as he moved faster. His breaths were panting with my soft cries for mercy.

"Trent," I breathed, biting my lower lip. He pulled out all the way again before rotating his hips to slide back in me. "Trent!" I cried, feeling myself release all over this nigga. Shit!

He pulled out, gripped my arms, making me turn over on my stomach. Both hands clamped down behind my back, ass up in the air, with his other free hand gripping my dreads. Then he slid back into me, still catching the end of my first orgasm. Maybe second. Shit, I don't know. His hand slid to the back of my neck, holding me steady as I nearly screamed, mattress muting my sounds. All you could hear was skin slapping skin. Occasionally he would let go of my neck to grip my ass, slapping it hard. That rough shit was my weakness. He moved hard, fast, and steady, keeping pace before pulling out suddenly. I could hear his breathing, shaking and labored.

"You good?" he asked in a low voice.

I glanced at the door, seeing the girls were still standing there. listening to us have sex, before I slid down on the bed, gripping my pillow.

"Nah," was all I said, voice barely above a mumble.

"What? Nothing smart to say? No smart-ass comment?" he snapped.

I turned over on my back, spreading my legs, and shook my head. I was good, nigga.

"Thought so." He got up without any other word, slipped on his pants and shoes, leaving the shirt off, and walked out. I watched the girls scatter about, laughing like they weren't just listening to us have sex. Even Jordyn's weird ass poked her head through, trying to see what was going on.

I couldn't move. I didn't want to. Nigga had fucked me silent. Body was still jerking from the orgasm.

"Daaaamn, nigga," I let out slowly with a laugh, pulling the covers over me, smiling hard as hell. "Shit . . . Got me sitting here talking to myself. Fuck."

Grandma Glasses

Jordyn

"Jordyn! Answer the fucking phone! Told you to keep this shit in yo' room!" Tia snapped, throwing the phone hard against my room door, making me jump. "Tell yo' lame-ass friends not to call so fucking early!"

"I'm sorry," I mumbled, half asleep as I got out of my bed to get the phone. Rubbing my eyes, I opened the door, grabbed the loud cordless phone, and automatically answered, not even meaning to do so. Everyone was knocked out in the apartment, getting ready for class tomorrow. It had been one wild, crazy weekend to say the least, but it was back to business as usual. Glancing at the clock, I saw that it was almost four in the morning. Ugh.

"Hello?" I answered with a yawn, slipping back in the bed.

"What up?" a male voice said, and my eyes snapped opened.

Elijah. What the—? No, no, no. You weren't supposed to really call me.

"Do you know what time it is?" I snapped, pulling the covers over my head with a frustrated sigh.

"Only time I get peace and quiet. I didn't want to call you when I was around a bunch of people. Be glad I'm even calling you, because I got a bunch of other bitches I could be fucking with. Besides, you up. You wouldn't have answered if you weren't so chill with that attitude," he said.

I opened one eye to look at the phone in confusion before hanging up. I tossed the phone on the floor after muting it, just in case he tried to call back. You'll never hear me say this throughout the book, but fuck he think this is, talking to me like I should be glad I was in his presence? I had enough shit on my plate. Didn't need to hear a selfish, egotistical, cocky son of a bitch on my phone talking like that to me.

So, when I woke up a couple hours later, I showered up, got dressed, and ate an apple for breakfast. Typical morning for Jordyn, nothing fancy like Tia, who takes hours in the bathroom to flat-iron her hair, or Jade, who blasts Jay-Z in her room every morning just to get her mind right. Me, I walked around with my headphones in my ear, listening to the next music piece I had to play, and a book in my hand, reading. I was ready for the day. Elijah was still on the back of my mind, but at this point, I didn't care. He should have probably gotten the point that I wasn't interested. If he had so many girls, so many other options, he could freely talk to them and completely forget about me.

I wore my usual sweats and hoodie, switching from class to class before finally finishing up around one, meeting up with Rita and my only male friend, Terrell. We sat in the cafeteria together in the corner, keeping to ourselves as we enjoyed a small lunch.

"You need to experience a relationship, Jordyn, at least one time. How can you have sex and not be emotionally attached to the guy?" Rita asked.

"Easy." I shrugged, chewing on my food. "Emotions complicate things. Relationships are designed for people who want to carry the weight of someone else's feelings on their shoulders and into their lives. I don't want to do that. I have my own emotions, my own life that I need to worry about. Sex is just a natural stress relief. It's pleasure and passion, raw and natural, for the body to release onto another. It's the act of doing it that I focus on, not who I'm doing it with," I stated matter-of-factly.

"So, when's the last time you relieved your stress?" Terrell asked as Rita turned her nose up at him.

"Nigga, you a sick freak, and you got a girl-friend!" she snapped as I laughed.

"It's been a while. I know I'm way overdue. Just hasn't been on my mind lately." Besides I had toys that I used, but they didn't need to know that. No one did. Not even you, the reader.

"You such a fucking robot, Jordyn. Actually, you're like a nigga in a woman's body. Fuck with no feelings. One day you're gonna get caught up," he said.

"I doubt it," I stated. "Not impossible, but I highly doubt it will happen."

"Mm-hmm," Rita mumbled, chomping on a fry before her eyes went wide as if she remembered something. "So, back to what this nigga Elijah did last night," Rita said suddenly. "Now I have to meet this nigga. I can't believe you hung up on him and didn't mention me."

"You can have him. I swear you can," I stated. "He's too much for me. Too wild. Told you when I first met him he was all over the place."

"So, how you know he won't call again?" Terrell asked, leaning back in his seat.

I'd known Terrell the same amount of time I'd known Rita. Met them when I first moved down here for college three years ago. I knew he had some sort of crush on me back then, but I really just looked at him as a brother, and he ended up getting a girlfriend who I rarely heard about. Probably one of the nicest guys I knew, but he could be a little too passionate at times, especially when we debated, but if someone was talking about me and he was standing there, he would always stick up for me, no questions asked. I liked that about him.

"I'm pretty sure he won't call back, but if he does, I will pass your number over to him gladly," I said, taking a bite out of my salad. "It's been a crazy weekend. My roommate Jade walked in with that guy Kodak that all the girls like—"

"Oh my God, she did what?" Rita broke out, and I laughed. "The one she got into a fight with?"

"Yeah, she walked in the apartment last night with him, and they were literally all over each other. He barely said hey before grabbing her and taking her to the room."

"So that nigga did lie."

"I heard she had herpes," Terrell said, confused, taking a piece of my pizza.

"No, that nigga lied. I bet you he did that to keep anyone else from getting to her. It only makes sense. I remember when she first transferred over here with her sister. Niggas was sweating her hard. So, of course when Trent gets a hold of her, he's not trying to share her with the yard."

"You put waaaay too much thought into that," Terrell said, and we both laughed. Even I thought that was a bit too much, and I overthink everything.

"Whatever," she said, glancing at her phone. "Shit, I'm late for this dumb-ass exam. I'll catch you bitches later. Jordyn, don't forget to send this Elijah my way. I'll take care of it."

"No problem," I said, watching Terrell get up.

"I gotta go pickup my girlfriend." He sighed.

"How's Lyric doing?" I asked. Never met her before, but I loved that name.

"I'm done with her. Been done for about a year, but she still trying to hold on to me. You know how that is," he let out as I nodded.

As soon as they both walked out, I finished up my salad before deciding to head to the library to work on my papers. Midterms don't stop for anyone. Everyone on the yard was prepping up for homecoming next week, and I wanted no part of that. Flyers were being posted up, parties were being promoted, and events were trying to form up. I would be in my room watching TV that weekend and every weekend. Last time it was homecoming, there was a shooting. I didn't want any part of that.

"Jordyn!" someone called out as I turned around. Ugh. It was Leon, a guy in my class who constantly ragged on me for no reason for the past three years. We always shared at least one class every semester; never failed. He was tall, light-skinned, lanky, with short dreads sticking out of his head underneath a 'fro. I turned around and kept walking, but he caught up with me with his friends with him. "Why you walking so fast with yo' scary self? Come here."

"Can you just leave me alone for a day, Leon?" I pressed as he wrapped his ugly, lanky arm around my shoulders.

I couldn't stand this guy. Every time I walked in the classroom, he cracked a joke. Now the whole class felt like they could say something to me, knowing I wouldn't speak up. Can you believe it's bullying in college? Like, it didn't make sense to be surrounded by these grown adults and they were acting like it was high school.

"My day is always fun when I get a chance to fuck with you, Jordyn," he joked, pulling at my hair as I pushed him back. I knew all the signs. I was smart, had a 4.0, for crying out loud. He liked me, always had, and didn't know how to channel that attraction into something positive, so like a kid, he acted out. He was constantly touching me, tugging at my hair, and sticking his finger in my ear. Yeah, even that.

"You going out this weekend?"

"Why?" I asked.

"Because not once have I seen you at a party," he said, following me to the library steps.

"Yeah, and you never will," I retorted, one hand gripping my books and the other holding onto my violin case. Quickly walking inside the library, I passed the metal detectors and kept moving, not once looking back. He wasn't going to follow me in there, and he damn sure wasn't going to wait around there for me.

I let out a huge sigh as I hit the third level where the reference books were. Nobody went up there. I sat all the way in the back corner on the floor up, against the wall, and just smiled. Being alone was like my natural drug. My natural high. Smell of papers, books, and sound of silence literally turned me on.

I stayed in the library the rest of the day and throughout the evening, just doing homework that probably wasn't due for another month, working on final papers, studying ahead of the class, writing music, and even taking a small nap. By the time I walked out, it was going on nine o'clock at night. I could hear chanting not too far off—the Greeks showcasing their skills to the onlookers, trying to outstep each other.

For some reason, my mind went to Elijah suddenly. I was wondering if he was still trying to call me. Rita would definitely have fun with him. He was perfect for her: wild, country Atlanta boy. Mmm. Definitely couldn't handle being around him for no longer than five minutes without getting annoyed. I kept walking, holding my books tight and keeping my head down as my violin case hit my leg repeatedly with each step.

Walking the back way to my building, I saw a couple making out as I passed by. I rolled my eyes before spotting a group of guys smoking and playing spades outside their dorm. If I didn't know this was a well-respected college campus, I would think we were in the straight upscale projects of Atlanta, where everyone knew everybody. Fights were bound to happen, and everyone was sleeping with everybody.

Keeping my head down, I crossed over the grassy field before stepping onto the parking lot of my building, hearing music blasting extremely loud from a truck. Looking up, I saw that familiar black truck with the black rims, dark tinted windows, and the driver's door open. The moment I heard his voice, my heart dropped into my stomach.

"Aye, baby, you look good as fuck! Come here!" Elijah yelled out to a girl who walked by, smiling hard at him before coming up to the truck. He sat on top of this truck, dreads hanging freely as he started talking to the girl.

I pushed my glasses up quick as I tried to slowly creep past him. Maybe he wouldn't see me. Why was he even there, anyway, in front of my building of all places?

"You gon' come fuck with me and my niggas, beautiful? I only put bad bitches on my team," he told the girl, getting her number.

"Nigga, I'm the baddest bitch you'll ever meet on this campus," she said in a fake voice, laughing.

I snorted out loud with a roll of my eyes, trying not to laugh at how stupid she sounded. Guess I was too loud, because Elijah looked up in my direction as I walked past a few cars.

"Hold up, hold up," he said to the girl. "Aye! Come here!"

I stopped dead in my tracks, watching him walk over toward me like an idiot, dreads moving, legs wide as he gripped his jeans to pull them up. The girl stood by the truck, hands on her hips as she watched with an attitude.

"So, you hang up on me, don't call me, won't answer none of my calls, and then try to walk past me like you don't fucking see me? It's like you ain't even trying to fuck with me like that."

"Noooooo, really?" I said sarcastically with an innocent expression. "You think?"

"Don't do that, shawty," he said, flipping his dreads out of his face. "Not with the attitude. I really hate that shit about females."

"Yeah, well, you don't have to put up with it, trust me." I tried walking off, but he grabbed my arm, stopping me.

"Stay right here. Hold up," he said, walking back to his truck to the girl who was trying to stare me down.

I just watched him continue to talk to her, looking him over. He was so flashy in his choice of outfit. He wore a long-sleeve, multi-color shirt that had DOPE on the front, straight-leg jeans that were so low he might as well not even have them on. He had flashy, matching multi-color shoes, and I watched him tie his dreads back and put a fitted cap on that was flipped up.

"I'ma call you tonight, beautiful, a'ight? Don't let nobody know you saw me, just between you and me," he told the girl, kissing her hand as she nearly collapsed. She nodded like a puppet, eyes wide and smile even wider, before running off to her building, probably to get on her phone and tell everyone she just met the one person I didn't know.

Wait a minute. Why am I still standing here?
I shook my head and started walking toward my
dorm, with him coming up close beside me.

"You gonna tell me your room number?" he
pressed as I stopped, looking at him. I was so
sick of this.

"What do you want, Elijah?" I asked.

"Ahh, so you remembered my name." He
smiled, looking me over. "Even in these bum-ass
clothes, I can still see yo' sexy-ass body and that
fat ass." He was licking his lips as I backed up
with a dropped mouth. He was so blunt it was
unbelievable. "Shit, you don't even wanna know
half the nasty-ass shit I would do to yo' body,
girl. You not gonna wanna fuck with nobody else
but me."

"You think that's attractive?" I pressed. "You
coming on to me like this in a sexual manner?"

"I mean, maybe you can't handle it because
you a virgin, and I understand that. I'm willing
to step up"—he put his hand on his chest for
dramatic effect—"and take yo' virginity from
you. I will treat it with care and make sure you
have the time of yo' life." He smiled, flashing his
pearly whites, trying to keep from laughing. I
didn't crack not one smile.

"Really?" I pressed, head tilted to the side as
I kept my books close to my chest. This guy was

so stupid. I don't even see what girls saw in him, what Rita would ever see in him.

"Maybe you not used to a mothafucka like me coming straightforward like this, but I'm not into the games, and I'm not into wasting time. I see you, that ass, and I want it. You know? I like a nerdy bitch every now and then. I'll even fuck you with the grandma glasses on, shawty. You not the best-looking bitch, but I can get with it. Can show you everything I know, teach you how to please a nigga like me. I usually get what I want, and since you still have yo' innocence about you, I'm trying to be a little patient, but I want that shit too, shawty," he said, sticking his tongue out.

I almost threw up. He was so disgusting, and what he just said was even worse. The tattoos on his face didn't make it any better. Nothing was going to make this conversation any better, except for me ending it.

"Okay, first of all," I started, putting my violin case down, "stop calling me a bitch. I'm a grown woman, and I have a name. That's Jordyn with a Y. Secondly, I wouldn't let you take my innocence if you were the last nigga on earth," I stated, feeling my northern roots come out.

"Thirdly," I said, looking him over purposely while pushing my glasses up, "I'll have you know, Elijah, Mr. I'll-do-nasty-shit-to-yo'-body"—I pointed hard at his chest as I looked up at him, meeting his wide eyes—"not only am I not a virgin, but you wouldn't know what, how, or where I like to be touched, fucked, bit, slurped, kissed, slapped, or licked if I showed you." I moved closer so I could make my point and be done with this. "I fuck niggas like you for fun, for laughs, for pleasure, and for a joke that only I get. You understand? Don't ever in yo' life"—I locked eyes with him hard so he wouldn't miss a beat—"come at me the way you just did, because then I'm going to really hurt yo' feelings. Learn to speak fucking English, and stay the fuck away from me, *breh*," I ended, mocking his southern drawl. "Got it?"

I didn't even give him a chance to say anything; just picked up my stuff and walked off. "I happen to like my grandma glasses by the way!" I let out without looking back. I was sick of this fucking city and the people that lived there.

Together Or Nah?

Jade

"What's the move tonight?" my friend KJ asked as my crew and I walked the yard. All of us always met up around the same time after our last class of the day, grabbed some food, smoked a blunt, and chilled. These niggas right here, Chris, KD, and Mo? All of 'em made me feel like my dudes from back up north. That's why we bonded so well. KD was from Atlanta, but he had the heart of a northern nigga nonetheless.

So, yeah, it was a Wednesday afternoon. I hadn't spoken to Trent since we last fucked. Shit, I was still trying to recover from it. Y'all read what happened. Fucked me crazy. He got what he wanted at the end of the day: for me to shut up. Yeah, shit was going around constantly about me on the Internet, but I deleted my profiles on all social networks. Not that it helped. Trent was still running his mouth, though, but that was okay. Nigga could do that. I was over the whole situation; tired of arguing, yelling, and fighting with this gay nigga. Just let him do him and let me be. Good dick will do that to you; calm a crazy girl like me down.

"I was supposed to meet DJ in the gym, but I don't think she's there yet. I don't know who's in there really, but we can chill in there for a few minutes to figure out the next move," I said, checking my phone for text messages. "I really want me some wings. Like, I've been craving wings for days, nigga. Seriously," I said, flipping my honey locs back.

"Probably pregnant by that nigga," Chris joked as I playfully hit him.

"Not pregnant by nobody. Just a fucking fat-ass." I laughed.

"Ayo, Jade, what up?" a guy yelled out from in front of his boy's dorm. I didn't know who the fuck he was, but I gave him a heads-up anyway, slick famous on this yard because of the post and how I handled myself at that party. Nobody was expecting me to come at Trent the way that I did by hitting him. Regardless of how I looked, how ratchet I turned out to be, I handled it. That's all most people saw really at the end of the day.

"May have to start being yo' bodyguards," Mo joked as we crossed over behind another dorm. "Niggas is straight thirsting off yo' ass, B."

The Carter Boys: A Carter Boys Novel   137

"I know." I smiled. "Isn't it wonderful?"

"Ahh, shut yo' ass up." KD waved me off as we all laughed. I could always count on my boys to have a good ol' laugh with.

The yard was quiet, with people still in class. A few were posted out on steps and benches, but for the most part? Everyone was either in class or inside somewhere. It was a pretty day, too. Sun was out, balancing out the cool air, so it felt like it was mid-70s. I wore white ripped jeans, showing more skin from the holes than most jeans, a Knicks T-shirt with the matching Jordans, gold bangles lined up my wrist, with my locs free-falling in whatever direction. Orange rod was going through my eyebrow, and my tongue rings were orange; nipple rings, too, so of course no bra for me. Little to no makeup, eyebrows recently done by me, and I felt good. Shit, I looked good. These broads out there basic as fuck compared to me.

"So, you ain't spoke to dude since Sunday?" KD asked. I shook my head.

"Ohhh, I forgot to tell you!" Chris said, hand on my arm as he started laughing to himself like he was preparing for a joke. "This nigga so-called found himself trying to check me, Jade."

"Who are you talking about?" I laughed, confused.

"Yo' boy! Trent! Pretty boy K," he said as the boys started laughing. I didn't. Mind was racing, trying to figure out what his definition of *checking* was. "So, look, I'm sitting there chilling in the student center right? This nigga comes out of nowhere, pulls up a chair at my table with his homeboys standing by, and start talking to me."

"What!" I shrieked with a laugh as I looked at him. Nearly tripped not paying attention to where I was going. Gym was a few yards past the main buildings on the yard, so we were dipping and ducking in between buildings and walking sidewalks to get to it.

"What that fuck nigga want?" KD asked with an attitude.

"Tried to ask me what was my status with you. Why was I sitting outside with you that night? Am I trying to talk to you? I mean, nigga was straight bugging out over you. So, I told him, 'That's my girl. We cool like homies, nothing more. Why? Wassup? What's the problem?' And he was all, 'Oh, I'm just making sure I ain't fucked nothing up with you and her since I smashed. Wasn't trying to step on nobody's toes or nothing.'"

"Nigga is a straight bitch," I mumbled. Classic female move.

"I'm like, 'Yo, if you trying to get at her, dude, just talk to her. She's not all mean and shit like you making her out to be. She's actually chill as fuck.'"

"What he say?" I asked, feeling like I was in high school all over again as I readily eyed Chris for that response.

"Dude was just like, 'Nah, I'm straight on that. I was just trying to smash.'"

"Ahhh!" Mo laughed, waving it off. "Nigga was checking for you, ma. He likes you, and you probably like him too. All this shit y'all doing is just how y'all show your attraction for each other."

"Nah." I laughed slowly. The idea in itself was stupid. I was about to say something to argue that further when I heard a loud howl from behind us. We all turned around, seeing niggas in blue surrounding the Greek walk, doing their fraternity call before chanting.

"Oh, you know what's supposed to be happening tonight, right?" Mo said excitedly. "They doing the Meet the Greeks shit. Block party on Greek Row."

"The what?" I questioned, seeing more people representing different Greeks walking up, one being Trent. Moment I saw him, I felt chills go through my body just thinking about that night. It was a shame I didn't have too many girlfriends, because I was ready to dish those fucking details to anybody who would listen. I even almost attempted to tell Jordyn's lame ass, but she wouldn't get it. Sex was probably outside her thought capacity.

"Meet the Greeks, where each house throw a little something, and we walk and stop, checking out the brothers, and they may have some music or food. Same with the girls. You know, back there behind the school, all them houses lined up. Whole neighborhood about to turn up tonight. You going?" Mo said excitedly as we all looked at him, giving him that *nigga, fuck outta here* look.

"Nah, I'll pass." I chuckled with my hand up.

"Dem Carters Boys supposed to be out there too, so shit might turn into a straight-up concert," Mo continued as my eyes popped up. I missed them at the club last time because I was in the middle of fighting a ho, but I did like a few of their songs. Can't even hate on Atlanta music like I want to. Shit sucks, but let them play it over and over, starts to ride after a while.

"Oh, shit. I didn't know that," KD let out, pulling out his phone. "Let's go see what they talking about."

"Fine." I sighed, linking arms with Chris as we walked back toward the Greek walk seeing most of the student body surrounding the spectacle of a scene.

"Ladies! We want all the sexy ladies to especially stop by our place!" Trent called out as I eyed his attire: dress pants, dress shirt, tie, frames, and black shoes. Nigga cleaned up nicely every time. He had a black tote bag with the long strap, looking like a true corporate-ass nigga. Stood tall and addressed the crowd like a natural public speaker.

"You know as always we do our red light specials," he continued, winking at a few freshman girls. I rolled my eyes. "But we having some music guests stop by and perform a little something for you. Fellas, you can come meet with each brother, and feel free to ask questions, inquire about our organization, what we stand for, what we're looking for, and how we can help you attain your future by joining us."

"I wanna join," a girl teased as she licked her lips at Trent.

"Well, come see me personally, beautiful. We can make some arrangements," he countered smoothly as she damn near fainted. I knew he was flickering those hazel eyes at the girls. I bet you he was.

"Will we get hit in the face by a bitch, like you did at that party last weekend, if we join your organization?" KD yelled out as I nearly died with laughter, hitting him hard. I could hear a few people in the crowd laughing as Trent turned his attention toward us, eyeing me hard before looking back at the girls in front.

"Nah, but if you come at me with another slick-ass comment like that, I will do to you what I should have done to that bitch at that party," he snapped as the crowd nearly came to a hush mode.

"Nigga, shut yo' lame ass up." I laughed with a shake of my head. "Come on. I don't have time for this bullshit."

"Ain't that the girl with the herpes?" I heard someone whisper as my boys and I walked off, making the biggest scene of a lifetime.

"Don't show up nowhere near the house!" Trent yelled out to me. "You know what's going to happen if you do!"

I turned around, still walking as I smiled. "Fuck outta here, punk-ass nigga, I'm not going nowhere near yo' li'l gay parade!" I turned back around and kept walking. "Goofy mothafucka. I got better things to do."

"Like what?" Chris pressed as I looked at him.

I looked at Mo and KD before we all obnoxiously fell into an easy laugh.

"We going to that nigga house tonight?" KD
laughed.

"You know it," I said with a smile. Damn. I
was trying to have a peaceful, no-more-fighting
school year, but he kept on trying me. Good dick
only gets you so far. Shit was wearing off with
me. Now I was ready to fuck up some shit.

So, of course, you know me by now. I didn't
take no shit from nobody. I changed clothes and
decided to wear all black for the occasion: black
leggings, with black Jordans and a black hoodie,
gold hooped earrings, and my blond locs pulled
up with a few hanging in the front and the back.
Nigga, I was on one that night. Piercings got
changed to all black, and I already had a drink or
two, so I had a nice li'l buzz.

Tia was already out at the block party with
her ho clique, and Jordyn? Well, shit, I don't
know. I popped over in her room, seeing she was
aggressively typing on her laptop and writing
stuff down in a notebook, listening to her classi-
cal music. I knocked on wall to get her attention.

"Yeah?" She took the headphones out as
she looked at me through her glasses, nose
scrunched up. All she had to do was get them
eyebrows tweaked and throw a little makeup on,

change up the wardrobe, and she could be the baddest bitch on the yard. Her gray eyes already did enough for her anyway.

"You not stepping out tonight?" I asked.

"No," she mumbled, putting her headphones back in.

Okay then.

I walked out and met up with the boys as we started off to the backwoods neighborhood. That's what we usually called it, the backwoods, or if you lived in the Gaino projects, we usually just said, "over there by Gaino." All of that shit was back there. Soon as you stepped off the yard, it was the straight hood. You could tell the difference between a guy who went to school here and one who lived in the backwoods. Every time they walked on the yard, they stood out like a red dot on a white paper. I said I was going to get me a thug-ass country boy to fuck with for the winter, but I was just over that shit. I'd been through that phase of wanting to mess with thugs and hood niggas. I was over it.

"Oh, shit! Look at this, yo," Chris mumbled as we looked around in the lit-up neighborhood. Streetlights were on, flashing bright on all these cars lined up, people walking the streets. You could smell grilled meat, alcohol, and hear the thirstiness of the hoes that night. Girls came out in flocks, wearing their shortest shorts, tightest leggings, and baddest weaves. I mean, girls was on it that night. Some who were trying too hard to impress the sororities dressed like it was *Mr. Rogers' Neighborhood.*

Bitch, it's not that serious.

Every house on the block was having something, or at least sitting out enjoying the vibe. Even if they weren't a part of Meet the Greeks, they were out there trying to get it in like everyone else.

"Let's go," I said, leading the way. "I want to cuss this nigga out just for fun. Just because I can. You making weak threats at me? Nah."

"Why don't you just admit you like him?" Chris started as I snapped my neck to look at him sideways. "I'm saying, you haven't stopped talking about this cat since whatever happened Sunday between the two of you."

"What you talking about Sunday?" KD asked as I sighed.

"Not important. Let's just keep walking," I concluded, stopping for a car to drive by, blasting their music.

"Shawty with the dreads! You looking good as fuck!" the driver called out as I waved with a smile. I loved it.

We stopped at multiple houses, grabbing plates, mingling, and collecting numbers. Some were connects for weed, others were niggas trying to fuck something. Even with all this shit going around about me, for some reason it just made dudes want me more.

So, you know we saved the best for last. Walking up to the big-ass, two-story red house, I could see it was a huge crowd outside, with a bunch of niggas standing on the porch. It was so packed that a few people were standing on the curb because there was no space to stand in the yard.

"How y'all ladies doing tonight?" I heard someone on the mic say. I tried straining my neck to see who it was as girls started hollering out, screaming.

"You so damn sexy, Jodie!" one girl called out as I nearly gasped.

Carter Boys. One of the biggest Atlanta groups hitting the stage as of now. They were starting to get national recognition but still took the time out to do local shit like this.

"Ahh, this about to be a straight-up freak show, son," Chris complained with a smack of his teeth.

Jodie started to sing a soft, melodic tune, taking a girl's hand, pulling her close up against him. Nigga was smooth. First glance, he looked like a straight thug: dreads loose, shirtless, jeans sagging low as fuck, with tattoos covering his whole entire body. There was even some on his face. But when he opened that mouth, started singing freak shit to the girls with his brothers rapping alongside, it was a wrap.

"Aye," Jodie started, looking at Trent with a smirk. "I may have to take a couple of girls from yo' li'l party, twin."

"Take me!" one girl called out as I maneuvered in the crowd, trying to get a better look at the boys. Damn, you could tell they were brothers. All of them fine as hell.

"Take me, Jodie! I want you to sing to me while you fucking me!" another girl yelled out as my mouth dropped. Damn! Bitches was thirsty.

Taking another closer look, I realized it was my roommate, Tia. Ho-ass. When I tell y'all this nigga sat this girl down on the chair on the porch, mic in one hand, as he started serenading her . . . Her hand was touching his body, looking like she was about to cry, with him moving his hips in a sensual way. Shit, even his brothers started taking girls from the crowd as more people made their way over once they found out who was there.

"Man, this ain't no fucking Meet the Greeks," Mo complained as I laughed.

Looking back up, I caught Trent's eyes as we stared at each other before he started making his way over to me.

"Whoa! Shit, shawty." Jodie laughed, backing up from the girl, who was trying to bite his stomach. "You not ready for all that, baby."

The music continued to play, and everything was going on, but my eyes stayed on Trent. That's all I saw; no one else. I backed up, getting into the street, as he stepped off the curb, hands shoved in his sweatpants pockets. He was shirtless, with frames on his face. Pretty boy K—always had to show off that body.

When he stood in front of me, before he could open his mouth, I just went in. "Nigga, I don't give a fuck who you are. You can't tell me whether or not I can come to a house party. And leave my friends alone! Nobody asked you to be questioning them and shit like you checking for me, nigga," I snapped, hands crossed over my chest. Boy, I was ready to lay it in on him that night.

Trent just stared at me with tired eyes as he leaned on the front part of a black truck, no facial expression.

"You done?" was all he said in a low voice as the crowd suddenly went wild.

I looked back, seeing everyone was jumping in unison to one of their club anthems. Even niggas was getting into it, dancing, hitting the moves Atlanta was known for. The Carter Boys was on the porch killing it right now, with Jodie singing the hook.

Fuck it. I can't even enjoy myself without this bitch nigga in my face.

"No, I'm not done," I continued, hands now on the hips. "Who told you to come up to my friend, asking questions about me, nigga? That was a bitch-ass move!" I was clapping my hand for effect. "You got to be the biggest bitch on the yard if you checking for me through them!"

He gripped his forehead like I was stressing him out. He hadn't seen nothing yet.

"Oh, you tired, nigga? You tired, yo? Because—"

"Shut the fuck up, Jade. Like, shit!" he let out as my eyes grew wide. "You talk too fucking much. All you do is run that mouth. For no reason! You don't even know why I came over here."

"To start some shit! I know you. Make up some more lies about me and then run and tell yo' li'l friends. I know how—"

"You wanna be my girl?" Trent asked in a tired voice as he looked at me, eyes matching the voice.

I couldn't move, just felt my stomach do all kinds of flips. He just stared at me, no facial expression, waiting on an answer. I took a deep swallow, feeling my nerves numbing my body. I wasn't expecting that. Wasn't expecting the answer I gave him either.

"Okay."

I looked down at the ground. It felt like high school, or middle school. Neither one of us wanted to speak, but somebody had to make the first move. Trent stood up straight, directly in front of me, nodding his head before walking back to the house, leaving me standing there, confused as hell as to what just happened. I looked around, seeing a few girls who were watching it play out. Their mouths dropped. The girl that spit at and hit the nigga in the face at the club was suddenly his girlfriend. I came ready to battle, and instead I ended up putting myself in the arms of the enemy.

"So, y'all dating or nah?" a nosey chick asked as she chomped hard on her gum, eyeing me with jealousy.

"You wanna mind yo' fucking business or nah?" I retorted. She rolled her eyes, turning back around.

I watched Trent walk back with a plate full of food from the grill as he leaned back on the truck, handing it to me. No words, no eye contact. Shit, I took the plate with no words, no eye contact.

"You can say thank you, Jade," was all he said.

"One, I didn't ask for it, and two, I don't have to say shit," I let out, picking through the food to see what I wanted.

"Why you feel like you have to battle me on everything?" Trent asked, scrunching his face up with an attitude. "You can't have a normal conversation like a grown-ass woman? You have to—"

I started to walk off in the opposite direction. He said that shit the last time, and it rubbed me the wrong way. Tossing the plate full of food aside on the street, I kept moving until I felt his hand grab my arm, turning me around. We was damn near in the middle of an intersection as more people started walking the streets around us.

"I rather you bitch at me than walk away. Don't ever walk away from me when we're talking. Disrespectful-ass shit," he let out as I cocked my head back.

"I don't like how you talk to me. How you talk down to me is disrespectful, Trent. Do you not hear it?"

"You call me gay, a bitch, a female, everything but my name every time you see me. You get talked to the way you act, Jade. You act like a fucking child, I'll treat you like one. Period."

I snatched my arm back as I backed up from him, eyes never leaving his. "So, why did you ask me to be yo' girl then, nigga? Shit don't add up if that's how you feel about me."

"Why did you agree?" he countered.

Damn. I should have saw that one coming. We stood there in silence, staring at each other; clearly pissed off, but neither one of us wanted to move.

"Nigga, I'm done talking to yo' bitch ass," I mumbled, looking past him, attitude hard, with my hand in his face to keep him from speaking.

He sighed, stepping closer to me as he took my hand to bring it down. Holding on to my waist, he pulled me gently toward his body. I looked off in the distance, trying not to break face, keeping a mean face on, but inside my body was throbbing. Responding so physically toward him, it was crazy.

"Don't cuss me out when I do this," he murmured, leaning in and kissing me softly on the side of the face. He waited for my reaction before kissing me again as I closed my eyes.

Shit, what was it about this pretty-ass boy? I couldn't stop him or myself. When he looked at me for a reaction again, he gently cupped my chin, pulling my mouth toward his as we kissed.

He was nervous. I could feel it. Or maybe I was nervous. Our mouths danced like they'd been doing it all their lives. It was different from us sucking face on Sunday. This was sensual, passionate, a lot of emotion from each of us toward the other.

He pulled back slowly, licking his lips, but he never let go of my waist as I stared at him through heavy eyes.

Damn, Trent.

"When I saw you with dude yesterday near the student center, and I saw you laugh and smile for the first time? I felt some type of way knowing I have not once made you do either of those things with me."

I felt everything in me just soften up the hard shell that I kept so closely intact.

"Seeing you smiling in another nigga's face didn't sit right with me, so yeah, I went up to yo' friend. I'm not the type of nigga to share; I'm protective over me and mine. I just don't know how to come at you because you like to challenge me on everything. Argue and hit a nigga where it hurts. So, tonight? Can I just have one night of peace? One night where you can look at me like a woman looks at her man? No fighting, no attitude, just chill. Let you get to know me, and I can get to know you."

I nodded dumbly, feeling so numb and help-less.

I never had someone talk to me the way he just did. If this was him running game? Well, shit, then I lost. I had no words.

Just Be Ready

Jordyn

Thank God it was Friday. I had grocery shopping to do, papers, homework, books I wanted to read; so much I wanted to get done. I didn't know what was going on with my roommates, but suddenly Jade and Trent had become a thing. Rita couldn't stop talking about those two, and Tia wouldn't come out of her room, and if she did, she became so mean, more nasty than usual toward me. Whoever she was mad at, I almost wanted to go off on them because, I didn't like being her constant target. Elijah hadn't called me back since, and I was grateful. Rita was, of course, upset I didn't get a chance to mention her, but she got over it. He was an asshole. I couldn't even imagine myself being around him no longer than five minutes anyway.

I was in my car heading to my favorite gas station to fill her up for the weekend. Had no plans other than to buy a few drinks, relax in my room, and write music. Everyone else was going out to party for the night as usual. It was a football game the next day with a big-time rival, so everyone was running around, trying to prepare for that. Like I said, I didn't care. I came to school to get my degree and move on. Shame I didn't have as much sex as I would like to, because I was definitely starting to feel like I was way overdue. Last guy I had sex with became so clingy that it turned violent. That was why I waited so long before I did anything. Now? I was definitely feeling like it was time. Maybe because my batteries died in both vibrators, and I was too lazy to buy another pack. Who knows? Maybe I could go out and find someone. Rita wanted to set me up with one of her guy friends, but I didn't want anyone that I had to look at on the yard. Had to be someone off campus—out of sight, out of mind.

So of course—God works in mysterious ways—whose truck do I see once again at the gas station? This time it was only one black truck, black rims, tinted completely, with no music blasting. I pulled up to the pump in front of it, praying it wasn't Elijah. It was freaking eleven o'clock in the morning. What the hell was he even doing there? I checked myself in the mirror before stopping myself. What in the world did I care what I looked like? It was my usual getup, only this time Nike shorts and a hoodie with my hair up. I put my glasses on as I stepped out, counting my money.

I tried my hardest not to look up when I heard the truck door open and close.

Jordyn don't look, not even a glance in that direction. May just be another guy you don't know. . . . Fuck it.

I looked up, seeing Elijah staring down at his phone, looking like he just woke up; locs pulled back, basic T-shirt with sweats, slip-on Nikes with colorful socks, gold chain, and diamond stud in each ear. Tattoos stood out on his dark skin against the white shirt as he looked my way, lifting his head up. I just gave him a short smile. No need to be mean if he wasn't coming at me disrespectfully like last time.

"What's good?" he said from his truck as I walked around my car.

"What are you doing here?" I asked curiously. "It's so many other gas stations in Atlanta."

"Fuck kind of question is that?" He laughed. "I just dropped a few chicks off at yo' school. Needed some gas, so this is the one I stopped at. Not trying to follow you or nothing, I stopped calling yo' ass after how you did me the other day."

"You did that to yourself," I mumbled, walking past him to go inside.

He followed behind me, no doubt watching me walk. I WAS surprised he had nothing blunt or obnoxious to say. Usually he was loud and over the top, but right now? With those sleepy eyes, he looked like he was just trying to wake up.

We both walked to the back at the drink section, same exact place where we first met. I couldn't help but smile to myself. This was crazy. I couldn't even believe I kept running into this guy.

"What's so funny?" he asked in a low voice, looking at me with a serious face.

"Nothing," I said, shaking my head as I grabbed a bottle of Smirnoff. I needed to be passed out beyond drunk so I wouldn't think about sex. It was all my mind had been on ever since Trent walked in with Jade that night, scooping her up in his arms like she was his everything.

"Aye," he started, turning toward me with his head down. "My bad about how I came at you, shawty. I thought about everything I said to you, and wish I could do it all over again."

"It's fine," I mumbled, staring hard at the Smirnoff. He continued to talk, apologizing and explaining himself, but I tuned him out, looking him over. His tattoos threw me off, but overall,

I could see he was in shape. I could even make out a print in his sweats. Damn it. I needed to have sex badly. I couldn't handle this dry spell I was under. I apologize to you, readers, but there were some days where I craved it like a drug. Usually I could handle it, but battery-operated toys only went so far with me.

I pushed my glasses up with a lick of my lips as I tuned back in.

"So yeah, you know, my bad," he concluded, sounding sincere. I watched him grab a can of Four Loko and a Starbucks iced coffee. Interesting.

"Do you want to have sex with me tonight?" I asked. He nearly snapped his neck to look at me, dropping both cans to the ground, causing them to burst immediately. "Oh my God, I'm so sorry," I said, quickly backing up as the contents spilled everywhere, mixing together. He just stared at me, eyes wide, as I quickly put my drinks down to grab napkins.

"Marco!" I called out. "*Ven aquí!*" I watched the contents spill into the aisle as I tried dabbing it down. Marco came rushing out, and I quickly told him I would pay for it. Elijah just continued to stare at me, slowly smiling. "Why are you looking at me like that?"

"Shawty, you gave me a fucking hard time all damn week because I'm trying to fuck, and then you come out of nowhere, after you made me look like a bitch, and hit me with that question?" he let out.

"I'm sorry," I said, pushing my glasses up as I finished helping Marco with the mess.

We walked to the counter. Elijah paid for everything, including my drinks and gas, which was nice. Not needed, but nice anyway. When we walked out, he stopped me with a hand on my arm as he looked in my eyes.

"You serious?"

"I'm serious," I repeated, no smile, nothing. "I haven't had sex in a while. I don't feel like going out to look for it, and I know we don't ever have to see each other again. I'm not looking for nothing serious, and I hope you aren't either."

"Fuck no," he spat out, smiling hard as he dug in his pocket to pull out his phone. "Shit, you don't have a phone. Damn, Jordyn with a Y. I won't be able to come over until late, late tomorrow night, shawty. Like two or three."

"That's fine," I said, making a mental note.

He just smiled, flashing his white teeth as he stepped closer to me. "You sure you ready for this dick? Not to be blunt as fuck about it, but I don't play no games. Girls are known to fall in love with me after the first round," he said, grabbing himself.

Ahh, there he was, the self-righteous, over-the-top Atlanta country boy I met.

"I mean, you fuck with me, you really not going to want to fuck with no one else."

"I think I'll be okay," was all I said, pushing my glasses up.

He dropped his head, laughing. "Do we need to go over some ground rules first?"

"Look at you," he said, smirking. "Sounding all professional and shit. Fuck yeah, no kissing on the mouth, but I'll make an exception for you. Just don't overdo that shit. I'm not into all of that."

"Okay." I nodded my head. He really thought he was . . . whatever. I just needed to release some stress—a year's worth of stress—and he was the only available guy around. Looking him over again, I watched him open up his thing of Starbucks iced coffee.

"You drink coffee?" I asked as he took a sip, closing his eyes.

"Every damn morning. I will fuck up somebody's day if I don't have coffee," he said, and I laughed. That was so curious of him.

"Interesting," I let out, watching him drink it like it was a drug. "What else?"

"No oral. I can't eat every bitch out, and I don't. What I do with this mouth, I can't share with the world, baby." He smirked, flicking his tongue out. I didn't even blink. "And no calling me up, asking about our status. No relationship talk, no baby this, none of that. I want this to be strictly sexual, you feel me? Too many bitches get attached to me, and I can't have that. I got too much I'm trying to do in life. Besides, you not even my type of girl I would go for anyway. No offense, but I get bad bitches daily, and you nowhere near that level."

"Well then, we're on the exact same page," I said in agreement. Nowhere near my type, and I had too much I was trying to accomplish to even catch feelings. "No kissing, no oral, and—?"

"I mean, you can suck my dick if you want, though," he cheesed, sticking his tongue out teasingly.

I didn't even smile. Just stared at him like a tired mother with her hyper child.

"And no relationship talk," I continued. "That's it?"

"Yep," he said before adding, "and take them fucking granny glasses off. You don't need to see what I'm about to do to that ass. You don't have nothing for me, baby?"

I just smiled, pushing my so-called granny glasses up as I headed for my car.

"Just be ready."

Duh, Nigga

Jade

"Hold up," Chris said, shaking his head in confusion. "So y'all go out now?"

"I mean . . ." I shrugged as I looked myself over in the mirror. Chris was laying back on my bed, with KD and Mo sitting on the edge, trying to smoke something. It was Saturday morning, and we were heading out to this game. Nobody knew about Trent and me. Shit, we were still a little confused on where we stood because that exact same night, we went right back to arguing, telling each other fuck it. Came at me the next day, and we tried to be civil toward each other, but we were both so controlling that we kept bumping heads. So, we ended up not speaking for the next two days, but we did text all last night, if that counts. Shit, I was so lost and clueless on how to deal with a nigga like Trent. Usually dudes just shut up and let me take control; Trent was acting like a bitch that wanted to wear the pants in the relationship.

"I don't know what we are doing right now," I concluded, turning around to look at my boys. "Nigga doesn't know how to talk to me the right way."

"Oh, and you talk to him like—?" KD started, and I laughed, dropping my head.

"What the fuck am I supposed to say? Nigga is a straight bitch. You know that. We all know that!" I laughed.

"Nah, you can't do that to that man. I don't even like him, but you got to soften up a little bit. Sometimes a man likes to feel like he's needed, Jade. Can't keep calling that dude a bitch, especially to his face."

"I mean, but he is one," Mo mumbled. I smirked, grabbing my shirt off the dresser to throw it at him.

"So, how am I supposed to come at him? I've been like this my whole life. I don't know how else I'm supposed to calm down and chill. Let the nigga be the nigga. What female does that? Not me."

"Every girl does that!" Chris laughed with his hands in the air. "That's why Northern niggas like Southern girls, because they're softer down here. They not so hard core, in yo' face, nigga this and nigga that."

"But that's why niggas down here like girls up there," KD countered, standing up for the Atlanta men. "I get turned on just hearing you talk, Jade. It's sexy as hell to see a girl handle her own."

"See!" I laughed, pointing at KD. "He likes it, so what makes you think Trent don't like it?"

"Because we in yo' room with you, getting ready to go to the game with you, while yo' man is out doing his own thing, not even trying to be around you. Think about that shit. Nigga gets pussy thrown in his face every day, but he steady coming after you, and you keep turning him down, even after y'all established a relationship. You too hard for him, ma. Tone all that shit down and just be his girl."

"I don't just want to sit there like a Barbie doll with no voice."

"You won't! I'm telling you." Chris laughed with a shake of his head. "Just be easy on that nigga. When you go to the game, sit with him and his boys. Just be his girl. That nigga will probably nut the fuck up if you even try to hold his hand when y'all walk."

"Ahh, hell nah." I waved him off as we all laughed.

"Aye, it's going to hit you that you like him more than you realize. Maybe you just need something to trigger you."

"To what?" I questioned.

"He probably realized he was feeling you when he saw you talking to me. You got to see something that he does for you to realize you like him just as much. You know? Something to make you feel some type of way."

"A'ight, Dr. Phil ol' ass," KD cracked as I laughed. I loved these niggas.

"Let me call this fool and see what he's trying to do." I walked out of the room as I dialed Trent's number, spotting Jordyn asleep in her bed. Bitch was a hermit. Never went out nowhere, never did anything.

"Yeah?" Trent answered as I looked at my phone.

"Nigga, most people answer the phone by saying hello," I retorted.

"What do you want, Jade?" he said, and my eyes lit up at his bitch-ass tone.

"Nigga, never mind. Don't even worry about it. I was trying to see if you wanted to come to the game with me, but—"

"Nah, I'm not going no more. Something came up. I'll hit you up later," he said before hanging up.

I looked at my friends, who were sticking their head out from behind the door being nosey, listening to the conversation. I just shrugged.

"Shit, I got the blunts rolled up; KD got the snacks. Can we hit this game up or nah?" Mo asked as I laughed.

"Let's go," I said, grabbing the keys.

"You could have at least asked that nigga if he was okay," Chris mumbled, and I rolled my eyes.

"Man, fuck that nigga. Let's go. If he was trying to hang with her, he would have done it by now, so no," Mo snapped.

"Exactly," I concluded. "Fuck that nigga.'

So, like always, I had a good time with the boys. Sat with my sister and her crew at the game, and she rolled deep—basketball team, the bisexual girls on the yard, and girls who just wanted to be around her popular ass. We always had a good time. So, of course once the game was over, we stayed a little bit longer on the yard, not once checking my phone. Didn't need to. Stopped by a nearby Wal Mart to grab some food for tonight, because we planned on blazing up in Chris's room.

We walked to my room so I could grab some clothes for the night, since I was staying over with him. Not weird. I usually slept in the living room, while he was in his bed. Nothing going on with us like that.

"Aye, the *Walking Dead* marathon is on tonight," Mo said excitedly as we walked up the stairs to my floor. "Y'all watch that shit?"

"Nigga, it's nothing but a bunch of zombies walking around eating people. I don't understand the hype around it," I reasoned, stepping out into the hallway.

"Nah, the show is straight, though. You should watch it," KD agreed.

"We not watching that in my room," Chris concluded. I laughed, slapping hands with him. "Show is stupid. I've seen a couple of episodes and fell asleep every time."

"Man, y'all just don't know. You gotta watch it from the beginning," Mo argued as we cut the corner.

The moment I saw Trent standing by my door, leaning against the wall, my heart started to pound. He was texting on his phone, with a duffle bag strapped alongside his body, looking like he was about to go work out in his basketball shorts and shirt.

"This nigga here," I mumbled as we walked toward my door. Trent and I locked eyes. "What are you doing here?"

"I've been calling and texting you all fucking day. Where you been at?"

"Nigga, I went to the game with my friends, and now we about to go back to his room and watch TV," I stated simply as I opened the door to my apartment. "I just came to grab some clothes for the night."

"So, you spending the night in his room?" he questioned, looking confused as he looked from Chris to me.

"Aye, look, it's not like that," Chris said with his hands in the air. "We just be chilling. It's a couple of us. I mean, you can join too if you want."

"Fuck nah," Mo mumbled, and I smirked. I set down my stuff from Wal Mart as Trent continued to look at me, still trying to play like he was confused.

"Look, don't even worry about it. We about to go. Jade, chill with yo' nigga. I'm not trying to cause no problems between y'all two," Chris said, backing out into the hallway as my eyes grew wide.

"So, y'all smoking without me when I bought the shit?" I pressed, clearly agitated.

"We'll save it until next time," KD let out, eyeing Trent, who kept his eyes on Chris. "Go do what you gotta do. We'll hit you up tomorrow."

"Fine," I mumbled, watching them walk out as the door closed. Trent and I stood awkwardly in the quiet apartment. Ugh! I couldn't take this anymore.

"What's the problem, Trent?"

"I mean, do you want to be with me or nah? It seems like the last two days, you still acting like the same bitch I met before."

"Oh, so I'm a bitch now." I laughed to myself as I unpacked my groceries.

"Answer the question. Do you want to be with me? Do you want to be my girlfriend?"

"Why you asking it like it's a fucking privilege, like an honor to even be considered your girl?"

"Just answer the question! Yes or no?" Trent snapped, almost making me jump.

I rolled my eyes. "I mean, duh, nigga," I mumbled, walking over to the stove to turn it on.

"So, why you can't answer yo' phone? Why I gotta wait outside yo' apartment just to see you? Why the fuck were you even thinking it was okay to spend the night with another nigga?"

I stayed quiet, realizing my fault and mistakes of the day. I didn't even want to look at my phone to see he'd probably been calling, texting, and leaving voice messages. Damn. I felt like I couldn't do nothing right with this nigga. Every step I took, it pissed him off.

I grabbed my phone off the counter and decided to look, seeing the very first text from him was an apology for how he spoke to me on the phone earlier. Damn.

"My bad," was all I could manage to say as I looked up at him.

Trent was still standing by the door like he was ready to walk out, hazel eyes hard as he stared me down.

"Are you hungry?" I asked, trying to change the mood as I molded the ground beef into two thick pieces. "I'm making burgers."

"What you got going on with that short nigga?" he pressed, and I groaned in frustration.

"Nothing is going on between Chris and me. Damn, Trent, just relax. If you don't want me to spend the night with him, I won't do it. Not like we in the same damn room anyway."

His jaw dropped and his eyes grew wide.

Ahh, shit. Here we go. The bitch is ready to come out of him.

"That's not the point! You should know not to—" He suddenly stopped himself as he dropped his bag on the floor with a sarcastic laugh. "I can't believe I gotta explain how the fuck you're supposed to act as a fucking girlfriend. Can I use your shower? I just left the gym, and I want to shower and change."

"Fine," was all I could say.

By the time this nigga even started the shower, the burgers were already cooking and ready to be flipped, I'd been changed into a T-shirt with panties, and my hair was wrapped. I slowly crept up to the bathroom door, hearing the water going, and just listened. He was singing to himself, maybe rapping. Nigga was definitely in there talking. I smiled, just listening to him before the water cut off. I quickly went back to the kitchen, flipping the two thick burgers, and started to cut up the tomatoes and lettuce. I knew he was going to take his time getting out because he was high maintenance like that, so I had his plate ready and waiting as I went into my room, slipping underneath my covers, enjoying my homecooked burgers while watching videos on You Tube.

"Yo, these niggas is straight wildin'!" I laughed out loud, watching two trannies get into a fight on the train with two straight niggas. Of course this shit was in Atlanta.

"What are you watching?" Trent asked as he stood in the doorway, shirtless, light caramel body glistening as he bit down on my burger. I almost choked on a piece of meat, forgetting the nigga was even in my apartment in the first place. I was kind of glad he didn't have any tattoos. Might ruin the details of his pecs and abs.

He walked in, glancing at himself in the mirror before sitting down on the small bed next to me, smelling so good.

"These niggas in Atlanta got into a fight on MARTA." I laughed. "Fuck y'all got going on down here?"

"Like that don't happen in New York."

"I mean, I ain't never seen no shit like this," I lied, knowing this could happen anywhere in a major city. "Look at this," I told him as I pressed play. I started the video over from the beginning and watched Trent's reaction at the part where the tranny was completely naked, boobs and dick flashing everyone on the train.

"Ohhhh, shit!" Trent coughed as I fell onto his shoulder, laughing uncontrollably. "I thought he was a bitch."

"I did too!" I giggled. "Look at this video right here. My sister sent this to me the other day." Just like that, we fell into an easy conversation, watching hood fights and prank videos on You Tube. By the time we got sick of the videos, it was going on midnight. Neither one of us was tired, but we didn't leave that bed. So, we lay there in the dark, just talking. The only light was coming from the kitchen. None of my roommates were home yet, which was shocking, at least for Jordyn.

"How was the game?" Trent asked softly as he grabbed my hand, playing with my fingers one by one.

"It was straight. We lost as usual, but the band was on point, though. You should have came."

"Nah, that's the exact reason I don't go," he stated, holding my hand in his.

Damn. I felt myself softening up just being around him. Had a way of calming me down. So, I turned over and sat up, looking down at his body before kissing his shoulder gently.

"I apologize for today," I said quietly. "I should have answered your calls and text messages, and never even thought about spending the night at my friend's place."

"I don't get how you even thought that shit was an option after I told you about how I am."

"Because"—I sighed, dropping my head as I saw he was still upset about it—"I do it all the time. I have more male friends here than girlfriends. Chances are you going to see me with those niggas every day. I'm going to be in their room, or they're going to be in mine. It's just how it is. Not something I'm changing. I eat with these niggas, chill with them, hang out outside of school with them on a regular basis. Talk on the phone, all of that. Even my dudes back home. Some of them are coming down for homecoming weekend." I was leaving out a small detail that my ex was coming down, but I'd deal with that when he got there. Had I known I was going to end up dating the nigga who I got into a fight with, I would have never told him about it, because now the reason why my dudes from back home were coming down was to fuck

Trent's ass up. Didn't know how I was going to tell either of them, but somehow I had to do it before shit got out of control.

"Are we good, nigga?" I pressed, seeing he was just staring at me, light bouncing off the right side of his face since he was closest to the door.

"We good for now," he mumbled as he pulled me to lay on top of him, my body straddling his. Large hands gripped my thighs gently. I leaned down and kissed him, feeling like we were sealing the deal to the official start of our relationship—not coming from an angry place, not coming from an emotionally tired or stress-filled argument. None of that.

"I'm sorry for how we started off," he said against my mouth, wrapping his arms around my body to pull me closer. "Sorry for the club, the bullshit on the Internet, all of that."

"Nigga, and yo' comments about dark-skin women. You don't fuck with girls like me, remember that?" I pressed, and he smiled.

"I don't, but—"

I sat up so quick to look back down at him. "Son, really, though?" I snapped as he laughed, pulling me close to him once more.

"I'm sorry for saying that too. My mama dark-skin, so nothing against y'all. You are a beautiful black woman, and I am looking forward to seeing where this relationship goes, a'ight?"

· I smiled and just kissed him once more, holding both of his hands, with our fingers intertwined.

"We are going to upset a lot of people by being together," I told him, realizing the situation we'd put ourselves in.

"I know," he said, kissing me, letting his lips stay longer on mine.

"Can't believe I'm going out with yo' punk ass," I mumbled with a smile as I sat up. "At least you got good dick and bomb head game."

"Ahhh, told you, baby. What I tell you about that Kodak moment?" he boasted, blowing another one of his gay-ass air kisses with the lips out.

"Nigga, chill." I laughed. "Told you I'm not with that."

After having my way with Trent, I was knocked out peacefully in my small twin bed with my legs all over him. Door was closed shut, windows blinds were down, and it was pitch black. The only small speck of light in the room was from our phones charging nearby on the floor together. Usually I find it hard to fall asleep next to another body. I may be the only girl who does this, but I never fully let myself be comfortable around a man in the bed if we're sleeping. I become a light-ass sleeper when I share the bed with anyone other than my sister. Yet, for some reason, with Trent? I felt comfortable enough to allow myself to fall into an easy, deep sleep.

So, why am I sitting here talking to y'all if I'm supposed to be asleep? I'll tell you why. My eyes nearly split open at the sound of someone screaming out. Sounded like a man, but I wasn't sure.

"Fuucccck!" the voice let out in a deep, low tone as I sat up, looking around my dark room. I glanced at Trent, seeing he was moving his head a little bit.

"What the fuck is that?" he questioned in a groggy voice.

"You have to be quiet," I heard a girl say with a giggle.

"What the fuck you doing to me?" the guy cried out in a low groan.

My mouth dropped as I hit Trent in the arm.

"What did I do?" he snapped.

"Someone is having sex." I laughed. "I thought it was my roommate, but it can't be. It must be down below us."

"Who is yo' roommate? Not that glasses-wearing girl?"

"Yeah!" I laughed before we fell silent. It couldn't be Jordyn, because she was a virgin.

She looked like she would freak at the sight of a dick, so I knew it wasn't her. I listened, hearing the guy moan, literally sounding like he was being tortured.

"Yooo, that is too fucking funny." I chuckled. Rarely do you ever hear the guy moan and groan and make all the noise; he was too busy focusing on pumping iron. But this nigga was definitely getting fucked.

"Shit, tell them mothafuckas downstairs to shut the fuck up," Trent snapped as he turned over in the bed, pulling the pink sheets over him completely.

I laid back down next to him with a smile. Whoever the girl was, she was giving that nigga the business.

No Period?

Tia

"Hello?" Porscha answered, sounding tired, as I closed the door to the bathroom. It had to be like five in the fucking morning, and I was sitting on the toilet with my pants and panties down, hoping and praying hard as fuck right now. I kept the sink running so it could drown out my conversation. Even though everyone was asleep, I still wanted to be careful.

"Bitch!" I snapped. "You are not going to believe this shit. Maybe I'm just acting scary as fuck right now."

"What happened? Elijah called you back trying to get some? That would be shocking, and worth this damn phone call at five in the fucking morning," she retorted as I heard a male voice in the background. Her boyfriend probably, who she stayed cheating on.

"No, I was supposed to get my period this week. Shit hasn't happened yet. I always get my period on the same fucking day. The eighth or ninth of every month," I told her, feeling myself panic as I looked down in between my legs. If I could force that shit to come out, I swear I would have, because the last thing I needed was to be fucking pregnant right now. Only nigga I fucked without a condom who I *let* cum in me was that lame-ass nigga Jahiem Carter. Every other nigga knew how to pull out, but for some reason, he decided to shoot that shit in me—twice! I couldn't say nothing, though, because I knew it was happening; but at the time, I thought it was Elijah. Fuck! How could it be, if the nigga said he was getting a condom in the first place? I didn't even think about half the shit I should have thought about.

"So, what are you trying to say? You a few days late? That shit happens after you have a bunch of sex right before your period. When's the last time got some? Don't say it was Elijah." She laughed.

"Bitch!"

"Oh, shit!" She laughed as I buried my face in my hands, stomping the floor repeatedly. She didn't even know what really happened. How could I tell my friend I got raped and didn't realize it? That I fucked the wrong nigga?

"Girl, you may just be late. I wouldn't even trip. Give it two weeks. Sometimes periods act like that when you're under a lot of stress, and you have been acting crazy as fuck lately, so just chill."

"You right," I said, turning the sink off as I pulled my panties and pants up. Don't know what the fuck I was expecting to happen there. "I just pray to God I'm not." I looked in the mirror. I had my scarf on, with my weave braided into two pigtails. No makeup on; small, slanted, almost Chinese-looking eyes red from lack of sleep. Only thing that had been on my mind. Period. Where was my period?

"You probably not. Just give it some time. Damn, you just had sex with the nigga what? Last week?"

"Yeah, it's been a week, and it hasn't happened yet. This is—oh, shit," I said in a shaky voice. "I can't. I refuse to be fucking pregnant."

"You not. Calm down and take yo' ass back to bed. I'm going to back to sleep," she said, hanging up.

I opened the door, hearing a noise as I stopped to listen. It wasn't Jade and Trent, because they were knocked out cold. What the fuck? I could have sworn I heard a nigga's voice coming from

Jordyn's room, but her lame ass . . . she didn't even have any friends. I closed the door to the bathroom and opened my door to the room just as I heard the sounds of a nigga moaning.

Ahh, hell nah. Who the fuck she got in there? I closed the door to my room and started walking toward hers. *Not in my damn apartment you not, bitch.*

Freak Flag Fly High

Jordyn

"Hear the drums, they swing loooow, and the trumpets they gooo," I sang along with Jason Derulo as I pulled up in front of my building. Cutting the car off, I sighed as I looked at my bags. Maybe I overdid it with the shopping, but I was getting paid big bucks to play at a double wedding the next week, so it was okay. It all balanced out.

Walking up to my room, I thought about Elijah, wondering what he was doing that was so important that he had to only come at two or three in the morning. I didn't know if I could stay up that late. I tried staying in the library, but they closed at midnight, so I hung out with Rita until she decided to step out. Now I was heading to my room, and I would just wait—waiting to release all this stress, all the issues in my life, all the emotions I kept bottled up, onto one man that night. Elijah had no clue what he was in for.

Opening the door to my apartment, I could immediately hear the familiar sounds of sex happening in Jade's room: the consistent knocking noise of the bed, and her calling out Trent's name. Looking at the time on the clock, I saw it was barely past one a.m. Great. I had to sit there and listen to them now.

I set my stuff down, tossing the keys on the counter as I cut the lights on in the kitchen. As I unloaded my groceries, the door swung open and Trent stepped out, smiling at something Jade said, while pulling up his boxer briefs. Body was glistening in sweat as he closed the door, heading toward his bags that sat next to the front door.

"What up?" he greeted casually as I eyed his body. Not one mark on that light brown skin, not even a bruise. What kind of childhood did he have?

"Hi," I mumbled, looking away after catching a glimpse of his dick print. I could feel my lower body respond as I mentally told myself to calm down. *In time, Jordyn.* Hopefully Elijah was half the man Trent seemed to be.

He grabbed whatever and walked back to her room as my eyes followed him. Body was perfect. Face was perfect. He was like the exact male model of the perfect black man: educated, spoke correctly, handsome face, with pretty bright brown eyes that stood out, and definitely your typical masculine man. Meanwhile, I had to look at Elijah, who probably dropped out of high school to chase a dream of living life on the streets. *Fantastic.*

In the meantime, I took my time to clean up my room, playing a little music to drown out the noises of my roommate next door until they fell asleep. Taking a long shower, I washed my hair, blow-dried it out, and slipped on a T-shirt and shorts with no bra, no panties. Even slipped on my contacts so he wouldn't say anything about my wide grandma glasses that were so reliable. Digging in my red shoebox I kept on the side of the bed, I added two brand new vibrators I'd bought that day, plus some massage gel and cute handcuffs. Box was filled with sex toys that I'd collected over the years.

Was I a freak? I didn't think so, but I did enjoy sex. Ever since I saw my first porn, I felt like I wanted to experiment with everything, and I had for the most part. Figured out what I liked and didn't like. Glancing at the clock, I saw it was going on 3:30. I was just about to give up when the house phone rang. I quickly grabbed it off the hook and answered it.

"Hello?" I smiled, feeling excited. I could already tell it was him by the background—loud music, him yelling out to someone with that obnoxious laugh.

"Aye, what up? Come out here. I'll be there in about ten minutes, baby. You ready? You not sleepy, are you?"

"I was just about to give up on you," I told him.

Elijah just laughed. "Ahh, don't do that. You might miss out on something good, baby. Be outside. I'm pulling into the entrance of the yard now. I gotta take this call," he said, and just like that, he hung up.

I quickly slipped on some shoes, grabbed a long cardigan out of my closet, and walked out, careful not to wake anyone up. I could hear Trent snoring in the room next door, and Tia's TV blasting from down the hallway. Good. Hopefully everyone minded their own business while I got mine. Looking myself over as I walked down the hall, I smiled. Plain white T-shirt and black shorts, hair cascading down past my shoulders in loose curls, no glasses, showing off my deep gray eyes bouncing off my cinnamon brown skin. Looked more Mexican than anything, but the eyes and hair gave it away that I was more.

I could feel the cold air as I walked toward the main doors, seeing his truck pull up through the window. Moment I opened the door, that air hit me so fast that I almost thought about going back inside and closing the door until he got there. It was too cold for what I had on.

"Bruh!" he yelled into the phone as I rolled my eyes, watching him close the car door. "I don't want to have to go from New York then California all in the same fucking day. I want to at least chill somewhere overnight. We got Miami to hit up too, promoting a club that just opened up down there." I watched him walk toward me as I licked my lips. He was definitely Rita's type, but in some aspects, I could see why girls would fall for him with his tall, slim, toned frame wearing a red hoodie, low sagging jeans, and these fancy red high top sneakers, with his dreads pulled back in a messy ponytail.

He smiled at me with those bedroom eyes as he licked his lips. I couldn't get with the tattoos on his face, but I guess it was what made him who he was. He was cute in a dangerous, violent, chocolaty, obnoxious kind of way.

"Where yo' bra at, shawty?" he teased, pulling at my nipple as he walked in the door.

I quickly covered myself and gave him a small smile as I turned around so he could follow me, still talking on the phone.

"Where are we going to have this at?" he asked on the phone.

I signaled for him to be quiet as I opened the door to the dark apartment. I quickly took his hand, guiding him to my room, and closed the door softly, locking it.

"Nah. Yeah, let me go. I just got back to the crib. We'll talk when I wake up, a'ight? Yeah. A'ight, bet," he said, hanging up.

Elijah looked around my room with a huge grin. "I don't know why they give y'all these small-ass beds like they don't think people be fucking in here."

"Cheaper. Costs less to buy the smaller beds," I reasoned as I sat down on the edge of my twin bed.

He took off his hoodie and kicked off his shoes, revealing fresh, neat Polo socks.

"Aye, I'm about to take a shower real quick since I just came from the club. Where the towel and stuff at?" he asked.

After giving him the things he needed, I sat and waited some more anxiously. It was going on four o'clock and I hadn't had any yet. I didn't want him there when everyone woke up. Just wanted to have sex, kick him out, and sleep.

So, when Elijah walked back in, towel wrapped around his waist, dreads hanging loose in his face, he closed the door behind him, locking it. He was smiling hard at me. My eyes immediately went to that toned body, covered in art.

"Why do you have so many tattoos?" I asked curiously, eyeing his neck, which was covered.

"Been through a lot of shit, baby. This right here"—he pointed at a small black bruise, and then another one right on the side of his stomach—"I was shot here, so I tried covering that shit up with artwork. Once I got that first tattoo, I couldn't stop." He smiled as he moved closer to stand in front of me so I could see. Body was completely tagged in names, scriptures, a tattoo of a cross that hung around his neck, everything. His whole life story.

"Who are these people?" I asked, pointing at the names, Trenton Michael Carter and Olivia Keisha Carter, along with a birthdate.

"My other halves," he said in a low voice, watching me look his body over as I lightly touched his wet brown skin, outlining the names with my finger. "I'm the second oldest of a triplet."

"So, what's your whole name?"

"Elijah Jodie Carter."

"That's pretty neat," I said, letting my hands run through the tattoos as he stood in front of me.

"You still don't know who I am?" he questioned.

I looked up at him, confused. "Why don't you just tell me, because you keep saying it like I'm supposed to know. Are we related? If we are, this would be a great time to stop this."

"Nah." He laughed slowly. "Nah, we not related. I hope not. You got me hard as fuck looking at those damn eyes, girl. Damn," he mumbled as I giggled.

"Well," I said, standing up in front of him. Towering height was not an issue for me. "Shall we start? I remember: no kissing and no relationship talk, right?" I walked over, cutting the lights off.

"We can kiss. No oral, though. I see how you purposely left that shit out. I'm not going to eat you out, and don't try to get me to do that shit either," he stated.

I smirked, walking back over to him. I could barely make out an outline of his body, but the moment I felt his arm, I grabbed it and gently coaxed him up against the dresser, gripping his chin as I lightly kissed his lower lip, tugging gently with a sensual pull and pluck. I heard him moan.

"I'm serious, Jordyn," Elijah said against my mouth.

I pulled the towel down.

"I'm not eating you—"

"I only let girls do that, so you don't have to worry about that," I said, cutting him off. His mouth grew so wide I almost let out a small laugh before slipping my tongue inside his mouth to be playful, ignoring the no-kissing rule completely. Bet he wasn't expecting that. I slipped my shirt and shorts off. "You ready?"

"Shit, hold up."

I bent down, with my hands sliding down his body so that I was eye level with his dick, gripping it with one hand as I took it in completely. I hoped he wasn't going to talk the whole time.

His hands came down on my head as he pushed himself inside me farther. I loved doing this. It kept a guy harder a little longer and allowed me to have a little fun, hearing guys respond like wimps. His thighs were jumping as I pulled out, playing with the head.

"What the fuck, Jordyn," he breathed, looking down at me. "You get down like that?"

"You have no idea." I smiled, standing up as I wiped my mouth. "Go lay on the bed. Now."

Almost tripping on his own two feet, he laid back on the bed, and I tied his hands together. I needed to make this night count because I didn't plan on having sex with him again.

"What you doing, baby?" he moaned as I straddled him, one thigh reaching over his body to sit comfortably on his hips before sliding directly down on him. He was a lot bigger than I expected, but no worries.

"Oooh, shiiiiiiiit. Wait. Untie me, Jordyn. Untie me, baby, please," he begged as I slowly started to work, using my muscles to play strictly at the tip.

My hips were grinding slowly as I smiled to myself. Eyes slowly closed in relaxed concentration. I was feeding my body and soul that craved to be touched, and released in pleasure. I flipped my hair back as I looked up at the ceiling, playing with my own self, rocking my hips faster on him, booty bouncing back on the beat. I let my mind just escape to another place where it was just strictly pleasure. Elijah felt so damn good in me. I couldn't believe I'd waited this long. I slid down, pushing as far as I could go, hearing him whimper in response, fighting to pull apart the tie.

"Please, baby, let me go," he begged.

I shook my head, smiling down at him. I wanted to see his face, so I reached over, cutting the lamp light on, and he was so far gone, it was almost hysterical. Sitting up, with my hair hanging down, teasing his skin, I began to squat down on him. I held on to his chest with one hand and started to move at a steady pace. Booty was bouncing, slapping hard against his thighs as I blew a kiss at him. I reached behind me as I kept moving, and touched his thigh, waiting for the right moment before I hopped off, realizing he had no condom on.

I had to keep telling him to be quiet before he woke up my roommates, because he was so loud that music probably wouldn't have helped drown him out. He was barely hanging on.

"Ahhhhhhhhhhhhhh my gaaaaaaaah," he moaned, eyes nearly turning white with a roll. Drool was hitting the corner of his hanging mouth. Wrists were straining against the ties. His body was tensing, muscles clenching, as I slowed to roll and rotate my hips on him with a flick of my hair.

Elijah jerked at his tied hands, veins popping along his arms and neck. I began to stroke faster, slamming down on him every other second.

"Slow down. I don't want to—fucccck!" he let out, head going back as I moved even faster, realizing speed was his weakness. "Shawty, fuck you doing to me?" he called out like a wuss.

I smirked. Moment I felt his thighs jerk with aggression, I slid up just as he came, shooting out like a water gun. Dick was jumping as he continued to release.

"You gotta untie me," he breathed.

I smiled, sliding down as I cleaned him up with my mouth.

"Ahhh come on, baby, damn!" he groaned.

I licked him clean and smiled to myself, knowing it was my turn. I could get mine with no problem.

"Let me at least taste it," he begged, licking his lips sloppily. "Nigga mouth dry as fuck. I'm hungry, shawty. Lemme just—Shit, lemme touch som', feel you or som', please!" he pleaded desperately.

"Thought you don't eat every girl out," I breathed, moving my hair off my shoulders. I reached over, moving his locs out the way and wiping sweat off his forehead. He just lay there. How was he already sweating?

"I don't, but you got me wanting you in every way possible right now," he stated.

I smiled. "I only let girls eat me, Elijah. I was being completely serious when I said that," I mumbled, reaching down to grab my box full of goodies. Now the real fun began. "Have you done anal or no?"

"What, shawty?" he whined, head dropping back on the pillow in defeat. "Nah, I never did that shit."

"You want to?" I pressed, grabbing the gel. I'd only done it twice, but he was the perfect size to do it. Not too big, not too small.

"You into girls?" Elijah asked, avoiding the question as I started to massage his chest slowly. His hands were still tied above his head.

"Yes, I'm bisexual, if that's what you're asking," I told him.

He groaned again like he was in pain.

"Are you okay? Am I too heavy? I can—"

"Nah, that's my fucking weakness. Shit," he let out slowly, closing his eyes. "God damn, Jordyn. You like girls too? Fuuck, where you been at my whole life?"

"Around." I shrugged with a smile as I kissed his chest. "Are you willing to try it for me, Elijah?" Our eyes locked as I continued to kiss his chest, loving the feel of his dark skin against my lips. He smelled so good; clean skin, nothing salty like the last guy.

It had been sooo long. I had so much I needed to do before the sun rose. I placed my breast in his mouth, and he gladly took it, playfully biting before sucking. My hair was covering us both as I hissed in response to his sudden wet mouth circling around the sensitive nipple with ease before I pushed more into him. I bit my lower lip in with my eyes closed as I felt that tongue work.

He might be able to eat me, but I didn't want to risk it. Last time I let a guy do it, I nearly fell asleep. Waste of my time.

He let go, licking his lips as our eyes locked again.

"Give me that mothafucking mouth, girl," he demanded.

I giggled before kissing him, cupping his face as we let our tongues dance.

"Untie me. I can't handle all this shit you throwing at me, and I can barely touch you."

"Say please," I commanded softly.

"Come on," he groaned, and I giggled again. "Why you playing with a nigga like this?"

"Say please, mami," I said, letting my Spanish accent come out. I lightly let my tongue lick from his chin to the upper lip in a playful manner before kissing him completely again. For some odd reason, I liked the way he kissed me. Maybe I just liked to kiss him. I don't know. I had been drawn to his lips the moment he stepped in the room, the time he said no kissing, I ended up kissing him just moments later, just naturally, like it was meant for our lips to lock.

"Say it, Elijah," I pressed.

"I ain't saying that fuckin' shit," he let out.

I smirked. "Oh, but you will," I said, getting up slowly. I straddled him in the reverse position, and literally in fifteen minutes, maybe less, I had him calling me everything but my name. Hair was bouncing, ass facing him so he could get a view. I had the lights on so he could see everything. A woman riding him like he was my only ride, and speaking in Spanish; Elijah didn't know what to do when I did that. By the time he broke free from the tie, his arms just collapsed to the side as he came—for a third time, I might add. I got mine around the same time he got his last, and rode that out until he begged me to stop. I know after a certain point, a man will start to get sore after too much fun, so I stopped immediately when he said to.

Getting up, I tied my hair back as I wiped sweat from my face. Body felt so loose, so relaxed. I was definitely going to get a good sleep. I looked at Elijah, who just lay there, hand on his dick, as he stared at me.

"Are you okay?" I asked.

"Fuck no, I'm not okay," he mumbled.

I walked over to my mirror and took these stupid contacts out of my eyes. I hated them. Reaching for my glasses, I put them on, and slipped on a simple T-shirt.

"I hope you didn't wake anyone up. You were pretty loud," I added as I gathered his things, bringing them closer to him. It was time for him to go; going on seven o'clock, and I didn't need anyone waking up to see him there.

"Fuck them," he spat with an attitude as he sat up, shaking his dreads loose. When he stood up, he walked over to me, pulled my hair down, and kissed me, glasses on and everything.

"Baby, I can barely stand up," he said against my mouth. I smiled, thinking about his reaction when I pretty much forced him to do anal. He loved it. Once men get it out of their head that it's not a gay-man thing and see that I'm all woman and it feels just as good, then everything is okay. "Jordyn with a Y," he mumbled as he slowly looked my face over, moving a stray hair out of my face. "I see I wasn't prepared for you like you told me to be."

"You weren't," I agreed with a small nod.

"What haven't you done?" he asked curiously as he continued to stare at me with this intense look, smoothing back my curly hair.

All I kept thinking about was that he needed to go. I didn't have time for this sentimental talk, but it was kind of cute to see him a little shocked by me.

"I don't know." I shrugged, hearing a door open from outside my room. "Elijah, you have to go," I whispered.

"Let me stay the morning," he mumbled, kissing me softly, light smacks echoing in the room as I sighed. There was something about the way he kissed me.

"When I say you fucked the life out of me, shawty? I can't drive right now. I can barely move. I don't even know who the fuck I am right now."

"Elijah, I'm serious." I giggled as I wrapped my arm around his neck, pulling his mouth deeper. He was so dramatic, yet I couldn't stop kissing him. My eyes closed as his hands came to my lower back, gripping my booty with ease while he dipped his head to the side of my face, then dropped to my neck. He pulled my body closer to his as I relaxed in his hold.

"Ain't neva met a girl like you," he said softly against my ear before facing me as he cupped my chin gently, tipping my face to look at him before kissing me again.

I giggled against his mouth, feeling him smile before our lips combined once more. His other hand slid down the natural line of my booty before gripping in between, like it was his, holding his property that he seemed to claim. We stayed as we were until someone knocked on my door.

"Jordyn?" Tia said, trying to open it.

My heart started to beat as Elijah looked at the door before sighing.

"Huh?" I answered back, helping Elijah get himself together.

"Who the fuck you got in there with you? I heard a nigga's voice," Tia snapped.

Elijah's face scrunched up. "Tell that bitch to mind her busi—"

I covered his mouth as she started aggressively trying to open my door, doorknob jingling like crazy. "Nobody. Go back to bed. It's the radio," I lied as I looked at Elijah with pleading eyes before letting his mouth go. I was the target in this house, and him being there would make it worse if they ever found out.

"I know you ain't got nobody in there," Tia continued with a snort. "Ain't nobody trying to fuck with yo' lame ass anyway. I'm going back to bed."

Elijah nearly opened the door himself before I grabbed his arm.

"Who the fuck is—"

"Elijah," I hissed.

He sighed, tucking in that lip to keep from saying anything further.

"Bruh, these hoes don't have no fucking tact about themselves, I swear," he groaned.

I smiled, surprised he even knew what "tact" meant.

"Here," he said, reaching in his jean pocket, pulling out a white phone and its charger. "Take this."

"I don't know how to use—"

"Learn. I don't have time to wait on you to get here so you can answer yo' house phone. Learn how to use it. I'm going to be out of town all week, and probably next week too, so I won't get a chance to come back over until I get back."

"You want to come back?" I asked, shocked.

He scrunched his face up like I'd asked a stupid question, causing me to laugh.

"I see how you are, so I gotta come at you a little differently, but best believe, shawty, you not about to get me screaming like no li'l bitch again. You got lucky tonight," he stated, slipping his shoes on. "Walk me out."

Another Sunday

Trent

"What up?" I dapped hands with my brother Talin as we came in for a quick hug. It was too cold to play ball on this Sunday late morning. The sun wasn't even out, and it was past eleven o'clock. Wind was blowing, so we decided to meet up at Talin's house to chill. So far it was just me, since I lived the closest. The rest were on their way.

"What's been good with you?" Talin asked, wrapping his locs up as he sat on the couch.

"Same shit, different day," I said, watching his wife walk out of the room, yawning, small pregnant belly starting to stand out in her tank. Toni was like the only female I knew that could match a nigga's attitude, word for word, vibe for vibe. Light skin with dreads, and didn't take shit from no one. Usually quiet and kept to herself, she kind of reminded me of Jade in a way—if Jade didn't run her mouth constantly.

"Nigga, what you smiling for?" Talin asked, hitting me on the arm as Toni waved at me.

"You want something to drink, Trent?"

"I'm good, mama," I told her, using her nickname as I hit Talin back. "You remember the girl I got into it with at the club? That video where she hit me?"

"Yeah," he said, changing the station to ESPN, getting ready for Sunday football.

"She's my girl now," I mumbled.

Talin looked at me, eyes wide, just as two trucks pulled up, honking their horns.

"Nigga, she's what?" Talin laughed as I watched the rest of the Carter siblings pile out of the trucks with food in their hands. We all brought over something, since we planned on watching the game over there, to take the stress of cooking off Toni.

"Aaaye! What's good! Where li'l mama at?" Jahiem asked as he stepped in, screen door pulled back with everyone coming in behind him.

"Nigga, fuck you so loud for?" Toni asked as she walked over, hugging each of the brothers while taking a few bags. "Y'all trying to eat this now?"

"Hell, yeah," Ontrell said.

"Nah, wait until the game," Shiloh argued.

"Hi, girly," Olivia greeted as she hugged Toni. "Girl, I swear you're getting bigger by the day. Look at you! You're only just getting started, too."

"I know. I'm already waiting and ready for this baby to just hurry up and come on out so I can be done with this process," Toni said as the girls went into the kitchen.

"Rise up, mothafuckas!" Ant called out as he closed the screen door behind him. "Game day!" Nothing but Falcons fans in this house. We ride hard for our team.

Everyone started talking at once, trying to get a word in. Talin wanted to know what was going on with Jade and me. Elijah was strangely quiet as he texted on his phone, sitting on the floor up against the couch, and the rest were just talking over each other. Fucking chaos, until it got around that I was now dating the girl who had hit me in the face. That became the number one topic in the house at the moment.

"Hold up, so you asked the bitch out? How the fuck did that happen? You liked her?" Ant went in as I sighed. *Here we go.*

"Nah, the nigga probably felt bad for her. Maybe the pussy was good, and—"

"No, of course he liked her," Shiloh argued as I stayed quiet, letting them speak on the shit they knew nothing about, only assumed. Again, Elijah, who was the most hyper and energetic, was the quiet one in the room, just observing.

"So, when do I get to meet her? I'm going to let you know, I already don't like her, and I hope you don't expect me to treat her with respect after how she did you," Olivia said with an attitude as she sat down next to Elijah on the floor.

"So, why the fuck would I let you meet her then if that's the case?" I snapped. "All of y'all don't know what the fuck is going on. You just assuming."

"Bruh, how you fucking with a ho that hit you and spit on you in front of everybody? That shit don't make sense," Jahiem argued. "It's like you want her to make you out to be the bitch. She probably controls everything you do, or walks all over you."

"Nah, we—"

"Why y'all giving him a hard time? Toni is just like this girl—"

"Nah, Toni and you known each other forever. Been around the family for years, nigga. This is different. This bitch might be half man or some shit the way she was acting on that video," Jahiem joked as they laughed.

"Y'all don't have to worry about meeting her," I let out. "I'm the one that fucked up, not her. She would have never acted that way if I didn't say what I said about—"

"It doesn't matter. No woman should act that way," Olivia said.

I looked at my sister, my own flesh and blood. I loved her like no other, but she was two-faced like a mothafucka, and I had no problem telling her that on several occasions.

"You was the one telling me to apologize to her last weekend, Livie!"

"Yeah, but I didn't say go date her! Elijah, say something to him! Please!" she argued.

Elijah looked at us, shaking his head. "Yo, I might be in love with this girl," was all he said.

We stared at him. Even Toni cut the sink off in the kitchen and came walking over to the living room, eyes wide. Elijah stared at us with a small smile, shaking his head as if he was shocked himself. "I met the girl I'ma be with for the rest of my life."

There was silence. Nobody knew how to react, but nobody wanted to be the first to laugh at him either. Until they did.

"Nigga, what?" Jahiem let out with a laugh.

"I just had the best sex of my life, bruh," Elijah started in a low voice. "And she's a bitch who like other bitches, bruh. You know I love a bisexual ho. I think I love her. On everything—"

"Ahh, what?" Ontrell waved off as I laughed, throwing a pillow over at him for wasting everyone's time. "Nigga, you ain't in love."

"I am. I can't stop thinking about her, and I'm already thinking about the things I'm going to do to her when I see her."

"Nigga, shut up!" Jahiem cut in as we laughed. "You in love with the pussy, nigga, not her."

"Same thing in my eyes."

"Nooooo," we all said in unison as we started to go in on him.

Soon as the game started, everyone got comfortable in the living room. Blunts had to be smoked outside out of respect for Toni, who wasn't allowed to take a hit, only it was too cold to be smoking, so everyone kind of just chilled, ate wings, meatballs, and pizza. Beer bottles were lined up everywhere, and there was good-ass conversations in between the game, as always.

"Aye, you ever heard from that chick we met at that party?" Elijah asked Jahiem, who started cheesing like crazy, mouth full of food.

"Nah, but if I see her, though," he said, shaking his head, "I'll see if I can get another dose of that head game, nigga. Shit was too good. You missed out."

"Nah, I ain't missed out on shit. You could tell she was a fucking ho that's been ran through too many times," Elijah stated.

Olivia rolled her eyes. "You guys need to settle down. I'm not understanding why some of y'all have kids and only one brother is married," Olivia started as we all groaned. "I'm just saying, what do you get out of sleeping with multiple women?"

"They're men, Olivia. They will do what they wanna do," Toni reasoned with a shrug as she propped her feet up on Talin. "Niggas pass up on the good girls and end up settling down with the ratchet bitches. Especially in Atlanta. They're known for that."

"How would y'all like it if some guy did that to me?" Olivia reasoned as we all fell silent.

"Mannn, that nigga is going to get *got* on sight, my nigga. Real shit. You already know we don't play that," Shiloh said with all the seriousness in his voice.

"Soon as you get a boyfriend, it's going down," Ant said as we laughed. Olivia just shook her head.

"Nah, I mean for real, though. I'll settle down," Jahiem said. "I'm twenty-seven. I'll find me a nice girl when I'm around thirty-five, maybe. Get me a young ho."

"I'll settle down with one of my baby mamas eventually," Ant let out. "Just right now, our music thing is taking off. You know how much pussy we get thrown our way on a regular basis? Shit is hard to turn down."

"Hell yeah," Elijah agreed. "To the point where hoes will be waiting by the fucking car, room, bed, stalking yo' ass. One girl followed me through the mall the other day, all the way to my car, taking pictures nonstop."

"I'll settle down when I'm forty," Ontrell said, and I laughed.

"Oh, no! You out of everyone should take your relationship seriously. I don't even know how Tyree is still in a relationship with you after all you put him through."

"Because that mothafucka ain't going nowhere. He see I'm making money and getting big now, so who would leave that? Nigga caught me fucking with a bitch the other night, and what happened? The next day we was at the mall, buying up some shit. He's good; I'm not worried." Ontrell waved it off as I shook my head.

"One day you're going to wake up and that nigga is going to leave you," Toni warned him. "Then what?"

"It won't happen." Ontrell shrugged, and I laughed, hitting him in the back of the head.

"Bruh, you a ho," I let out as we all laughed. "Fucking niggas and bitches like it's nothing."

"Aye, real talk, I think he probably get more bitches than me, because girls be wanting to know what it's like to fuck a nigga that go both ways," Elijah said, and Ontrell laughed.

"I just can't believe y'all," Olivia said, shaking her head. "Well, at least wrap it up. I don't want any more nieces and nephews no time soon. Talin's should be the last one until y'all get married."

"We about to have a bunch of these li'l niggas running around here," Talin said excitedly as I laughed at the expression on his wife's face. Toni brought his head closer to her as she lovingly kissed him on the side of the face.

"Nigga, we not having another child after this," she stated simply, and we laughed. "Sorry, but no."

After all was said and done, we left the house, saying our good-byes. I wasn't going to see my brothers for another two weeks, since they were doing a mini tour around the country.

I called up Jade, who I now felt comfortable saying was my girl, to see where she was at. Couldn't believe I broke down and made her my girlfriend, but I guess it was true. You can't help who you like. Even if she was a hard, tattoo-covered, pierced-all-over, slick-mouth-having chick who I couldn't stand most of the times, when she smiled and laughed at me, I told myself that shit was all worth it at the end of the day. Hated that she had all them fucking tattoos, though, but I liked her. Fuck could I say at this point?

"Hello?" she answered with music in the background.

"Where you at?"

"In the room, doing some cleaning up. I need to make a few errands, but it's too cold to ride MARTA right now, and my sister is busy at practice."

I smiled, realizing she either forgot I had a car, or that was her way of asking me without making it sound like she needed my help.

"Sucks." I sighed, pulling up at a red light. "Maybe it will warm up before it gets dark, baby."

"Nigga, bring the mothafucking car and come get me," she snapped, and I smirked. I wouldn't expect her to respond no differently.

When I told her I was parked in front of her building, she stepped out, wrapped up in a long-ass pullover with Timberland boots, leggings, and a long shirt. Everything about her was nothing I'd seen before, from the way she walked to the way she just looked at me. Had a way of looking at me like I was the biggest bitch in the world, and then could look at me like I could solve all her problems and be the nigga of her dreams. Shit drove me crazy.

Her dreads were up, with a few hanging down in the front as she opened the car door, slipping inside.

"Shit, nigga, it's cold as fuck, yo," she said with a shaky breath, putting on her seatbelt as I looked her over. Definitely beautiful. Naturally beautiful for a dark-skin girl. I wasn't going to tell her that, but she was sexy as shit with those slanted, dark brown eyes.

"Why are you looking at me like that?" Jade asked as I smiled at her, puckering my lips out, knowing she hated that shit. "Son, I swear on everything, you gotta chill on that shit. I hate that." She laughed before kissing me.

"Can't believe you're my girl," I said with a shake of my head. "Should be an interesting relationship."

"Hell yeah," she agreed with a small laugh as I pulled out.

Noelle: The Sweetest Girl

"Oh my Lord," I groaned in frustration as I turned over in my bed, using the thick pillow to block out the sounds of music and laughter from next door. I couldn't do this. I had just freaking moved to the house that day, barely finished unpacking, and already wanted to move out. I closed my eyes tight, trying to tune out the noise from outside, gripping the thick blue pillow tighter over my head.

"Bruh! Fuck that shit! Nigga had it coming! When I see those bitch niggas he roll with on the street, I'ma pop on them too!" one said with a loud laugh. "Hit 'em like, *Pop*! *Pop*! *Pop*! They not gonna ever see it coming!"

"Nigga, you is a fool, bruh!" Another laughed as I sat up in the bed, looking at the time on my digital clock: 2:43 a.m. Monday morning. I had work in a few hours, and these hooligans, these fools, these boys wanted to be outside like it was a Friday night and nobody else lived in this neighborhood.

I turned around to look out the window, peeking through the blinds and seeing at least ten people sitting on the lit porch, smoking and drinking. A few were hanging out in the driveway, sitting on cars, blasting music with a couple of girls, barely dressed like it wasn't cold outside. I sighed, laying back down on the bed as I covered my face with the pillow, wishing I could get some sleep.

"Aye, tell that mothafucka we about that life! Fuck that shit. We about it, my nigga. Straight run up on you, take you for everything you got, fuck yo' girl and yo' mama, and be out!"

"Yo, turn that music up, baby!" one called out, and the music became even louder.

I started to feel the bass of the rap song in my chest as I let out another sigh. I couldn't take this no more. I just moved there earlier that morning, first time in Atlanta, and already I had to deal with this. I was coming from Albany, Georgia, and I was definitely not used to all this noise and hoopla in the middle of the night. I liked quiet, silence, and a good night's sleep, not this crap.

I got up, patting my head through the scarf as I slipped on some shoes. I grabbed my long, thick cardigan, knowing I only had on a tank and some shorts underneath, and stepped out of my room. I was so close to calling the police, but I didn't want to be labeled as "that neighbor," you know? I moved past the boxes in my living room and opened the front door, stepping out. The cold hit me so hard I almost thought about going back in, but I was out now.

The streetlights were on, barely lighting up the streets as people walked along the sides, with obvious teenagers clearly sneaking in and out of houses. I looked to my left, seeing the small party on the porch, smoking, still laughing it up like it was daylight. *Hell, no.* I stepped off my porch, wrapping myself tighter within my sweater as I walked over to their yard, all eyes slowly making their way to me. It looked like something straight out of a rap video—guys posted up, jeans sagging, bottles everywhere, smell of weed hitting me hard—and I could hear dogs barking. No doubt it was a pitbull.

"What up, sexy?" one called out, blowing kisses at me.

"Ohh, shit. I like my bitches dark like you, baby. Damn! You just moved in here?" another asked, hopping off the porch as I continued to walk.

Girls were already eyeing me like they wanted it to be a problem. The last thing they wanted was a problem with me. All of the guys had their eyes on me greedily as I took the first step onto the porch and held my position, looking around for an authority figure. They looked too young to be hanging around there at night—like in their early twenties, late teens.

"Who lives here?" I asked, arms crossed over my chest.

"Aye yo, cut the music off!" one of them called out as he stood on the top step. The music came to a complete stop. I could hear the girls who were cuddled up with a guy smack their teeth and snicker to themselves.

"What did you say, baby?" the guy with the short dreads asked as he took a pull on his blunt. He was tall and lanky with a sunken face, like he overdid it with more than just weed.

"Who lives here?" I asked. "The owner of this place?"

They looked at each other just as another person came to the door, opening up the screen, joint in hand as he stepped out, shirtless. I nearly had to catch myself as I cleared my throat, giving him a look over: tall, light complexion, with tattoos all over his body, teardrops on the side of his face, low eyelids that made his eyes look sleepy, dark pink lips, and jet black curly hair that sat low and tapered on the sides. He looked so mean, so serious, like he was incapable of smiling and probably could scare anyone off with just one look. Not me. I needed my sleep, and I was a firm believer in killing someone with kindness.

"What's the problem?" he asked in an extremely deep voice as we locked eyes.

"You live here?" I pressed.

He stayed quiet, just looking at me. Didn't even blink. Nobody spoke. It was almost like the world had come to a stop when he stepped out.

Whatever. I formed a bright smile on my face, despite my tired body, as I extended my cold hand out to him.

"Hi. My name is Noelle. I just moved here to Atlanta today."

He just stared at me as my hand stood by itself. No shake, nothing. I could hear the guys laughing amongst themselves, but it didn't faze me.

"What's your name?" I asked politely.

His face didn't change; eyes didn't blink as he continued to stare at me, occasionally taking a quick up and down look at my body. Despite how uncomfortable I was starting to feel, I smiled through it, taking my hand back as I intertwined it with my arm across my chest to keep warm.

"I just ask can you guys cut the music off, or maybe take this get together inside? I live just right there," I said, pointing as they all looked at the house next door. "I have work in the morning, and I haven't been able to go to sleep yet because of the noise. So, if it's not too much to ask, can you please cut it down?"

It was silent. All the guys were looking at me, barely sober themselves, but the one who stepped out just stared, no expression on his face, no sympathy, nothing. Suddenly, I felt a cold breeze hit my thigh as I turned around, seeing one of the guys lift up my long cardigan take a peek.

"Excuse me!" I snapped, snatching my sweater out of the guy's hand as he laughed.

"My bad, baby. You got a fat ass, though," he slurred.

"Nigga, why you had to—"

"Aye!" the guy who stepped out of the house snapped, making everyone flinch at the sound of his voice. "Y'all get the fuck on. You shouldn't be at my shit anyway."

"We were just chilling, though. We weren't even that loud," one guy argued.

The guy cut his low eyes toward him, giving him a deathlike stare as the guy got up, head dropped in shame. Amazing. Everyone started to make their way toward the cars parked in the yard or alongside the house, while others walked the streets.

I smiled as I looked at the guy again. He hadn't taken his eyes off me.

"Thank you so much," I said, excited by the fact that I could get some sleep. He just stared before turning around and going back in the house, closing the door behind him.

Whatever.

Moment I went back to my place, I nearly jumped in my bed. Silence. I had my first day of work the next day and grocery shopping to do. My friend from back home was coming to help me unpack soon. I felt good. I guess I should have introduced myself a long time ago, but now that it was quiet enough, I could hear my own thoughts.

My name is Noelle. I'm twenty-five years old, a college graduate with a degree in fashion. Ultimately, I want to move to New York, but I thought Atlanta would be a great start. I didn't have many friends in Atlanta, but I had enough not to consider myself alone. I'm a country Southern belle at heart—church on Sundays, home-cooked meals, and definitely didn't believe in sex before marriage. So, of course, I rarely date. It isn't hard to get a guy or boyfriend, just hard to keep them once they realize I'm not having sex before marriage.

Now, on to my looks. I am, as my daddy says, God's precious piece of chocolate. I am dark-skinned, with matching dark brown eyes, elegant bone structure for a model, and straightened hair that falls past my shoulders. It's not natural; I've been relaxing my hair for years, and it works wonders for my hair. Just have to know how to take care of it. Overall, I'm just your average country girl, big-time daddy's girl, and probably one of the nicest people you will ever meet. It's hard to get on my bad side, but once on there, it's hell to pay. I can get crazy, downright ugly if I have to, but I hate showing that side of myself. I really do. So, a lot of times, I ignore ignorance directed toward me because it's not worth it at the end of the day.

The next morning, I woke up in a rush, trying to get ready. My closet was full of heels and cute flats, and one pair of Jordans my daddy bought me for Christmas one year. Still had yet to wear them. I had a cute black pencil skirt with a cute matching top tucked in. My hair was smoothed into a ball, an I wore pearl earrings and necklace. I definitely needed to finish unpacking, because I hated having to dig through my boxes to find my clothes.

I grabbed my water and bag of grapes as I walked out, keys jingling in my hand. I'd almost forgotten about the night before until I stepped out onto the yard, seeing the same mean-looking guy walk a girl out of his house, arm wrapped around her neck, kissing her. Cute. I quickly rushed to my silver Honda Civic, put my things inside, and rushed back in the house. Couldn't wait to get my day started. I was working at a modeling agency in Atlanta, doing a few things behind the scenes of a photo shoot, answering phones, basic office chores, but it was in the industry I wanted, so I was happy regardless.

I walked back out, locking the door as I glanced back over at the guy, who stood shirtless once again, smoking as he looked over at me after the girl backed out of the driveway in her car. Had to admit to myself he was cute in a rough, I'm-a-thug kind of way. Not my type, but I did find him attractive. Nice body, if it weren't covered in crap. He just looked so mean, so unapproachable. Opposite of me. I just waved politely and continued to my car, not looking for a response or a wave back.

"Aye!" he called out.

I looked up, opening the driver's side door, waiting.

"My name is Shiloh Carter," he said in a low voice.

We locked eyes. He still had no smile, not even a twinkle in his eye; just took a pull on his joint as he stared hard at me.

"Nice to meet you, Shiloh," I said sweetly before dipping into the driver's seat, closing the door.

Weeks Later

Tia

"Move out the way!" I snapped, pushing past someone to get into the bathroom stall, where I bent over, puking my fucking life into the toilet. I felt so sick. It had been going on for the past two days. Didn't know what the fuck I'd eaten, but I was done. Stomach was sore from squeezing tight just to throw up.

"Girl, you need to go to the clinic," Porscha said from behind as she held the door closed. "I don't know how many times I told yo' ass to take a pregnancy test. You might just be pregnant. You already said you missed your period."

"Don't wish that shit on me," I snapped, wiping my face as I gripped the nasty-ass seat. I was supposed to be in class, but I kept having to leave just to be hung over in the bathroom stall. All I kept thinking about was Jahiem. Nigga pretty much raped me—and with no condom. I told no one about it, not even Porscha. As far as she knew, I fucked Elijah and it was the bomb. That was four weeks ago. I hadn't seen those niggas since. Now that it was a Tuesday morning, with homecoming just around the corner, I felt like shit. I hadn't had sex since that night.

Hearing a toilet flushing next to me, I silently prayed I wasn't pregnant. Only nigga I fucked without a condom that came in me was Jahiem.

"Oh, shit," I mumbled as I leaned over again to release more vomit, head throbbing, body sore, face hot. I should have been in fucking bed. Just the thought of being pregnant with his child made me want to . . .

"Porscha, I need a wet paper—" I bent over one last time to get out the rest of the vomit, coughing hard as I wiped my mouth, tears coming down heavy. "I need to be in my room," I cried softly.

"Girl, here," she said, tossing the paper towels over the door. "I can't go in there or I'm going to be sick with yo' ass. We need to get you to the bed. I don't even know why you left the house this morning anyway if you was feeling like this. Are you done?"

"I think so," I mumbled, trying to stand up.

She opened the door, holding her breath as she helped me stand up. "If you are pregnant, just think about whose baby you're about to have," she said excitedly. I looked at my friend with tired eyes. "Girl, you about to get that money, bitch. You having Elijah's baby!" she whispered loudly, trying to make me smile.

I just looked at her, eyes swollen red from crying, weave a hot-ass mess, and the only thing on my mind was finding this nigga Jahiem and telling him off. If I was pregnant, not only was he paying for an abortion, but he would pay for my expenses, traveling fees, emotional distress, all of that. Nigga better borrow the money from his brother, because I was not fucking playing around with none of these Carter Boys no more. I was done that night after seeing how they got down. So, if he didn't get with it, I was calling rape. He fucked with the wrong ho, nigga.

"Girl, take me back to the room so I can tell you what really happened," I let out.

Her eyes grew wide. "A'ight, come on," she said, pushing her fresh braids off her shoulder. "And what you mean, what the fuck really happened? Did you fuck him or no? You damn sure left me on the curb, so I was expecting you to get the best dick of yo' life, trick."

"Girl," was all I could manage to say as we walked out of the bathroom and headed straight for her car. I needed to smoke a blunt. All I needed to do.

Soon as we got in her car, she drove up to the clinic on the corner store just outside the yard and bought a pregnancy test. After telling her the truth of that night, I could only imagine how I was going to react if the test came back positive. My heart was already pounding, stomach rolling, and nerves in my throat as she set the bag in my lap.

"I can't believe yo' ass is having a baby," she squealed in excitement, and I hit her on the arm. "What? I can't be excited for my main bitch?"

"Nigga, I don't want this fucking baby, and we don't even know if I'm pregnant or not, so stop saying that shit. I'm not ready to be a damn mother."

"You just saying that because you know it ain't Elijah's baby," she retorted as we pulled up to my building. "I mean, at least Jahiem is cute. You could have done worse."

"He is worse! I didn't want his no-name ass," I snapped, getting out of the car with the bag in my hand. I felt like I had to throw up again.

"Well, was the sex good? I mean, I'm sure he wouldn't be better than Elijah, but was the dick good?"

"I don't want to talk about it," I said, holding my stomach as we walked inside the building.

When we got to the quiet apartment, I went straight to the bathroom to throw up again before deciding to just say fuck it and take the test. Porscha stood outside the door, popping on some gum as she checked her Instagram.

"If you are, I know exactly where these mothafuckas gonna be at tonight, so you already know I have no problem rolling on them like, *nigga what*?" she started.

I smiled. That's why she was my bitch. I took the stick out of the wrapper and did what I had to do, then waited. Looking in the mirror, I saw that my eyes were red, blond weave was a mess, and just overall I looked like I could possibly be a fugly bitch without makeup, when I knew that wasn't the case. I never allowed myself to look like this.

"Mm-hmm, I'm on Jahiem's page right now. Nigga is a ho for sure," she mumbled as I waited for the test results.

Shit felt like it was taking forever, so I walked out of the bathroom and went straight to my room with her following me.

"He got a lot of shirtless pictures . . . sexy-ass body, though," she continued, laying back on my bed as I leaned against the desk, chewing on my nails in anxiousness and anticipation.

"He do have a nice body," I mumbled in agreement. Flashbacks of us intertwined on the bed, kissing, and . . . damn! His lame ass almost got me with that dick. Almost had me fooled.

"Girl, was the sex good, though?"

"I mean, it was a'ight. Better than what you expect from a whack-ass nigga like him. He was straight." I waved it off, knowing that was probably one of the best dicks I had in my life. I wasn't going to give him that satisfaction.

"Well, it says they're going to be at club Mojo tonight. Girl, I don't even know where the fuck that is, but we will roll up there if we have to. Bust them fucking doors down and demand that nigga pay for everything, including gas money just to drive there."

"I may not even be pregnant. Quit speaking that shit into existence," I snapped as I wrapped my hair up.

After waiting another fifteen minutes, I finally found the courage to go look at the test before telling Porscha to look at it. My body was numb, almost felt like I was going to pass out just looking at this shit. It was not the first time it happened, but it was the first time I'd been throwing up like this. First time I actually remembered a nigga shooting in me, and me letting that shit happen.

"Okay, so you ready?" she asked with a huge grin as she looked at me, hanging in the bathroom doorway. "I have it in my hand now."

"Just read that shit!"

"A'ight, damn." She laughed as she looked back in the bathroom.

The moment she gasped, I nearly dropped to the floor, eyes watering up as I gripped my head. When she looked back at me with wide eyes, I immediately went back into my room and fell onto my bed, crying.

"Tia, it's not all that bad. We just need to go find this mothafucka and make him pay for the abortion. You got plenty of time to get rid of this baby."

"Well, where the fuck is club Mojo? Is that where they're going to be at tonight? Nigga, that shit sounds like a gay-ass club!" I snapped angrily, wiping fresh tears from my face. Mind was racing with so many thoughts. Would he even remember me?

"It's down there in middle Georgia. Shit, girl, that's over an hour away," she let out, looking up at the ceiling as if she was calculating something in her head before looking back at her phone. "We are going to have to take turns driving if we're going to make it back before morning for class tomorrow."

"So, we're really going to go find him?" I pressed as her eyes grew wide.

"Uh, bitch, yes the fuck we are really going to find him," she retorted, mocking my voice. "If this nigga had sex with you after you said you didn't want to, and then got your ass knocked up . . . are you one hundred percent sure he's the daddy?"

"I wish he wasn't, but yes, I know it's his baby," I admitted before my mind went to Trent and how I'd slept with him the night before. *Oh my God.*

"Well, then we about to fuck this nigga's night up. Get some sleep, and be ready by seven, because that's the time we're leaving," she said, walking out. "See if you can scrape up some money for gas, too!"

"Okay," I replied as I closed my eyes, thinking. I was pregnant by a nigga I never meant to have sex with. Just needed to get this baby aborted and get back to my regular life. I was not trying to be a fucking mother at this age, especially not by whack ass.

So sure enough, later on, I felt myself get a little better after some much-needed rest. My attitude became a lot better knowing I could easily get an abortion and be done with this shit.

My life wasn't ruined after all. It wasn't over just because I was pregnant. I was going to force that nigga to take me to the clinic that weekend. I wanted this sucker out before Sunday. So, while waiting on Porscha to scoop me up because it was going on nine o'clock at night and she was late as fuck, I did my hair, put on some makeup, and made sure my outfit looked cute. I wore a cute long-sleeve red maxi dress, with my honey-blond weave falling in wavy curls and a cute swoop bang on the side. Eyebrows were perfectly done; eye makeup was sultry, red lipstick and drawn-on mole on that upper lip. I mean, shit, if I was about to step to the nigga talking about "I'm pregnant," I wanted to look right, you know? Couldn't look busted and step to a nigga like, "I'm pregnant with yo' baby." Regardless, I wanted to look like a nigga should want me to have his baby, okay? Never leave the house looking a mess.

I packed a small duffle bag just in case we ended up having to get a hotel for the night, and met my main boo outside in the parking lot. Porscha was dressed up in a cute body con dress, with flats on so she could drive. Her long braids were up in a cute ball, and her eyebrows were filled in to perfection.

"You ready to go hunt for a fuck nigga, bitch?" she asked.

I laughed, getting in the car with her. "How much did you get?"

"He sent me two hundred, so we can kill that off the top. Go by some 'rellos and a few drinks so we can get this shit started," I said, checking my face in the mirror.

"Bitch, you are not about to drink or smoke with yo' pregnant ass."

"Girl, bye. I'll be back to normal before Sunday, so I can do what I want. Not trying to have no damn baby. Haven't even told my daddy, and don't plan on it," I let out. "Damn, we look good."

"I know it," she said, and we both laughed.

I grabbed the blanket that she always kept in the car and wrapped myself in it as she pulled off into the dark night. Last stop before we hit the road was the corner store. Already had the weed, just needed the 'rellos, and a few drinks and we were set. No traffic, no anything; highways were smooth sailing.

So, as I was taking a pull on my shit, I was checking Instagram, seeing these niggas post where they were at. In the midst of that, I did look at pictures of Jahiem out of curiosity, trying to put his life together based off one profile. For the most part, he smoked, drank, partied, and posted pictures of himself being shirtless in the gym. Either that or he posted outfits he was wearing, all name brands, with a clean shoe game. *Whatever*. Nigga was still lame. I clicked on one of the videos and waited for it to load, just to hear how this nigga sounded.

"Yeah, we out here!" he yelled with a crowd of people behind him. He smiled with his light-bright ass, dreads all over the place. "We out here in Miami! I love this fucking place, bruh. I swear the girls down here on something else!" he yelled out with a laugh as the girls screamed. "Yo' boy Jahiem from the Carter Boys. We doing big thangs, man!"

"Girl, what are you doing?" Porscha laughed as the video stopped. "Looking at yo' baby daddy?"

"Don't try me," I stated, and she laughed harder.

I just pressed on another video of him, looking like he was laying in the bed.

"Aye," he started in a low voice as he took a pull on his blunt before blowing smoke out into the camera. "Bed is lonely as fuck right now. This is one of them nights I wish I could come home to a girl and just chill, watch a movie or some shit, ya feel me? Who trying to come over and keep me company? Because I'm feeling lonely as hell."

"Ahhh," Porscha cooed as I read the comments below. Nigga had over fifty thousand likes alone, with girls nearly thirsting off this video, knowing he wasn't going to respond. "At least he's cute, and the dick was so-so."

"Yeah," I mumbled as I thought about the baby inside of me. Shit was probably the size of a pea, but regardless, it had to go. "All I need him to do is take me to the clinic. He don't even have to do that. Just pay for that shit and we can be done. Don't have to speak to each other again."

"Better hope he remembers you first."

"Oh, I'll make him remember me," I stated, determined, as I took another pull on my blunt.

We drove, listening to Tinashe's mixtape, singing along to every word before switching it to Jhené Aiko. I had a good buzz going, and I felt myself loosen up the closer we got to our destination. By then it was going on eleven o'clock, and after a couple of stops for a place to eat and use the bathroom, we finally made it to club Mojo. Shit was huge! Parking lot was packed, with everyone outside waiting to get in. We could barely find a damn parking space, so we had to park across the street near the gas station like most people. Shit was a two-story building, almost like a warehouse in the middle of nowhere. Straight country. If people thought Atlanta was country, they hadn't seen the rest of Georgia—straight cotton fields and peach trees, like, for real.

"Girl, I can't believe we drove down here!" Porscha laughed as we grabbed each other's hands, trying to run across the street without getting hit. "Do you spot the trucks?"

"Yep!" I pointed out four black trucks parked on the side of the building. "Right there! How much does it cost to get in? I'm not trying to wait in no fucking line tonight. We might as well go straight for VIP."

"Oh, these bitches down here," she said as we looked at how the girls dressed. You could tell we stood out from Atlanta, because these girls down there were at least a year behind. They looked straight ratchet, while we looked classy and sexy with it. They were still wearing cut-off jean shorts and half tank tops to the club, like that shit was cute, or leggings and a tank top with stiff-ass weave. *No, bitch. That's not going to fly in the A. Get it together.*

We crossed the parking lot, walking as I watched niggas' heads turn. Booty was sitting right in this all-red, body-hugging dress. I knew I was getting stared at. Walking straight past the regular line, we paid to get in as VIP, and the moment we walked in, my mouth dropped. Definitely wasn't expecting it to be as upscale as it was.

"Girl, look at this!" Porscha shouted over the music as I looked around. Everything looked like that shit was in chrome or crystal-clear decorations. Booths were lined up, multiple stages and dance floors. There were separate rooms for VIP, with giant beds that you could see through a window. I immediately spotted the Carter Boys. Their whole camp took up most of VIP.

"Shit, I know y'all not from around here looking like this. Where you from?" a guy asked, toothpick in his mouth.

Porscha and I glanced at each other with a knowing look.

"From Atlanta," I said sweetly to him.

"Damn, y'all look good as fuck, though, bruh. Come here! Y'all want a drink?"

"Nigga, what you think?" Porscha pressed as he smirked.

"A'ight, follow me, baby," he said, turning to walk off. We followed.

So, yeah, we got a little sidetracked and started to turn up a bit—maybe a little too much. Next thing I knew, we were turning up on the dance floor, twerking for our lives, okay? I mean, the music was on point, niggas was looking good. It was almost like not having to worry about competition because really, there was none when it came to girls down there. That was, until I started seeing people I went to school with. Soon as word got out that the Carter Boys were down there, I could see the Atlanta crowd trying to creep in. Whatever. By that point, I was past the point of being drunk. I was damn near fucked up. Felt like if I was killing my baby, why not speed that process up quicker?

"You need to go talk to him!" Porscha yelled at me over the music.

I looked at her, shaking my head hard.

"Girl, we did not drive all this way so yo' ass can get scared! You need to say something to him!" she yelled.

"I can't!" I whined, and her head cocked back. She was just as drunk, but she still had her sense about her. So, she grabbed my arm and forced me to the side of the club, opening the doors to the VIP section. It was like a lounge back there. Different set of music was playing, and everyone was on chill mode. Only type of seating were king-size beds and couches, with a few tables that had bottles all over them. Money was spread out on the floor, nearly covering the wood. As we closed the door, all eyes were on us.

"Where that nigga at?" Porscha mumbled, looking around as she held me steady.

I couldn't handle facing anyone. My heart was beating so fast. If this nigga didn't recognize me, or pretended like he didn't know me, I didn't know what the fuck I was going to do.

"Damn, y'all look good. Wassup?" one guy said as he came up to us. "Where y'all coming from?"

"Atlanta," Porscha said sweetly, getting side-tracked by the guy as I looked around, seeing naked girls dancing around the Carter Boys toward the back. I spotted Jahiem laying back on the bed, with a naked girl on top of him, kissing him, and her hand inside of his jeans. He smiled like a big kid, eyes closed.

"There he go," I told Porscha, pointing.

She grabbed my arm and marched over to them. I locked eyes with Anthony, who immediately remembered who I was.

"Whoa, shit, ain't you that girl we brought at the house?" Anthony pointed out as Jahiem opened his eyes to look at me. His mouth dropped before he nearly pushed the girl off him to sit up.

"I knew you would come back. And you came all this way to see me. I told you she was going to come back for this dick! Didn't I say that? Where my money at, Ontrell?" Jahiem laughed as Ontrell handed him fifty dollars.

"Nah, nigga, she's not back to fuck yo' sorry ass," Porscha snapped as my head dropped in shame. I felt like I was about to throw up again. "She's pregnant, and it's your baby."

"Ohhhhh!" they all said in unison as Jahiem backed up, shaking his head, eyes wide in horror.

"Nah, I don't remember that, bruh." He laughed. "It ain't mine."

"So, you didn't fuck my bitch without a condom then?" she pressed.

"She's a fucking ho! Just because I fucked her don't mean—"

"Nigga, you got me pregnant!" I snapped, tears in my eyes. "You think I want you to be the one? Nigga, I swear on everything I wish I wasn't standing right here right now, but you're the fucking daddy. All I need is the money to get the abortion and we can be done!"

"Man, I ain't giving yo' ass shit!" he spat, stepping up to me like he was ready to do something. "All you hoes are the same, just trying to get money out of me."

"Nigga, you don't have shit that I want! Nigga, I put this on everything: you are the lamest nigga in this sorry-ass group!" I yelled, pointing at all of them. "You think I want you to be the one after you fucking raped me?"

"Raped?" nearly everyone in the room let out as they looked at Jahiem, whose mouth dropped, eyes wide. That's what did it. That set him off.

"Oh, so I raped you now? After you told me it was the best sex you had in your life? Huh?" he yelled, moving closer, hunched over like he was really trying to gear up for a fight. "You—"

"Aye, hold up," Elijah said, coming in between, gripping his straight leg jeans up. He took a pull on his blunt before blowing the smoke out. All these niggas were approaching me like they were trying to buck at me.

The fuck? I felt myself about to throw up again as I looked at Elijah. He was the one I really wanted, not this whack, pale-ass nigga.

"We got to calm down. Nobody raped yo' ass, shawty. You came in that house willingly, trying to fuck something."

"I didn't consent to have sex with him!"

"But you didn't stop that shit, either, regardless of who you thought it was. Don't throw that rape word around like that, or it's really going to be a problem, you feel me?" Elijah said with all the seriousness in his voice as he stared at me with cold eyes, smoke shooting out of his nose, dreads hanging. Never seen a nigga look meaner than this. "I'll show you what the fuck rape really is if you trying to take it there, so chill the fuck out. I'm the one you don't want to piss off; you understand?"

I didn't say a word, but I felt my nerves swallow my body whole as I nodded.

"Get the fuck on, because we don't have no business with you. You disturbing the peace."

"Nigga, we not going nowhere until this nigga pays for her abortion!" Porscha demanded as the rest of the brothers stood up. Everything charismatic about them disappeared, and their street roots were starting to show.

I looked at Jahiem, who just stared at me. I wanted him to never forget this face, because this wasn't the last time he was going to hear from me.

"Nobody is paying for shit, baby. We not about to tell you again. Get the fuck on, or it's going to be a problem I know you not trying to have," Ontrell threatened.

"You know it's your damn baby!" I yelled at Jahiem while pointing at him. "You know you didn't use no fucking condom on me!"

"I don't know shit." He smiled with a shrug. "Sorry, but you got the wrong nigga. We fucked, but I know you fucked plenty of niggas before me, and plenty after me."

"Nigga, but you never pulled out! Twice!" I cried as Porscha dragged me out.

"Girl, come on. Fuck him. We'll find a way to pay for that shit. It's not like she's asking yo' ass to be a damn daddy and take care of it. She just needs help getting rid of the shit," Porscha called out as she opened the door back to the main club.

"Fuck it. I'll get rid of the baby my damn self. Let's get some drinks," I let out.

I started to drink away the pain, drink away the feeling of vomit, as I lived it up with random niggas. Porscha decided to let go and have fun; boo'd up in the corner with some nigga before walking off to VIP once again with him. I stayed on the dance floor as the club continued to get packed, and partied. When the Carter Boys came out to do a little performance, I didn't even look Jahiem's way. I was all in some drunk-ass nigga's face as I clung onto him to keep from falling.

"Damn, you look good, girl," he said against my ear before shoving his tongue inside it.

I giggled at the sensation, trying to playfully push him back, while at the same time bringing him close to me.

"We don't get a chance to show middle Georgia some love!" Elijah yelled into the mic as I turned around, placing my body against the man with his arms wrapped around me, swaying side to side. "So, tonight? We doing a little som' special!"

The crowd was going crazy as I felt this nigga start sucking on my neck. Glancing at the stage, seeing Elijah bring a girl up there as he sang to her, I looked at Jahiem, who had his eyes on me.

Good, nigga. I want yo' dumb ass to look.

"Let's go in the back," I told the guy with a slur.

"Aye, nigga, you gotta share," his friend said, slapping my ass hard.

"The more the better, because I'm a fucking ho, right?" I laughed with my head back, knowing I probably looked a hot-ass mess. "I need to be fucked like right now, nigga. Let's go."

"Now?" the guy repeated, shocked.

I nodded, licking my lips as I ran my hands down my body, trying to be sexy.

"Shit, okay!" He laughed. "Aye! Come on, bruh!" he called out to his friends as he picked me up, swinging me over his shoulders—all because I was a fucking ho. Well, why not do what hoes do best then?

He, along with three other niggas, took me into VIP and laid me back down on the king-size beds. I could hear them fighting over who was going to go first, who was going to record, and who was going to watch the door, as I felt myself slipping in and out of consciousness.

When he put me on his shoulders, I think all the contents in my body had shifted, because now I was feeling like . . . shit. My head was throbbing, and I was already throwing up a little bit in my mouth. I felt so sick. Moment I felt a hand on my thigh, trying to slide my long dress up, I started to regret what the fuck I was allowing to happen. Feeling the cool breeze hit my legs, I felt them spread me apart just as the door opened.

"Aye, nah-uh, bruh. Get the fuck out of here," I heard Jahiem snap.

"She said she wanted it!" the guy argued as I felt myself fade, the sound of Jahiem arguing slowly dying out.

Damn, what the fuck did I just put myself through?

Next time I opened my eyes, I felt the warmth of covers over me before feeling like I had to throw up. I sat up quick, sliding over the edge of the bed, seeing a trash can already in place as I let it out. Coughing and spitting, I continued to vomit. Head was throbbing, body was sore, and . . . I sat up, looking underneath the covers, seeing I had on basketball shorts and a shirt. My hair was tied up, and looking in the mirror, I could see my makeup was a fucking mess. Lipstick was smeared all over, eyelashes were falling apart, everything. I looked around the nice room, seeing no one. Just me. What the fuck happened, and where was Porscha?

Just as I tried getting out of the bed, the door opened to the room. Jahiem stood there, shirtless, with a water bottle in his hand and headphones wrapped around his neck. He had basketball shorts on, no socks on his white-ass feet, and his locs were held down by a black scarf cap, coming down to his shoulders; almond-shaped dark brown eyes, with tattoos going across his lower stomach and chest. Teardrop tattoos on the right side of his face stood out hard against the vanilla-like complexion. I saw he was starting to grow a beard now, which made him look like he was in his thirties. Nigga looked like an ex-high school football player. I didn't see how I could have mistaken him for Elijah that night, because his body was a lot thicker than Elijah's.

"Where is my friend?" I asked, voice damn near gone. "What the fuck happened last night, and—"

"Don't worry about all that," he said, cutting me off. "How much is this abortion shit, so we can go ahead and knock this out the way?"

"Just over three hundred," I told him, and his mouth dropped.

"Shit, well, to make sure you don't keep the money for yourself, I'm going with you so I can pay for it."

I lay back down on the bed, sneezing back to back before pulling the covers over me.

"Yo, wipe all that makeup shit off yo' face. Take all of that off."

"Fuck you care for?" I snapped in a raspy voice before sneezing again. I didn't want him or anyone to see me without makeup. I'd been wearing it for so long that I almost didn't trust my own face—even though, I mean, don't get it twisted, a bitch was cute. I just never really showed a nigga that natural beauty.

He came over, taking the trash can, and went into the bathroom. I watched him dump all of my contents out in the toilet. Soon as that smell hit my nose, I gripped my stomach. This shit was never-ending.

"I need it," I let out, holding my mouth.

He came back, holding the can as I leaned over to puke again, not even waiting for him to set it on the floor. It was like I had a fucking hangover, but worse. I watched him walk in the bathroom, flushing the toilet as he grabbed some towels, wetting them before handing them to me.

"Wipe yo' face and mouth," he demanded.

I just stared at them. I didn't want shit from this nigga.

"Aye, we not about to sit here and do this shit. Take the fucking towel. Be glad I even brought yo' ho ass in here. I could have left you with them mothafuckas who were really about to rape yo' ass."

"Whateva, nigga," I said, snatching the wet cloth and wiping my face free of makeup. I pulled off my lashes, wiped off my lipstick and eyeshadow that was caked on. By the time I was done, the towel looked like a clay of brown shit with a bit of red, resembling my own vomit when I gave it back to him. He just looked at me like I was dumb, while I could barely look him in the face. I felt naked.

"Don't know why hoes wear all this shit on their face in the first place," he mumbled, tossing the towel in the trash. "Aye, you got another hour or so of sleep before we hit the road back to Atlanta. I'll get at you by the end of the week to take care of it. Set up the appointment; do what you gotta do," he said, walking out the room.

I lay back down on the bed, smiling to myself. I couldn't wait until I got this shit over with.

Robbed

Jordyn

"Ooooh," I let out as Elijah slowly pulled out of me, collapsing next to me on the side of the bed. We were breathing heavy, bodies covered in sweat. I looked over at the clock on my nightstand, seeing it was nine p.m. We'd been at this since seven o'clock. It was Tuesday night. This would be his third go-round, and my fourth time coming. Nobody was home, thank God, because we were louder than the music blasting.

I turned to look at him, seeing his eyes were closed, hand on his dick as he lay there in silence, dark tatted chest heaving. Dreads were loose over the pillow and his face. It had been few weeks now since the first time we had sex, already in the month of October, and every time, it was something different, something new. Still not the best I ever had, but he learned quicker than most men, which put him in my top five.

"You okay?" I asked softly.

He looked at me with those low eyes, slowly smiling. "Fuck nah. Every time I try and come over here, show you what I can do, you make me out to be a bitch nigga," he complained teasingly, and I laughed. "One day I'm going to catch yo' freak ass off guard, shawty."

"That will never happen." I smiled as we locked eyes, naked bodies lying close to each other.

He turned on his side to face me. "You hungry?" he asked, moving hair out of my face. "I need to smoke, and I want to eat, so you riding with me?"

"Now?" I pressed as he got off the bed, flipping his locs back. I sat up quickly, already thinking of the pros and cons of stepping off the yard with him. Normally when he was in town, we kept our business to my room. We never talked about hanging out or grabbing food.

"Yeah, shawty, come on. Get this shower going, baby," he let out, opening the door to my room as he stepped out, butt naked and all.

I smiled as I quickly reached for my glasses. I followed him to the bathroom, grabbing towels and lotions that he and I agreed on using together a while back. He actually liked my girly lotions, didn't mind smelling like a sweet flower, which I thought was funny.

"Shawty had a nigga like, damn!" he let out obnoxiously as he stepped back out of the bathroom, waiting on me to walk up. Dick was hanging on soft as he smirked at me. "Damn, Jordyn, you don't even realize how sexy you are, even with those granny glasses on, shawty. I can't believe I got you to myself right now."

"And how do you know you have me to yourself?" I pressed as we walked into the bathroom together, smirking at each other. I set the things down as he tied his locs in a loose ball on his head. Shower was going as I closed and locked the door. He eyed my naked body, lower lip tucked in like he was turning himself on all over again.

"You not fucking nobody else, baby," he said in a low but determined voice.

I pushed my glasses up before stepping in the shower with the pink shower curtains hanging. He came in behind me, closing the curtain, and immediately slapped my ass, making me laugh.

"Elijah, you need to stop," I said, still keeping my back to him. Both of us started washing up, and washing each other, as he lathered up my back and washed my hair, occasionally kissing my shoulder or my neck. I turned to face him, seeing his tall, muscular body soaked as his dreads fell loose to his shoulders.

"Why you got them fuck-ass glasses on, Jordyn?" he asked.

"I forgot to take them off." I laughed, closing my eyes tight as he took the glasses off. I could hear him step out then stepping back in, pulling my body close to his as we stepped underneath the shower head. He started kissing me on the lips. I was feeling the water between us as we made out, slipping tongues in each other's mouths. He might have been loud, at times annoying, and over-the-top dramatic, but one thing I would say? He was by far the best kisser. Out of anyone that I'd kissed, his mouth felt like it matched mine, movement for movement.

"I hope you not fucking with no other nigga," he said against my mouth, hands cupping my face as I opened my eyes to look at him. "I want to be the one and only nigga you dealing with on that level. If I ain't made that clear before, I'm stating it now. I'm the only man in yo' life, Jordyn."

"What about you, though?" I pressed, hands coming to his sides as the water steady continued to pour down on us.

Elijah let go of my face, eyes traveling over my features in admiration and awe, like they always did.

"I can fuck these bitches out here because they don't mean shit to me, baby," he stated proudly.

I rolled my eyes. Of course he could have sex, but I couldn't.

"I can fuck without feelings; you can't. Women can never do that. Don't fuck no other nigga, and I won't chill with another ho on that mental level like I do you."

"How you know I even have feelings for you?" I quipped, pushing him away.

He smirked. "Come on, Jordyn with a Y," he teased. "Shawty, you feeling a nigga."

"Whatever, Elijah." I laughed as I turned back around to finish rinsing off. He was so full of himself it was unbelievable.

After the shower, I blow-dried my hair and threw on some simple clothes—jeans, boots, a hoodie, and pea coat. His hair was in a ball as he threw on his jeans, black Polo boots, long-sleeve thick, black Polo sweater. Before I knew it, we were out, riding in his truck in the middle of the night, trying to find a place to eat. I had my contacts in because I didn't feel like hearing jokes about my granny glasses from him, and I brought my cell phone along so he could teach me some more stuff about the iPhone. I learned something new every day with that phone.

"Aye, what you got planned for this weekend, baby?" he asked as he turned the radio down, coming to a stop at a red light. He had one hand on the steering wheel, and he leaned to the side, with his locs in a messy ball. Tattoos on his neck were looking like they were crawling up to his face to match the ones underneath his eyes. "You going to the Classic, or any of the after parties?"

"I don't know. My friend Rita keeps telling me about the after parties. There was supposed to be one happening at the Gold Lounge," I said, looking at him.

"Yeah, I know about that. Shit is sold out," he told me, merging onto the highway.

"Something about the Carter Boys." I shrugged with a roll of my eyes. "Do you know who they are? Because it seems like everyone keeps talking about them like I should know. She wants to go so bad, but I guess if it's sold out, we probably won't be able to make it there."

"You don't know who they are?" he asked with wide eyes before nearly bursting into laughter. I was so lost. I missed the joke completely. "You for real, shawty?"

"Who are they?" I questioned as I stared at him and his tatted face.

"Ahh, man, you really don't know, baby," he said with a shake of his head. "You want to go to that party?"

"I mean, I guess, but there's no way in without a ticket."

"I got you and your friend," he said.

I smiled. That was sweet of him.

"You want VIP or no?"

"It doesn't matter, as long as we're in. Knowing her, she's going to want VIP, but it doesn't matter to me. What? Are you going to tell me a word to say to the security guy?"

"Nah." He laughed, placing his hand on my thigh. "You fucking foolish, Jordyn. Nah, I'm not going to tell you a word. I'll send someone for you, or get you myself if I'm not too drunk. You know you got to dress up and look good, right?"

"What are you trying to say?" I asked, moving his hand from my thigh, trying my hardest not to be offended.

"I mean, I know you. I been fucking you for a month now? Almost a month? You not that type of chick to get done up and look good. You just chill."

"I can if I wanted to," I said, watching cars whip by on the highway.

"What? You gonna walk in with yo' granny glasses on and grandma panties?" he asked with a laugh. "You got to come correct. These chicks that be in the club be looking like five-star meals, baby. If you're going to be around me, or near me for the night, you got to be on point."

"You don't think I will be?"

"Fuck nah." He laughed, and my mouth dropped. He quickly realized how rude he was coming off. "I mean, you look good. I wouldn't fuck with you if you didn't, but you can do better, baby. But that shit works, though, because I be looking at you as one of the homies sometimes. You like a girl I can kick it with, talk to, and fuck around with. I don't have to worry about other niggas coming for you in that way," he said, still not realizing how he was coming off. I just rolled my eyes. It was his polite way of saying I wasn't as attractive.

Whatever. Being beautiful and pretty was not something on my list of concerns when it came to my life. All of that stuff only lasts but so long anyway.

"You are something else, Elijah," I let out as we pulled up to a wing place. "Well, when I get there, I hope I know how to handle large crowds. People like to touch up on you, and—"

"If anybody touch you, anybody fuck with you? I will shut that shit down. You feel me? I got you," he said, looking hard at me. I believed him.

We got out, feeling the cold air snap against our bare faces. I quickly rushed to his side to keep warm.

"You want to eat here?" he asked, arm wrapping around my neck.

"Are their wings good?" I asked, looking around the suspect area. It was definitely not in a safe area for sure. The buildings next to this one were boarded up, and people were hanging out around the building, kids acting foolish on the sidewalks, and creeps walking all over the place. This whole area looked abandoned except for this small wing shop. I could see through the windows that there were a couple of people sitting down eating, and another standing in line.

"Yo, this spot right here, shawty? Man!" Elijah let out excitedly, opening the door for me as the bells chimed. "Don't nobody make wings like they do, baby. I'm going to order for you, because I want you to try the wings that I usually get."

"Okay," I said quietly as we walked up to the counter, eyes already on me as I kept close to him. One older guy who was sitting alone blew a kiss at me, sticking his tongue out in a disrespectful manner. I gripped Elijah's arm tighter as I looked up at him, seeing his eyes were on the menu.

"Aye, pssst," the guy whispered to me as I looked back at him. Hand was clearly on his dick as he shook it.

My mouth dropped as I buried my face in Elijah's arm to keep from laughing. What the hell was wrong with people these days?

"You good, baby?" Elijah asked against my head, kissing it.

"That guy over there," I mumbled, looking at Elijah as his eyes locked with the man sitting at the table. His demeanor immediately changed, and I could feel him stiffen up.

"What he do? Nigga was on some disrespectful shit?" he asked in a low voice.

"He just grabbed his dick in front of me and stuck his tongue out," I let out, trying not to laugh at how disgusting that was.

"Oh, word?" Elijah pressed, nodding his head slowly as we stepped up to the counter. The girl popping on her gum seemed to be star-struck by Elijah as she let out a goofy smile, but Elijah kept his eyes on the man, who stood up.

"What you looking at, young nigga? You ain't about to do shit," the man let out with a disgusting laugh as he walked toward the door.

"You right," Elijah let out slowly, looking back at the menu. His whole stance seemed to change. Even the look in his eyes, which was usually playful and silly, was replaced with a cold, hard stare. His jaw was tightening up, flexing. "Let me get number three, hot lemon pepper, extra wet, and get her the honey Cajun boneless wings, beautiful. Two fries, and two large strawberry lemonades."

"Will that be all?" the girl asked, putting on a sexy voice.

Elijah ignored the obvious come-on as his voice became even deeper. Definitely not the same annoying, wild Elijah I was used to dealing with.

"Let me get another order of those hot lemon pepper wings, baby," he said, giving me his phone and car keys. "I'll be right back."

I watched him walk out of the small restaurant, and I immediately gasped, seeing him run up on the older man before disappearing to the side of the building. When he did finally walk back in, he smirked at me. His dreads swung loose and free, and he was walking with that wide strut, gripping the middle of his jeans.

"My bad, baby," he said, going through a thick brown leather wallet. "My nigga that just walked out said the meal was on him, so I had to collect the money."

"Damn, nigga," the girl mumbled with a smile as she took the money.

My mouth dropped as I looked at the wallet in his hand, seeing the man's identity, his credit cards, and a wad of cash that Elijah stuffed in his wallet. There were pictures of his kids, everything.

I looked up at Elijah, seeing the last hint of coldness in his eyes before he looked down at me with a flirty smirk. "I can't believe you just literally robbed an old man," I mumbled, taking the receipt.

"I can't believe you never ate here before. These wings be on point, baby!" he yelled out obnoxiously, shaking his dreads. "They wings finna have you doing this," he said, licking his fingers, making smacking sounds as I laughed.

Noelle

"I need ground turkey, fruit, eggs, and milk," I mumbled to myself as I looked at the list on my phone. I stood in the middle of an aisle with my shopping cart at Publix, mentally going through the meals that I needed to cook for the week. It was Tuesday night, and the store was moderately packed with shoppers. I was just getting off work and already felt like I was ready to get home, cook, shower, and relax. I needed to prepare for the next day. It was supposed to storm really bad that night, so I needed to hurry up. I could already hear the sounds of thunder shake the grocery store.

I pushed the shopping cart, letting my four-inch heels click as I pushed my hair off my shoulders. I had on a long-sleeve dress that hugged my curves perfectly, hitting just below my knees, and a black trenchcoat. Makeup was done to perfection, hair hanging down, and I felt like a Barbie doll that was worth a million bucks.

As I pushed the shopping cart up and down the aisle, grabbing what I needed, I caught a few guys glancing my way. Ugh. My dating life was nonexistent at this point. I didn't know too many people in Atlanta, and the guys that I did seem to attract were definitely not in my league. My ex-boyfriend, Sean, lived up here, but he had no idea I moved to Atlanta, and I wanted to keep it that way.

"Excuse me, Miss?" someone called out.

I turned around, seeing an older, light-skinned man eye me hard, licking his lips.

"You are so damn beautiful. Can I get your name?"

"Noelle." I smiled sweetly, pushing the cart as he continued to follow me, trying to have a light conversation. I didn't mind. It forced me to hurry the hell up and grab what I needed to go. I could hear the thundering outside rumble the store as I quickly gathered the last-minute things.

I told the man politely I wasn't interested before checking out and rushing my things to my car. It felt like the rain suddenly wanted to pour down when I stepped outside, so I quickly bundled up as I opened the trunk, trying to put the thirty-something bags in the car. Rain was hitting me hard as I rushed to take the cart to the proper holding area, heels steady clicking. I needed to hurry up and get home.

So, of course, it seemed like bad luck wanted to play with me. Car wouldn't start for the next twenty minutes. I had to have someone help me jump-start it in the parking lot, in the freezing rain. When I did finally get on the road, traffic was everywhere you looked, so I decided to take the back roads to my neighborhood. I was trembling so bad, waiting on this heat to finally kick in and circulate in the car, when I pulled up to my place.

I could see Shiloh was home by the lights being on in his house and his fancy black Mustang parked outside. I quickly got out, feeling the cold rain hit me hard once again as I rushed to check my mail.

"Lord Jesus!" I let out in a frenzy, wiping my face as I quickly opened the mailbox, grabbing whatever was in there. A clap of thunder sounded off as streetlights flickered off instantly, causing the streets to be pitch black. Glancing at Shiloh's house, I could see the lights were off in his, too, meaning the power was out throughout the whole neighborhood.

"Not tonight, Lord," I mumbled, closing the box, not even watching where I was going or paying attention to how all over the place I was. I dropped my car keys.

"Fuck!" I let out, wiping my face as I bent down to look for my keys. I felt my heart drop in my stomach, realizing I was right next to the drain.

No, no no, please don't let this shit happen to me.

I grabbed my phone, turning the flashlight on as I looked around, seeing a shimmer of silver down in the drain. "What the fuck!" I screamed. How was it possible that I was having the worst night of my fucking life right now? My house keys and car keys gone, with rain water slowly pushing it further and further into the drain.

I looked up, glancing at Shiloh's house, wondering if he had a wire hanger. If my keys could hold on a little bit longer, I could reach down and grab them. I stood up, almost twisting my ankle in my heels before deciding to just take them off altogether, running directly to his place. My feet hit the soaked grass with determination as I stepped on his porch, banging on the door frantically with a fist. When I heard nothing, I started damn near kicking it as I looked back at the drain near my mailbox, hoping my keys held on.

Suddenly, the door swung open, and Shiloh, who stood with a hoodie, sweats, and shoes, came up on me with a gun cocked in his hand, cold eyes wide, like he was ready for war. My eyes were level with his weapon, and I shrieked in fear, backing up off the steps, almost falling back before he grabbed my arm.

"What the fuck are you doing banging on my mothafucking door like you got a problem?" he snapped in rage.

My heart was pounding. I'd never been so scared of a man in my life. My body was shaking so bad from the cold rain, and from fear of this man.

I guess he noticed how he came off, because he tucked his gun behind him, eyes softening up just a little as he glanced at my car.

"I just needed a wire hanger," I let out in a shaky voice. "My key fell down the drain, and I . . . I . . ."

He just stared at me: no expression, nothing. Just walked back in the house, closing the door behind him. I took a deep swallow as I rushed back to the drain, heels left on his porch. Dress was ruined, hair was soaked, makeup probably smudged all over my face. I looked and felt like a mess. I turned the cell phone light back on, seeing my keys were gone. Only spare I had for my car was in the house. *Great.* I hit the ground hard with my hand, feeling tears come down as I stood up. Couldn't believe this shit. First few nights in Atlanta had been hell. I just wanted to go back home.

I heard a door open as Shiloh stepped out with an umbrella and came over to me with a wire hanger already stretched out. Just the sight of him made me panic a little. I don't think I will ever get that vision of someone pointing a gun at me out of my head— the first, and I pray the last, time that will ever happen to me.

"I don't need it," I mumbled, walking to my car. "It's already down the drain." I sat inside my cold car, teeth chattering as another sound of thunder went off.

"Fuck, man!" I could hear Shiloh shout as he walked over to my car, tapping the window.

I opened the door, looking up at his low, dark eyes.

"Aye, you can chill in my house until you can get a hold of somebody or something."

"I'm fine," I let out, wiping my face.

"Look—" Another round of thunder went off, followed by a flash of lightning, making me flinch. "Fuck it. I'm out. You can sit in here or come in. By the time I get to that mothafucking door, if you not there, I'm not opening that shit up for nobody else. Understand?"

He didn't even wait for a response, just walked off, closing my car door himself. I quickly got out, grabbing my things, and followed behind him as the rain continued to pour down. I grabbed my heels off his porch as I walked into the warm house behind him, closing and locking both screen and wooden doors.

It was dark, and the smell of weed mixed with some type of burning incense hit my nose. I felt around for the couch, just as the lights flickered on and off before officially staying on. You could hear the power cutting back on as the TV in a room down the hall started to sound off.

I looked around, seeing the nicely decorated furniture, matching dark blue couches, glass coffee table, and bookshelf full of thick paperbacks. His sound system sat up with the flat screen TV. I stood there in my wet clothes as he walked down the hallway, only to come back with a towel and some clothes.

"Aye, you can change in the bathroom in my room," was all he said as I looked at him. He took his hoodie off, revealing his light, toned body with STAY TRUE going across his lower stomach in graffiti letters. His curly black hair was wet. He licked his dark pink lips, looking at me with those low-set eyes. No expression, just looking.

I grabbed the towel and walked to the back, where his room was, seeing a whole different type of vibe in there. There was African artwork on his wall and desk, books everywhere, a small Egyptian statue on his desk, and a kid-size basketball hoop that sat on the corner of his room, high up on the wall.

"Aye, hurry up," I heard him snap as I made my way to the bathroom. He was certainly not the friendly, outgoing type. I took a shower, washing away the dirty rain water, makeup, and stress of the night. Seeing he didn't have anything but men's soap, I ended up using that. Oddly enough, he had women's shampoo, so I washed my hair and soon stepped out, wrapping the towel around me. I was already feeling better after a hot shower, but I noticed the lights were off again. This was going to be a long-ass night. It was storming pretty bad outside, and the power was going in and out. I felt around for the walls, keeping the towel close to my body.

"I just need to find the bed," I mumbled, trying to use the moonlight from the window, but that wasn't helping at all. I placed the clothes on his bed before stepping in his bathroom, but seeing now that I was standing nearly butt naked in this man's bedroom, I wished to God I would have stayed in the car.

I could hear the sound of the power coming back, and the lights came back on. I spotted the shirt and shorts on the bed just as he came in his room.

"Aye, you—" He stopped in mid-sentence as we locked eyes for a brief second. His eyes traveled slowly over my body before he turned around, looking up at the ceiling. "Shit, my bad. I just wanted to know if you wanted me to get someone to break into yo' shit. I can have one of my niggas get in yo' house and unlock the door for you. Unless you want to call the owners and see if they can bring you a spare key."

"I'll call," I answered softly, slipping the shorts on. I sat on the bed, looking at his back as he stood in his red basketball shorts and red long socks, waiting for my cue to say it was okay to turn back around. "You can look."

He turned around, and my eyes immediately went to the center of his basketball shorts, seeing a definite rise. He put his hand over himself, trying to cover up his hard-on. I didn't know who was more embarrassed: him or me.

"My bad," he mumbled, looking at the floor, clearing his throat. "If you have to spend the night, you can have the bed. I'll sleep in the living room."

"Okay," was all I said as we looked at each other. "Do you have anything to eat?"

"Nah. I already ate," he said, walking out.

Great.

So, after calling the owners of the house and seeing they weren't going to be available until the following afternoon, I made myself comfortable on the full-sized bed. Stomach was rumbling to the point where it hurt. I hadn't eaten since that morning, and I was afraid to ask him for anything, so I was going to stick it out like a big girl—although I did call my daddy, crying, telling him what happened. It was the worst night of my life.

I eventually found the strength to get some sleep, already calling in for work the next day. With the heat circulating around the house, I found myself sleeping above the covers, because his heavy basketball shorts and oversized black shirt were making me hot. It wasn't until I felt a hand on my shoulder, gently shaking me, that I jumped out of my sleep, looking at Shiloh's dark figure standing over the bed, causing me to shriek once more.

"Aye, chill, chill," he started, setting a plate down. "I didn't mean to scare you. I figured you might be hungry, but I don't know how to cook like that, so this is all I got for you to eat." He turned on the lamp on his nightstand, showing the plate with two sandwiches. One was ham and cheese, and the other was peanut butter and jelly. Without a word, I took the peanut butter and jelly, eating it like it was my first meal after a year-long starvation period. I was eating in silence as he watched me, eyes roaming my body as I watched him. He really wasn't the talking type, and whatever he did say, it was usually something mean, aggressive, or abrupt: everything I stood against. I took the other sandwich and started to eat that as well, drinking the glass of water he gave me.

"You good?" he asked.

I just nodded, laying back down on the soft bed as he started to fumble around with his hands like he wanted to say something else but wasn't quite sure how to say it. "Aye, I um . . ." He dragged a hand down his face in frustration before walking toward the door. "My bad about earlier with the gun in yo' face shit," he mumbled, walking out and closing the door behind him.

Point Made

Jade

"But that's not the fucking point, Jade!" Trent yelled.

I rolled my eyes and continued to text Chris on my phone. Nigga was being a bitch again. I swear, us dating didn't make no kind of sense. We didn't belong together, like two wrongs making a bigger wrong. Shit wasn't working.

We were sitting in his car, parked in front of the science building, going at it because he thought I didn't respect him as the man in the relationship. Who the fuck says shit like that?

Nigga, it's barely been a month. I'm still getting to fucking know you.

It was stupid arguments like these that made me wish I never even agreed to go out with this fuck nigga. He wasn't my type, and I wasn't his. His friends didn't like me at all. I couldn't stand to be around him and his little Greek followers before punching one of them in the face. Course, he didn't like how close I was to my friends, but he refused to hang out with them because in his mind, they were lame as fuck, not on his level. Again, who the fuck says shit like that?

My sister and him got into the other day, and he wanted me to check her. *Like, nigga, really? You really think I'm going to check her when you clearly* . . . Don't even get me started. My sister had more balls than this nigga.

"Jade?" he called out, and I glanced at him. He cut the car off and switched his attention toward me as I went back to looking at my phone. It was Wednesday night, and this was how I was spending it. I could have been high right now. "I'm talking to you."

"I hear you, nigga," I popped.

"So, what the fuck is the problem? Why is it that you have to constantly come at me like I'm yo' enemy? Tell me so I know how to change that shit. How to fix it. I can't have you around me if you constantly want to fight and challenge me on every single fucking thing!"

"Lower yo' voice when you talk to me," I snapped in a low tone. "No need for all of that. I'm not trying to challenge you on shit. I don't even need you for half the shit you think I need you for. You do the most, thinking I'm supposed to respect you for it? I can handle myself in any situation—"

"I'm saying you don't have to! Let me take care of it. If a nigga steps to me, I don't need you jumping in, trying to defend me like you did the other day. I hate that shit!"

"Nigga, you weren't about to—"

"You don't even know me," he said, cutting me off. "Let me be the man and you be the woman. I get tired of having to tell you that. You talk too much; you act like a nigga. I feel like I'm dating a fucking nigga. Biggest turn-off. I get girls daily asking me why I fuck with you, and I just say I can't help who I like. I like you, but every day you give me more of a reason to fuck around on yo' manly-acting ass. All these women out here on my dick, and you the only one I want, but you can't even see that, because you too busy trying to grow a dick yo' damn self! Get the fuck out my car," he spat as my eyes grew wide. "I'm done. I don't want—I can't be with you. I thought I could make it work, calm you down a little bit, but I can't do that shit. Get the fuck on."

I looked at him, feeling my heart start to pound. He was serious. No. He couldn't be serious. When he stared at me with those hard, hazel eyes, he reached over and opened the door for me.

"Trent, wait—"

"Nah, no wait nothing," he said, shaking his head as he leaned on the car door. "I can't with this no more, Jade. What? It's been a few weeks? I thought I would at least see three months, but I can't make it past a month with you and that mouth. You stress me out for no reason. I don't need all of that. I'm trying to graduate in December, and you adding on more stress than what I need right now."

"I'm sorry," I said quickly, grabbing his arm, seeing he was serious. I might have just pushed him a little too far. Again. I had to keep reminding myself he was sensitive, or maybe I was just too . . . Nah. He was sensitive. I just didn't know how else to be other than myself. "Trent, I'm sorry."

"Yeah, me too. Get the fuck out," he said again as I gripped his arm. "We throwing something on the grill tonight one last time, and I don't want to be—"

"I will try harder this time. I'm used to being and doing for me, so when I have someone else who wants to take over, I just don't know how to react to that. I'm protective, I'm aggressive, and I'm harsh. I get it, nigga, but I realize I can tone it down for you."

"Tone that shit all the way down, Jade. Like off," he retorted. "Makes you look ugly as fuck."

I sighed, having to bite my tongue on that. I hoped he realized it wasn't just me who needed to tone it down. Half the shit he said to me was an insult in itself.

"I will work on it," I promised. I wasn't ready to give him up just yet. I liked the small times we did have together, when it was all smiles and laughs. He was a sweetheart. He really was. It did help a little bit knowing that I got the nigga on the yard that every bum bitch wanted to fuck with, and that he was related to a famous rap group in Atlanta. I mean, how could I fuck that up?

"This is your last chance. I'm not playing around this time. Come with me to this house and chill with my friends. Get to know them, and let them get to know you. Right now, they got a bad perception of you. They're not as bad as you think they are," he said, and I felt myself biting my tongue again. This nigga didn't even know half the shit I put up with when I was around his fake-ass friends. Yet, he wouldn't come nowhere near mine, and he hated that I even hung around them. Trent was the definition of superficial and materialistic. If it wasn't on his level, that shit was considered lame. I didn't like that way of thinking, yet he wanted me to be surrounded by a yard full of people that thought the same exact way. "Will you go? I'm not giving out no more chances to be with me, because this is it. I can't—"

"I'll go," I mumbled. All I heard in my head was my friend Chris saying, "Pretend to like the shit he likes. Most niggas do it for girls, so why not do it for him? Be cool with his friends.

"Yeah, I'll go," I repeated as we looked at each other.

He shook his head as he started the car and backed out. Silence. I looked myself over, seeing I had on boyfriend jeans that were baggy as fuck, a long, white droopy sweater, honey-blond locs falling anywhere they pleased, and I had just got my lip pierced the other week. Trent nearly flipped the fuck out. He hated it; acted like a bitch, and didn't even want to kiss me for a day.

I pushed my locs out of my face as I went back to texting Chris. They were all in my sister's room, having the time of their lives. I was wishing I was there. Ugh. Anything to save the relationship, though, right? Fuck it.

"Thank you, Jade," he said as he looked at me. I just nodded, staying quiet as he drove behind the school into the neighborhoods. "If they see what I see in you when we're together, then I know they will like you."

"I hope so," I said, trying to hide my sarcasm.

He just looked at me with that knowing look. He heard it in my voice, but he took my hand and kissed it as he turned the corner.

"See how you are now? Quiet, chill? Calm? I like this side of you. All that other shit can go," he said, and I smiled. Nigga was picking and choosing what he liked and didn't like about me. "Fuck you, Trent," is what I wanted to say, but I let the smile do all the talking instead.

"And I know you still probably mad, or maybe I'm making you madder by just talking to you, but know that I appreciate this, baby," he said, kissing my hand again. I stayed silent.

We pulled up to the house, seeing a crowd full of fake-ass mothafu—let me stop—seeing a group of his friends chilling in front of the yard with the grill going. I hoped somebody had some weed. I couldn't do this shit without it.

"Jade," Trent said, still holding my hand as we looked at each other. Those hazel eyes could do no wrong most of the time. "I know I may not act like it, but I do. I'm sure it's some shit I need to work on too that you're not telling me, but right now? Just be my girlfriend. That's all I want. Don't be my nigga; don't be my homeboy or whatever. I want you as my girl."

"Okay," I said with another fake-ass smile.

He just stared at me, probably wondering if I was being serious or not.

Nah, nigga, I'm being fake as fuck right now.

I wasn't being a bitch on purpose. His friends really were rude as hell, and for some reason, he didn't see that shit. So tonight, he was going to learn. I wasn't going to say a word. He wanted to be the man and stand up for me, then I would let him do it. See how far it got him.

Well, like I said, I was right. It wasn't nearly fifteen minutes in, these bitches were making snide remarks about me to my face, thinking I wouldn't catch it. His frat brothers were already on that "we not fucking with you," so they didn't speak at all. Only one that spoke was Armond, who sat down next to me on the porch as we passed a blunt back and forth. The sorority girls all looked the exact same: long weave, stuck up, trying to speak proper, knowing they were ghetto as fuck. It was all the same. I was smiling in every nigga's face as more cars pulled up.

Just about every organization was out there that night. I guess it was some sort of private thing for the Greeks, with me being the only one who stood out.

"Aye, so how long you been in Atlanta?" Armond asked as he passed the blunt back. I liked him. Nigga was a big, buff-ass nigga, but he was cool as hell. Not as pretty as the rest of them here, he was a bit more rugged.

"I moved here in late July, early August maybe?" I said.

"I can tell. Yo' accent is thick as hell," he said, and we both started to laugh, feeling that high take over. "I like it, though. That accent is sexy. Probably pull a lot of niggas down here with that shit."

"Damn right," I boasted, passing the blunt back.

"Oh my god! Bitch, you is too crazy!" A girl laughed, and I looked back, seeing the girls all together, laughing and talking, occasionally looking up at me on the porch with Armond. Trent was nowhere to be seen.

"You know they talking about you, right?" Armond said, and I shrugged.

"When is anybody not talking about me, yo?" I laughed. "I don't fit in with this crowd, but he wants to me fuck with y'all on that level, so this is me trying."

"Ahh, you ain't trying, nigga," Armond said with a wide smile as we both laughed. "That nigga is obsessed with you, though."

"No, he's not." I waved it off. He just looked at me, matching my red eyes. "He is?"

"Hell yeah. That nigga nuts up every time we say something about you. We give him a hard time every day, because you probably harder than that nigga, and he know it."

"Nah, I'm not harder than him. I'm just louder," I said, feeling myself about to defend my own nigga's manhood—the same manhood I attacked on a daily basis. Damn.

"Shit, we know. We just fuck with him like that. I seen him fight before. Nigga got hands like a mothafucka," Armond said, passing the blunt back. "He's just an easy target because he get the girls in the house. He's the one everybody wants, so it's funny to see him with a girl that gives no fucks about him."

"I do!" I laughed, already feeling bad.

"Nah, you rough on that dude. I bet it's hard as hell for him to come here, get roasted about you, and then go to you, and you jump on his ass. Nigga is dating the girl that hit him in the face. That shit is a blow to his ego, and you know like I know, he is sensitive as fuck about his image."

I nodded, thinking about everything Trent had been telling me. That was why he'd been bitching to me about lack of respect and wanting me to just sit and be pretty.

"He told you to talk to me?" I questioned, and he laughed.

"Nah, fuck nah. I really wasn't planning on fucking with you like the rest of them, but you smoke? I smoke," he said, shrugging. "I didn't want to smoke by myself, so shit—" He shrugged again. "You cool, though. I can see what he sees in you."

"Mmm," was all I said as we fell into an easy silence. I peeped the girls glancing back at me, one rolling her eyes like we were in high school and I was supposed to be offended. Shit, I was, but I was going to turn down for Trent. This was his night.

I stayed on that porch most of the night with Armond, talking even after the blunt was gone, watching people come and go. When it got to be late and everyone was turning in for class in the morning, Trent stepped back out, already dressed down for bed with red basketball shorts and a white tee, wave cap on.

"You want to stay with me, or you want me to take you back to yo' room?" he asked.

"Yo, stay here so I have someone to talk to in the morning," Armond said, and I smiled.

"Nah, she can't stay here!" I heard someone yell from the house.

"Nigga, shut the fuck up! Nobody asked you!" Trent snapped as I stood up, already seeing what Armond was talking about.

"I'll stay," I said. I had already made plans to hang out with my sister and friends in her room, but fuck it. I knew how to shut these niggas up one good time so they could leave him alone. "Where are your keys? My bag is in the trunk." I always kept an overnight bag in his car. Never knew where I might end up with him. At least that was what he told me. He kept one and I kept one, side by side.

So, after grabbing my bag, we went in the house to his room downstairs and pretty much chilled in there. He lay in the bed, watching TV, while I took a quick shower. Since I was the only female in the house, I already knew niggas had their noses wide open, despite them hating on me. I looked at myself in the bathroom mirror, wiping away the steam. I put on the cute, sexy red lingerie, since that was the color for the nights when I was with him. It was a lace bra and lace boy shorts. Hair was pulled up, tattoos were looking lovely against my arm, and teeth were pearly white. I liked my lip piercing, but for the sake of Trent, I took it out, praying to the man upstairs the hole didn't close up by the time I was finished with him.

"Baby?" Trent called out as I smiled at my reflection in the mirror. I looked sexy as shit.

"Yeah?"

"You good?"

I opened the door, seeing he was standing at the doorway, talking to one of his frat brothers. He glanced at me. Then he really looked at me, letting his eyes travel down and up, in that order, before smirking.

"Who you trying to get fucked by?" he asked as his frat brothers poked their heads around the corner to see, mouths dropped.

"Trying to get fucked by the nigga with that bomb ass pipe game," I teased, sticking my tongue rings out as I stepped out of the bathroom fully so everyone could see what only belonged to Trent. Sometimes, in a house full of dog-ass niggas, you only give one that bone while the rest watch him eat. Why? Because, if they see this nigga keep getting the best of the best, instead of fighting this nigga on a regular basis, they're going to try and figure out what the fuck he's doing, how he's doing it, and imitate this nigga so they can get that bone. Respect. While the rest of them starved, I was going to make sure my nigga ate. Yeah, I acted hard as shit, but let this dude put that dick in me, and I became a bitch on all fours, straight up.

"Ahh, shit!" He laughed while licking his lips, eyeing me some more. "You want it?"

"Possibly." I smirked as he scooped me up in his arms with me laughing, slick eyeing his jealous brothers, who stood with mouths dropped and eyes filled with envy. Point had been made. The look on their faces was them realizing the nigga they kept fucking with about me was the only one in the house about to get some, while the rest were sleeping alone in a dry-ass bed.

"Aye," Trent said, opening the door to the room. "Don't nobody come knocking on my shit. I'll try and keep it down."

"You could have brought some girls or friends over or something," one of them mumbled, eyeing me as I waved.

"Night, boys." I smirked as Trent closed the door to the room.

Next time I woke up, it was to the sound of laughter outside the dark room. I felt around for Trent, making sure he was next to me, accidentally touching his dick. Nigga woke up like it was a fire.

"What you doing, baby?" he asked, yawning with a stretch as he rubbed his nose.

"What the fuck are they doing out there?" I asked before laying back down against him. Damn, my body was hurting so good. Suddenly, my mind went back to the night before. Nigga came in me, talking about he couldn't pull out.

Fuck outta here with that bullshit. I needed to go to the store and take that morning after pill.

"Babe, get up," I said, shaking him out of the bed. "You got to get me to the store so we can buy the pill."

"Just give me like thirty more minutes," he groaned. Trent was just like every other black-ass nigga; not a morning person at all. I wasn't either, but um . . . the thought of having a baby woke me up.

"Trent, I am supposed to have my period in two weeks. Nigga, I'm fertile as fuck right now. Get up and come on before I push you off—"

"A'ight, damn!" he snapped without moving. "Shit, Jade, you can't drive yourself?"

"Fuck it. I'll make sure I wreck yo' car on the way coming back," I retorted as I got up from the bed. "Where's the money?"

"It's in my—" He sighed before flipping the covers back angrily.

Yeah, wake that ass up and come on.

We took a shower together with him still somewhat irritated at me, but all he needed was his coffee and the nigga was good. Yes, this man drank coffee. I didn't know a lot of black men that did, but apparently he did.

When we got in the car, letting it warm up, he sat quiet, still in his mood. I was scrolling through Instagram when I saw the promo flyers for this weekend. It was the Classic. I'd never been to one, but apparently that was the thing to go to down here every year. Atlanta classic. Shit, all I knew was it produced a lot of after parties. The one I wanted to go to was the Gold Lounge. I had the perfect dress for it, and plus I wanted to see the Carter Boys, seeing as I was technically dating one of them.

"Are you going to see your brothers perform this weekend?" I asked Trent, who started to back out, hoodie over his head, looking like a little boy who was pissed because he didn't get his way.

"Yeah," he let out in a low voice, eyes still looking tired. I wrapped the blanket around me, waiting for the heat to circulate as he drove with the radio playing throughout the car.

"People's station, V 103! Trying to give away some free tickets to see them Carter Boys this Saturday night at Gold Lounge! Caller one hundred, you're on the air now. Who is this?"

"This is Tiffany! Did I win?"

"Baby girl, you got the tickets!"

She was screaming as Trent cut the radio off. I looked at him, watching him drive, trying to put on a mean face, knowing he was too pretty for all of that. We pulled up to the nearest McDonald's, and he ordered his little coffee while getting us both some breakfast in the drive-thru.

"Baby?" I said as we waited in the line, still looking at Instagram. "Look at these bitches on yo' page coming at you. Why the fuck you even responding to half these broads?" Yeah, I was on his profile, watching the thirsty girls come at him. I had deleted my page a while back, but just started back up again now that Trent had me on his profile. He let it be known that we were together. Not saying I told him to do it, but it helped with the rumors he'd previously spread about me to come to a stop.

"Fuck you paying attention to that for?" he snapped angrily as he rolled the window down, paying for the food.

"I wouldn't if you weren't responding to these thirst buckets," I mumbled, commenting on one picture and tagging a particular ho who was talking about she can suck his dick better than his girlfriend.

Bitch, suck mine, and then I'll let you know if you can suck his.

He stayed silent, still in his morning mood, as we waited patiently for the food. Looking over at him, I smirked at his stale face.

"You are so cute when you get mad," I teased.

He glanced at me while pulling up to the second window.

"Here you go," the lady said, handing him the bags and coffee. "Y'all have a good day."

Nigga didn't even wait to pull out of the lot altogether. Just pulled into a parking space and went in on that coffee, taking easy sips while I dug into the bag. I usually didn't fuck with McDonald's like this, but I was hungry, and it was something about this particular one, almost tasted like real-ass food.

"You going to class today?" he asked, moving a loc out of my face.

I shook my head no. I wanted to be back in the bed. This cold weather turned me off from doing anything. You would think I would be used to it, coming from New York, but truth is, I don't fuck with the cold period. Don't care where I'm from.

"I want to go back to sleep," I told him in between bites. "I'll get the work from my niggas later on today. You going?"

"Nah," he said, shaking his head as I cocked mine back, shocked.

"So, what, you laying up with me all day?" I asked with a laugh, and he smiled.

"Don't think this shit is going to be a habit. I'm just ahead of the class right now," he lied. "I didn't get much sleep, so I want to catch up on that."

"And drinking coffee is going to help?"

"When I fuck you after we get back it will," he said blatantly.

I outright laughed before playfully throwing a napkin at him. "Nigga, you wildin', yo," I cracked. I leaned over the median of the seats just as he met me halfway and kissed me. I could taste that coffee on his lips.

"Can we get this shit so I can pop the pill and make sure we didn't conceive a baby?"

"Yeah." He laughed against my mouth before kissing it again.

Soon as we got back to the frat house, we did exactly what we talked about doing. I took the pill, we had sex again, and then went right back to sleep in the dark room. I was laying up underneath my man, phones on silent, with nobody disturbing us.

Definitely going to go ahead and chill on this story shit for now. I wanted to focus on this relationship and attempt to focus on school. Not the last you'll hear from me, but I'm falling back. Don't need or want any drama in my life right now. I'm good where I'm at.

No Babies Allowed

Tia

"So, are you ready?" Porscha asked me as I closed the door to my room. It was a Friday morning, and Jahiem was on his way to pick me up to take me to this first part of the two-day appointment. I felt like shit, but I knew it was all going to be worth it in the end when I got rid of the baby. I wanted to be right for the Classic the next day, and the after parties. Homecoming was kicking off Sunday, so I wanted to be right for that too. I mean, it was so much shit happening, I didn't have time to think about a baby. So, that night, I was going to get tore the fuck up, celebrating a baby-free stomach.

"Girl, I'm ready to get this over with," I said, digging in my purse for my vibrating phone. Looking at the screen, I smiled. "Hello?"

"Aye, come on. I got things I need to do. I'm out here," Jahiem said before hanging up.

I took a deep breath as I walked out of the empty apartment. Had to be no later than nine in the morning, but everyone was already gone for the day. Jade probably spent the night at Trent's again. Wonder if she knew he was related to the Carter Boys.

Walking down the hall, I checked my fit to make sure I looked decent enough for the clinic we were going to. I took my weave out, wearing my natural 'fro pulled back in a puff ball, a cropped Adidas hoodie with the matching sweats that hugged the ankles, matching Adidas shoes, gold hoops, light gloss, and light makeup. I looked good. I looked like I shouldn't be having no damn baby.

"You sure you don't want me to go with you?" Porscha asked as she checked her phone, knowing she had to go to work.

"I'm sure. Just go ahead. He's coming in with me, since the nigga think I'm going to take off with his money," I said as we pushed open the doors. I spotted his red Camaro parked in the front, blasting music.

Too early, nigga, too early.

"Call me as soon as you leave," she said, hugging me before getting in her car. I walked over to his car, slipping inside the warmth of the seat before closing the door.

"You good?" he asked.

I looked him over, almost taken aback. He wore all white, except for his black Polo boots—white shirt, white jeans, with a black Polo jacket over it. His dreads were pulled back, with the bottom hanging loose and free. Beard was trimmed to perfection, and his light-bright-ass face just stared back at me, dark brown eyes matching mine. He was kind of cute. We would have made a cute baby.

"Aye, fuck is wrong with you? Are you good? Why you just staring at me?"

"I'm fine," I mumbled.

"Where's this place at?" he asked.

I pulled my phone out, handing it to him. He put the directions in his GPS hooked up to the dashboard screen, and we were off. Silence filled the car.

"You did yo' research on these people?" he asked, merging onto the highway.

"No, I just looked at what was the cheapest," I said, and he looked at me like I was stupid.

"Whatever. Yo' body, not mine. Should have done your research instead of letting a motha-fucka give you something to take, thinking—"

"Can we not talk?" I asked, cutting him off. "I have so much on my mind right now, and you talking about this is making it worse. I don't feel good, I'm tired, and I really want to just be in the bed, but I want this baby out of me. Okay? We don't have to speak to each other or see each other again after this."

"Nah, we're going to talk, because this is my mothafucking car," he retorted as I sighed in annoyance. I swear I hate a lame nigga. Like a disease you can't get rid of. "You don't know me like that; I don't know you like that. Cool, we can keep it that way, but you should have done your research on these niggas before having me drive out here. What if that shit don't work?"

"Then I'll get the money on my own and try another clinic," I said, digging in my purse, realizing I forgot my snack. I was so hungry, but afraid to eat for fear of throwing it up. Yet, the moment my stomach growled, I knew he heard it.

"You didn't eat this morning?"

"I was afraid I'll throw it up," I said, realizing it was a mistake.

"Are you trying to eat?"

"No."

It was silent as he pulled off the highway and stopped at the nearest Burger King while getting on the phone, sounding like he was handling business. He got out of the car, telling me to sit and wait.

Looking down I saw Porscha had sent me a picture of a cute baby boy dressed up like a li'l thug nigga, matching what his daddy in the picture had on.

"Awww," I cooed, zooming in on the picture. She knew I wanted a boy. If I ended up being pregnant again, I wanted to have a boy. Wanted the daddy to be someone I was about to marry, and we live as one, as a family. Nigga would take care of us, making that money, doing what he needed to do to protect our family, while I made sure the home was straight. Food was on the table, and clothes were on our back. My other friend sent me a picture of a newborn outfit she took at her job the other night. Let me just say, my friends ain't shit. Half of them wanted me to keep the baby, and the other half didn't want me to but thought it was cute to send me baby pictures.

Watching Jahiem walk out with the phone to his ear, I eyed him once more as he delegated business. I wanted Elijah. This should have been Elijah—not Jahiem, not Trent, but Elijah.

"Bruh, she was bad as fuck last night, but on some real shit? I'm going to stop by after I finish doing what I'm doing here. Is that Harlem in the background? Tell her what's good. She need to hook me up with one of them bad-ass stripper bitches she be fucking with."

Jahiem closed the door, handing me a drink. "We gon' talk some more business later on when you stop by the studio. I got something I want you to hear anyway. See what you can write down from it."

"A'ight," he said before hanging up and looking at me. "I mean, I can't force you to eat, but—"

"You surely forced me to have sex with you," I mumbled, and he dropped his head before backing out of the parking lot.

"Didn't hear you complaining when I was giving you that dick," he retorted. "If I remember correctly, what did you say? Oooh, you fit so perfect in me," he mocked, changing his voice to a high pitch. "You fit perfect, baby. I do? Mm-hmm."

I covered my mouth, trying hard not to smile and throw up at the same time. "A little creepy you remember that shit word for word, but whatever, nigga. Yeah, I said it. So what? Didn't mean I wanted to have sex with you in the first place," I snapped back.

"I will never forget that. Never had a girl tell me that before," he said, getting back on the highway as the GPS started to talk. "Talkin' about, I fit perfect inside you. Ha!" He laughed as I rolled my eyes. "You partying with us at the Gold Lounge this weekend?"

"I don't want nothing to do with any of y'all anymore. I'm done. I'll party somewhere else."

"Ahh, I'm sorry to hear that," he said with a shake of his head.

I stayed quiet as I touched my flat, perfectly shaped stomach, thinking, constantly calculating, making sure I was one hundred percent sure it was his baby. It was a small chance it would be Trent's child, but I remembered him pulling out. I faked it with his ass anyway. Nigga's dick was weak. Only time I didn't fake it was with my ex-boyfriend, on occasions, and Jahiem. It was definitely his child. I didn't have sex with anyone else prior to Trent for at least two weeks. One used a condom; the other pulled out.

"Is this the place?" he asked, pulling up to a small building. "What time is yo' appointment?"

"Ten o'clock," I said, looking at the time, seeing it was ten minutes till. I started to take deep breaths as I got out of the car, looking up at the clinic. It did look a little broke down and busted on the outside, but it was in a nice city. North Atlanta always had the nicer shit, so I somewhat trusted it.

I stood at the door, waiting on Jahiem, who was pulling all of his locs back in a bun just as some man, some white nigga, nearly knocked me out of the way to get to the door, looking pissed.

"Aye! Aye, bruh!" Jahiem snapped angrily, stopping the man in his tracks. "I know you saw her standing there! Apologize, nigga."

"I'm sorry," he said quickly. "My daughter is in here, and—"

"We give no fucks, nigga. All you had to say was excuse me," Jahiem said as the man apologized to me again before walking in. "Shit, you ready?"

"Yeah," I mumbled, walking in with him behind me.

It had that clinic-like smell. All hospitals and doctors' offices had a medical smell. I couldn't pinpoint it, but it was a definite smell, and it almost made me sick. I went up to grab a clipboard to fill out the sheet before sitting down next to Jahiem, who was texting on his phone. We were the only black people in there, which already made me uncomfortable. Just because Atlanta portrayed itself to be an all-black city on TV didn't mean this shit wasn't still racist. This is the South. Will always be the South.

A girl was in the corner crying, with her stomach already starting to show, just as another came from the hallway, crying even harder, gripping her stomach. Her boyfriend was holding her as they went up to the front desk.

Looking around, I saw the kids' area, where they allowed the kids to play and be distracted, but luckily there weren't any here. I guess I spoke too soon, because as soon as the doors opened, someone walked in with two toddlers and a baby in her arm. I immediately felt my stomach flip as I looked at my own stomach. I couldn't believe I was actually about to do this shit.

"Why the hell did she bring a goddamn baby in here?" someone asked angrily as the mother went up to grab a clipboard.

I looked at Jahiem, who was oblivious to what was going on around him. I watched the kids play in the corner: blond-haired, blue-eyed cute boy, and girl toddlers, innocent to where they were and what was around them.

"You guys come here. Come sit next to Mommy," the woman said as she sat right next to me.

I felt myself about to choke on my own tears as I looked at her baby wrapped in her arms. He was sleeping, but when she pulled the blanket down some, revealing his cute baby falcons Jersey, I nearly lost it.

"How old is he?" I asked, leaning over as she smiled at me.

"Six months," she said as I watched him slowly move in his sleep, mouth chewing on that tongue.

Fuck, why did she have to bring a fucking baby in here?

One of the toddlers went running up to Jahiem, grabbing on his leg before showing him a toy truck he had.

"What you got, li'l man?" Jahiem asked, putting the phone down as he took the truck. I watched him interact with the baby with ease, playing alongside with him as his sister joined along.

"Is he your boyfriend?" the woman asked as I looked back at her, eyes watery.

"No, no." I waved it off with a small laugh. *More like a mistake.* "We just . . . one-time thing, and boom. Here I am."

"I know what you mean. I can't afford to have anymore. This was a one-time thing, and I'm usually against abortions, hence these three kids with me now, but I can't handle another one. Found out I was pregnant the other day, so I'm here to get the pill and be done with it. They are blessings, though," she said softly as our eyes fell on the baby boy in her arms. "Jesus, I need to fill this out. I know this is like the worst time to ask, but would you mind holding him while I fill this out?"

"Not at all," I said, knowing that was probably the biggest mistake I could have ever made. She placed him gently in my arms as I sat back in the chair, watching him sleep, that pale little white baby with stringy pieces of blonde hair. I looked at Jahiem, who was just watching me, face softening up by the second.

"Can you take my clipboard up there?" I asked him.

He nodded and stood up with the kids following him. Looking back down at the baby, I thought about my own. My baby. Thought about what my parents would say, my family, my friends. I couldn't have a baby. I had shit I wanted to do, a life to live.

Feeling the baby move, I adjusted the blanket as I started gently bouncing my arms to keep him still so he wouldn't fuss.

"Aye," Jahiem said as he stood in front of me, looking me in the eyes. "I'm running to the store down the street. This is a little too much for me to handle, so just call me when you ready for me to pick you up." He handed me the money rolled up in a rubber band.

I nodded, watching him say bye to the kids before walking out. Looking back down at the baby, I saw he was staring back at me; green eyes just looking, not crying, not looking scared, just staring.

"Tiana Greene?" the nurse called out as the lady put her clipboard down, letting me transfer her baby back to her.

I wiped my eyes, knowing I was crying like a bitch, but I was about to do some shit I knew I was going to regret later on.

"You ready?"

"Yeah," I sighed. "Ready as I'll ever be."

When I stepped back out of the office, I walked out, thanking the doctor before looking at the woman with the three kids.

"You okay?" she asked.

"Yeah," I said, nodding my head. We hugged, and I thanked her before walking out, getting on the phone to call Porscha.

"Hello?" she answered.

"Yeah, so, I'm leaving the clinic now," I told her, sitting on the curb. I felt like I was about to cry all over again. "Girl, it was some emotional-ass shit in there. A woman came in with her baby. I ended up holding it while Jahiem was playing with the two kids—"

"Why the fuck would she bring a baby in there? Why is she bringing kids in there knowing that—"

"I don't know." I waved it off as I sniffed, wiping my nose.

"Well, how did it go? This was just the check-up, right? Or did they just go ahead, get you the pill or prescription to—"

"I didn't do it," I let out before dropping my head. I could hear her literally stuttering, trying to find the words.

"Bitch, what?" she shrieked. "You didn't do it? Or you won't do it because you still got time?"

"I'm not going to do it."

"So, what about Jahiem?"

"I mean, fuck him. I'll raise the baby myself. I don't need, nor want him in this child's life."

"Oh my God, girl," she said with a laugh. "So, I'm an auntie?"

"Yeah, bitch, you are," I let out, and she screamed. "Let me call him so he can come pick me up."

"A'ight, but call me as soon as you get to the room so we can start looking at baby names."

"Oh, Lord. A'ight," I said, laughing.

I dialed his number, calling for him to come on, and the moment I got in the car, he started asking the questions.

"So, what they do?"

"The basic shit: see if I was pregnant, ask me about health-related stuff. I have to go in again after I take the pill for a checkup to make sure everything is good," I lied, remembering shit I saw on a brochure.

"So, you good then?"

"Yeah, I'll have my friend take me next time. Thank you," I managed to say, and he nodded. "You are no longer a daddy."

"Hell, yeah," he said excitedly. "Definitely wasn't ready for that, even if it was mine."

"Yep," I agreed, sinking into the seat as I secretly held my stomach.

What the fuck am I doing?

Both Ways

Tyree

Bougie Nigga

"Nah-uh, bitch, get in the car!" I yelled at my friend Niya as Tiffany unlocked the doors. Niya slipped into the back seat, and I sped off into the dark night. It was a Friday night, early October, and I was on the hunt, looking for a fuck-ass nigga named Ontrell Carter. Y'all reading this better buckle up and enjoy this ride, because you're about to learn firsthand how to catch a cheating-ass Carter boy in the act. Nigga thought I was playing with him.

"Nigga, what is all of this in the seat?" Niya laughed as she held up my metal bat. "You got bricks in here? You got all this shit back here. Fuck you need a belt for?"

"Girl, you already know he's crazy," Tiffany said, rubbing her pregnant belly as I stopped at a red light, mind racing, fuming. All I kept thinking about was this nigga fucking someone else other than me.

"Two years! I gave this nigga two years of being faithful, caring, understanding that he's now becoming this big-ass music star. Nigga, I dress you! I buy yo' fucking clothes, I cook for you, I suck yo' dick when you want it, and you can't—"

"You could have kept that last one to yourself," Tiffany mumbled.

"Whatever!" I snapped as I stepped on the gas. "Nigga keep thinking I'm playing with him!"

"I told you, you need to break up with his ass," Niya said. "Did you call his sister?"

"Fuck no. She a bitch too," I retorted while grabbing my phone to call Olivia. She was going to cover for his ass regardless, probably let him know I was on the way over to that ho's house. I'd been watching this nigga for about a week now, fucking with the same bitch, going to her house night after night when he was in town. Now that I knew where she was, bitch, it was a wrap. Simple.

"So, what are you going to do?" Tiffany asked.

"Bang on that ho's door and be like, 'Bitch, I came to collect my fuck nigga that you been sleeping with. Did you know he's a faggot-ass nigga?' Girl, don't get me started too early. I might not make it over there," I said, calming myself down.

Let me introduce myself while I drive on over to the east side where the fuck-ass bitches stay at. My name is Tyree. While y'all reading about these other punk Carter boys, you're about to see why and how I had to put up with my own. I'm twenty-two years old, college graduate, run my own business as a fashion stylist and personal shopper. I will have you dressed to a T, honey, okay? Won't ever let you leave the house looking a mess.

I met Ontrell through a friend of mine, and we sort of clicked. At first, I was all like, "Mmm, nigga is a little too rough for me," but he would take me out to eat, call me all the time, movie nights, and wasn't afraid to be public about his sexuality. He was the type of man that would say, "Yeah, I like niggas. Fuck is the problem?" Nobody could really say shit, because he had heart and power behind his words. Had no choice but to accept it and move on. Nigga didn't tell me he fucked females until he started cheating on me a year ago. So now, I had to sit there daily, checking my nigga's phone, wondering who he was talking to, checking his Instagram, steady hacking into his accounts and shit, checking his money, seeing where it went. Oh, yeah, I got control over all of that. Two years? I better have something to show for it. Now that he was coming out with this rap group with his brothers, he thought he was big shit.

Whatever. Back to me. So, anyway, I'm a New York native, Queens all day. Jamaican background on both sides. I'm cute, with a caramel brown complexion with no hair. Keep my head completely shaved. I hate hair on my body, face, and head. I don't care to dress like no bitch. I like men's fashion, and I feel like all gay niggas should be the same way. No sense in dressing like a woman. Not trying to be that. So, I keep my sense of style very New York, preppy, sometimes hippy, and very vintage. I have dark brown almond-shaped eyes; sexy, plump lips; and my body is perfection. Work out every chance I get. I could pull bitches if I wanted to, but they have nothing I want.

Now, for all of you who are reading this trying to stereotype me, don't get it fucked up, boo. I can switch it up and come at you like a straight-up nigga if I have to. I took boxing classes on a regular ever since I was a teen, and I learned how to fight. If a nigga step to me on that shit, I will handle you like a nigga. If a bitch come at me on some bullshit, I will handle you like a bitch. Just depends on the fuckery I get for the day.

Right now, though? I had on a hoodie with black basketball shorts, black Adidas, with the matching skull cap. I was ready for war. Ontrell had me fucked up if he thought he could keep doing this shit to me. As much as I loved him, it was only so much I could take.

"Are those it over there? The apartments she lives at?" Tiffany asked as I held the phone up to my ear, calling his sister Olivia. I hated all of them stupid-ass Carters. Olivia was cool when she wanted to be, but she was stuck up and wasn't capable of being one-hundred with you. Switched it up like a mothafucka. But who can blame her? Look who she was raised with.

"Hello?" she answered as I pulled into the apartment complex, cutting my lights off. I was in creep mode. I could hear her boyfriend in the background talking as she *shh*'d him to be quiet.

"Call yo' brother and tell him—" I could hear her sigh as I stepped out of the car. "Tell that nigga to come out so we can talk."

"I really don't—"

I hung up as all three of us walked up to the apartment building, seeing his truck parked right outside. I didn't know which door he was in, but I was definitely going to smoke his ass out. I glanced at Tiffany, who was holding the phone up, pregnant belly poking out through her shirt.

"Nigga, you about to record this?" I laughed as I waved to the camera. "What's up? This is Tyree! We about to catch my boyfriend Ontrell Jacob Carter cheating with some raggedy bum bitch. Nigga don't even like pussy," I snapped into the camera, sticking my tongue out, thinking I was cute.

"So, we waiting out here or what? How you don't know which door it is?"

"Because I don't," I snapped, walking up the metal steps. "Ontrell! Bring yo' ass out here! I know you in one of these damn doors!" I yelled out as I continued to walk up. "Ohhhh, Ontreeeeeeeeell!"

"This nigga is straight stupid." Tiffany laughed, camera up.

I started banging on the walls as I continued to pop off at the mouth. "Where the fuck is my boyfriend of two years? I know he couldn't possibly be fucking around with a dumb bitch that don't know he like dick!" I called out, hearing my two girls laugh.

The hallway was lit, with two doors on each side. I knew he went upstairs; I just didn't know where. I listened closely, hearing a female's voice. Moment I heard Ontrell speak, I flipped out, banging on the back door to the far right.

"Nigga, open this goddamn door!" I screamed, pounding on it as Tiffany laughed.

"Tell that bitch to come out!" Niya called out from behind me. She was my muscle. I told her I wasn't going to put my hands on a woman, so she said she would do it. Oh, but I would lay them hands on Ontrell as I had before. He knew he don't want that shit to happen.

"Ontrell Jacob Carter! Open this damn door!" I yelled, kicking at the bottom as I covered the peephole. He didn't need to see shit; just open the door.

Soon as the door swung open, I let out a gasp, seeing a big-ass nigga in his underwear, standing there looking like he just woke up, with a bat in his hand. "Oh, shit. My bad. I thought—"

"You thought what, punk-ass nigga?" the man said as I backed up. Nigga was twice my size in every direction.

"He didn't mean to knock on yo' door!" Niya yelled as Tiffany backed up on the staircase.

"I don't want no problems," I said, hands up, trying to check my attitude. "I swear I didn't even mean—"

"But you did that shit. You woke up my mothafuckin' kids, punk—"

The door next to his swung open as Ontrell stepped out, fully dressed. He immediately walked up to the man, dreads tied up as he pulled his jeans up.

"We got a problem?" he asked, face mean, eyebrows in as he mugged the big dude.

"Hell, yeah, we got a problem! You—"

"He said he didn't mean it, so take yo' ass back in the house!"

"And who the fuck—"

"Bruh, I swear on everything, you don't want it with me. You don't want no problems with me, bruh," he threatened as I backed up some more, watching my man defend me.

Shit, listen to how I sound. *My man.* Nigga was just cheating on me.

"He apologized. Now let that shit go. Let it ride, my nigga."

The man stared between us before walking back in his apartment, slamming the door shut, mumbling some gay slurs.

"There she go, Tyree!" Niya called out, running into the house after the ho. I started to go in after her, but Ontrell grabbed my arm.

"Fuck are you doing, Ty?"

"Nigga, what are you doing? I see you tried to rush and put yo' clothes back on. You fucking this bitch now? What happened to the last one?"

I snapped, mushing him hard in the forehead. "Nigga, you ain't shit!"

"I'm not over here doing what you—"

I put my hand up and went in the house after Niya, who was throwing hands to the bitch, repeatedly throwing jab after jab, with the girl crying for help.

"Yeah, beat that bitch ass! Fucking my nigga!" I knew he was lying, because the bitch only had on a T-shirt, nothing else, thinking she was cute, and it smelled like straight fish in there. Only females. I didn't understand the fucking hype about it.

Ontrell moved past me and nearly pushed Niya out the way to block her from hitting the young girl. Oh, hell no. Niya started pounding on Ontrell, who attempted to push her, but that was when I stepped in.

"Nigga, I swear you don't want it with me," I let out, mocking him and his country-ass accent. "Why you defending this ho? You love her? You love her more than me?"

"Man, why you doing all of this unnecessary shit, Ty?" he yelled, frustrated, as I kept Niya behind me, just in case he tried to get stupid again.

"Doing what, Ontrell? You laying up in the bed with a woman! Why do you keep doing all this

shit to me? All this unnecessary shit to me?" I
cried, feeling my voice start to shake as I looked
at the man I had loved for two years, almost
going on three, waiting for an answer.

"Because I can do that shit. I've been doing it.
You haven't left, and you will never leave. That's
just the reality of this shit, bruh. You not going
nowhere. Find someone better than me. I dare
you," he boasted cockily.

I just stared at him, eyes watered up. I had
fallen in love with this tall, masculine, brown-
skinned dread-head of mine, thinking we were
one day going to get married. He had tattoos
on the back, sexy-ass brown eyes, and lips that
could make me forgive him on just about anything. He was the perfect man in every sense of
the word, but he wasn't ready for a relationship.
Yet, I felt like I wasn't ready to let go, and I didn't
know why.

"Come on," Tiffany said, grabbing my arm.
"We need to go. He's not going to do no better,
obviously, so you need to come on."

"Take his ass on," Ontrell snapped while helping the girl to her feet. She looked beyond scared,
face bloodied up.

"Nah-uh. See, Tyree," Niya said as we walked
out of the house, feeling defeated. "We going

out to an after party for the Classic tomorrow. It's time you have your own fun, because clearly this nigga think he is your everything and that you won't ever step out on him like he do you."

"Clearly," I mumbled, feeling hurt beyond words. Then I thought about my shit in the back seat of my car. *It ain't over, until it's over*. I quickly rushed to the car, opening the back door and grabbing my knife.

"What are you doing?" Niya laughed as I looked at Tiffany, who still had her phone up.

"Bitch, you recording?"

"Yeah," she said, laughing.

"Get up close on this shit," I told her as we walked back to his truck. "Nigga wanna lay up with a bitch! You can stay with a bitch! Don't come knocking on my door, talking about you miss me and you love me." I stabbed the back tire with the knife hard before moving on to the next three, letting that air seep out. "Keep thinking I'm playing with yo' ass. I bet yo' ass is going to stay here with her."

"Ty!" Ontrell yelled as he rushed down the steps, hands on his head as he watched in horror. I was slashing each tire a second time, just in case I didn't prove my point the first round.

"Tyree!"

"Nigga, don't say my name no more. We're done!" I yelled, throwing the knife in the street as I walked off. "Got me out here chasing behind yo' ho ass. I got work in the fucking morning, and you got me out here wasting my time on you," I mumbled, opening the door to my car as I slipped in the driver's seat. "Come on, Niya!"

Jordyn

"So, he's going to be able to get us in?" Rita asked as she looked herself over in the mirror. It was going on eleven o'clock, Saturday night, and that was all anyone was talking about—this party. I almost backed out, but Elijah was so hard up on me not going because he didn't think I would fit in that I felt like I had to prove him wrong—again. I didn't think just because someone was beautiful on the out-side meant they were beautiful on the inside as well. Inside was where it really counted, but in this city, this society we lived in, everyone was so focused on beauty, body, perfection. So, for all the women who didn't think or give a shit about looking beautiful to others, this night was for them. It was a one-time thing for me. I wasn't going to make a habit out of this, because I just didn't care to spend so much time on how I looked for others.

"He said he could get us in. Usually he's good on his word." I shrugged, slipping on some heels, pretty sure I was going to bust my ass once or twice in them.

Rita looked back at me, smiling, hands on her hips. "Girl, you look good. I can't wait until I meet this nigga, because he is slick changing yo' ass." She smirked as I rolled my eyes.

"No one is changing me."

"You like him, don't you?"

"I like him as a friend, and nothing—"

"Don't give me that *friend* bullshit. We always share niggas when one of us gets one. You have yet to offer up this nigga to me," she snapped, and I sighed.

"If you want to sleep with him, you can," I let out with my hands thrown in the air. "I'm not stopping you."

"Good. I hope he's cute," she said greedily as I looked at my nails I'd just had done. I felt my stomach do some kind of weird flip at the thought of them having sex. I didn't have a problem with it; I just . . . I don't know. I definitely needed to find someone else besides Elijah.

"I still cannot get over how you look! Niggas are going to be weak when they see you."

"You think so?" I laughed as I stood up, smoothing my hair down. I wore a white, long-sleeve body con dress that dipped low in the front, showing off my breasts. I flat-ironed my hair so it easily fell just to my waist, with gold heels, gold earrings, and yes, I was wearing contacts. I wanted to wear my glasses so bad, but I planned on getting drunk, so there was no sense in having something on me that I might lose. My eyebrows were waxed and shaped, and Rita did light makeup around my eyes, supposedly giving me that sultry look. I don't know. I felt myself tugging at the dress that constantly kept rising up, hugging my booty.

Rita wore a red dress with the back out, and her long braids pulled to the side. Pretty sure she had on no panties, but I couldn't say anything, because neither did I.

"You ready bitch? I can't wait to finally show you these fucking Carter boys. The guy I'm talking to now is like their security so he's definitely going to let us chill with him in the VIP if Elijah doesn't come through."

"Okay," I agreed as we walked out of the quiet apartment. Everyone was already gone off to the parties for the night. Homecoming festivities started tomorrow, so it was so much happening, nobody wanted to be stuck on the yard. Hell, neither did I.

"Whooo! We about to get it in tonight! You bringing a nigga back to the room since I get to have Elijah?" she asked, looking back at me.

"If I see someone," I said, shrugging. "Is Terrell going?"

"Girl, you already know his bum ass is probably waiting in line like a bitch." She laughed as she playfully pinched my thigh. "Damn, Jordyn, I can't get over how you look."

"I've worn a dress before, Rita."

"Yeah, but not like this, chica. You definitely scooping a nigga up tonight, or a bitch. I don't be trusting half these girls in Atlanta, though," she said as we walked out toward my car, heels clicking in unison on the pavement.

The cold air swarmed my body as I quickly got inside the car, trying to warm up. Feeling my phone vibrate, I looked down, seeing it was Elijah calling.

"Hello?" I answered, putting him on speaker.

"Where you at, baby? You changed yo' mind?" he asked. I could hear in his voice that he was already drunk.

"We're in the car now. Why do you think I won't—"

"Heeeey, Elijah!" Rita cut in, glaring at me.

Here we go. Let me just focus on warming up this car.

"What up, baby?" he greeted as she smiled, trying to have a conversation with him. The background was so loud, filled with so much going on, I could barely hear him. "What Jordyn got on? She wore them thick-ass glasses?"

"No, my bitch is looking good. She said she trying to find some dick for the night since she's allowing me and you to have our own fun," she said.

My mouth dropped. I had to literally fight my inner hood bitch to keep from slapping her. I didn't even know I had an inner hood bitch, but who the fuck says shit like that?

"Oh, yeah?" Elijah laughed. "Shit, all pussy is welcomed on my dick. Hurry up and get here so I can see what you looking like, baby."

"Okay." She smiled before hanging up the phone for me. "He sounds cute as hell, girl."

"He's okay-looking." I shrugged, backing out of the parking lot. I rode in silence, with her doing most of the talking. I needed a drink. I didn't think I could handle the thought of them two having sex, yet I didn't have the courage to say not to, because it came off as me liking him, and that wasn't the case.

I stopped at the gas station closest to the Gold Room and grabbed a drink or two, literally popping it open before getting to the car. I was already hearing the cat calls from guys as I slipped back inside the seat.

"You trying to get fucked up, ain't ya?" She laughed as I took it to the head. I needed a buzz before I stepped out of this car again.

"I'm trying to get something," I replied, handing her the bottle.

She continued to talk the whole way until we got to the packed club. I had my buzz, and I was already feeling like the first guy I saw, I wanted.

"Girl! We are here!" Rita yelled excitedly as we got out of the car, watching everyone walk toward the building. I could hear the music bumping. I watched the people direct traffic and saw the line was wrapped around the two-story place in the heart of Atlanta.

"Call that nigga up, and I'll call mine. We'll see who gets to us first, because I'm not paying, nor waiting no longer than five minutes," she said.

I pulled out my phone, dialing Elijah's number, and he answered on the first ring.

"You outside?" he yelled over the music as we walked toward the front with a guy nearly tripping over himself from staring too hard at me.

"Yeah, I'm looking at the line now. Where do we stand?"

"What you got on? Aye, Nat! Go get 'em. They outside," he called out. "What you got on? What color?"

"I have on white; she has on red."

"I can't wait to see this fuck shit," he said, laughing as I hung up with a roll of my eyes.

"Someone is coming," I told Rita, who was still trying to get her guy on the phone.

I could hear the music change as the crowd went wild. Rita nearly shook my arm off as she squealed, "That's my song! Bitch, we need to hurry up and get in there. The Carter Boys are about to perform. We need to get in there."

"He's coming; just calm down." I laughed.

We stood out, looking at the line as girls eyed the hell out of me. They were dressed in different colorful ho-like dresses. I couldn't speak on it, because the way I was looking, I fit right in with them.

"Uh, excuse me, what kind of hair is that you got in your head?" one girl asked as we walked closer to the line. "What kind of hair, and how much was it?"

"It's mine," I answered, and her mouth dropped. Girls suddenly started coming up to me, touching my hair, asking me what I used and how I maintained it. They wanted to know what was I mixed with, and if these were my real eyes. It was crazy. One girl tried to literally argue with me about whether my eyes were gray. This was why I didn't come out, because of petty stuff like this.

"Aye! You Jordyn?" I heard a guy say. I looked up, seeing this huge, bald-headed guy step outside the door. I nodded, and he signaled for us to follow him.

"Girl, please tell me that's not Elijah," Rita mumbled, and I laughed.

The guards moved the red rope, and we stepped into the entrance of the club, hearing the rap music banging against the wall. The smell of weed immediately caught my attention.

"Are we in VIP?" Rita asked the guy excitedly. He nodded, and she looked at me like a kid in a candy store. "Bitch, who the fuck is this nigga? You think he knows the Carter Boys?"

"I don't know, maybe. I'm pretty sure he's like a club promoter, so maybe," I said, shrugging as the guy looked back at me, laughing.

We turned another hallway before stepping out into a balcony-like area, where there were lounges, couches, tables, girls dancing, and everyone literally on chill mode. I looked down below seeing the crowd was thick, dancing, moving around, hands in the air, just having fun. Down there was completely different from VIP.

"He's back there," Nat said, pointing.

"Oh, shit. Girl in the white dress is bad as fuck," I heard someone say, and I looked back at the guy, smiling. He signaled for me to come over, but I kept moving. I at least wanted to say hello to Elijah before mingling.

"So, where is he?" Rita asked as we walked all the way toward the back, where more lounges, couches, and tables were set up. I immediately spotted Elijah, sitting down with a girl on his lap and a drink in his hand. He was just about to tip it back when he spotted me. When I say he froze? Mouth was open, waiting for that drink he held in midair to hit his mouth, I just waved nervously at him.

"That's him right there," I said, pointing at Elijah, who hadn't moved, his eyes locked on me. Suddenly, Rita grabbed me again, gripping my arm as she pulled me in close to her. She was so fucking aggressive when she got like this.

"Bitch!" she hissed. "That's him! Jodie Carter! He's part of the fucking Carter—how could you not—Jordyn!" she shrieked.

My eyes lit up, looking at Elijah again. He hadn't stopped looking at me. Of course, he was shirtless, with his straight-leg jeans sagging low to show his red boxers. Dreads were loose, chains all over the place, eyes red, and a ring on each finger. So, he was part of the Carter Boys all along. I guess because I still didn't know any songs they did, it really didn't matter, but Rita was freaking out.

"Who y'all here to see?" Another guy with dreads walked up as Rita nearly screamed again. More guys started coming up to us like we were fresh meat, but I let Rita take over, as I scooted past to say hi to Elijah and to thank him.

His eyes were low while he watched me walk toward him. He forced the girl to get up from his lap.

"Hi," I mouthed with a wave. No sense in talking, because I could barely hear my own voice.

He walked over to me, smiling as his eyes wandered. It really did feel like it was just us two in there.

"E! Who is she, bruh? She got a twin?" someone called out.

He took my hand, pulling me toward him as we hugged. His mouth was against my ear, kissing it, and his arms slipped around my body.

"You look good as fuck right now," he said.

I let go as we smiled at each other, hand in hand, before Rita came walking up.

"I am your biggest fucking fan, nigga. You hear me?" She laughed.

I felt someone come up behind me as the rest of the group that was over there surrounded us, completely forgetting about the girls that were already there.

"You don't remember us? Gas station?" one said, and my eyes lit up. "Ahh, yeah, you remember, shawty. Damn, you might just be the baddest bitch in here. Are those yo' real eyes?"

I nodded as another brother stepped up, trying to talk to me. I felt hands all over me.

"Can I just get a drink?" I asked politely to anyone who would hear me out. They immediately started trying to offer me stuff, but Elijah shut everyone down, ending the chaos.

"Aye, y'all mothafuckas acting like you ain't seen a female before," he snapped as he handed me his cup. "Drink mine. Don't drink nobody else's shit but mine, because they act funny as fuck around here."

"Nigga, you act like we about to drug her." His brother laughed as I took Elijah's cup. Didn't know what it was, but I trusted him more than I trusted anyone else in there besides Rita.

"Come here," Elijah said, taking my hand as he led me to the balcony rail, overlooking the club. I took a sip of the dark liquid as he stood behind me, hands holding onto the rail on each side of me.

"You look good, baby," he said again, pressing his dick up against my booty as I smiled in the red cup before drinking more.

"Thank you," I said, looking back at him as he smoothed my hair out of his way, shifting it to the other side before resting his chin on my shoulder. I continued to drink, wanting to feel that next step, which was tipsy. He was already there; I was just trying to catch up. So, when he handed me a new cup that he was drinking, I smiled, took a sip, and closed my eyes, feeling the warmth hit my throat. *Damn, I'm an alcoholic.*

"Bet you weren't expecting me to look like this," I said.

"Fuck nah." He laughed, digging in his pocket to pull out a blunt. "Hell nah, I wasn't expecting you to look like this. Had I known, I would have never brought yo' fine ass in here."

"Why not?" I laughed, watching him light up the end of the long, brown stick.

"You know why, shawty," he said, taking a pull on it.

He held it out to me, knowing I didn't smoke, but what the hell. One time. I felt comfortable. I looked back at Rita, seeing she was in one of the other brothers' face, so I took the blunt, nervously holding it between my two fingers.

"How do I do it?" I asked as he blew smoke out his nose.

"Just pull on that bitch," he said. "Don't put your lips on it, though."

"That doesn't make sense, Elijah," I retorted, and he laughed.

He took it, showing me step by step before letting me try. I, of course, ended up coughing hard, handing it back to him as he laughed.

"Here, baby," he said as I watched him take another drag before cupping my chin, holding his breath. He pressed his lips against mine, blowing the smoke into my mouth, eyes never leaving mine before he kissed me. I started to cough as he laughed before raising his cup in the air.

"My girl Jordyn with a Y in this bitch!" he yelled obnoxiously, shaking his dreads as the song switched.

It almost seemed like a rap anthem, because suddenly, every guy in the building was rapping along to the song. I looked down below, seeing cups raised, guys citing the song word for word, just as someone handed Elijah a mic. He held onto me as he rapped to the song, voice going throughout the club before he started singing.

My mouth dropped as I looked at him, watching the effect he had on the crowd. So, he really could sing. I thought he was joking. I smiled as I swayed side to side, enjoying his hold, and watching the people below look up at us. Don't ask me what they were saying in the song; I just know everyone seemed to know it. Looking back, I saw Rita standing on a table, singing along with Elijah.

"Them Carter Boys! Give it up!" the DJ yelled, and the crowd went wild. "My nigga Jodie Carter hitting the ladies with that voice!"

He put the mic down as he held onto me with both hands, swaying with my body. "You enjoying yourself?" he asked against my ear, smoothing my hair down. I swear he loved touching my hair. He was absolutely obsessed with it. I nodded, taking a sip of my drink.

"You don't see nobody you feeling tonight besides me?" he teased as I looked up at him, head resting on his chest.

"Not yet," I replied.

He kissed the side of my mouth before taking another pull on the blunt. We stayed like this for a minute, tuning out everyone who wasn't us. I knew a couple of people kept calling his name, but he wasn't listening, and I was almost at my limit of drinking. Didn't want to be up under him all night, because I was starting to feel like that might just be dangerous for me.

"Aye, we about to hit y'all with that new Tinashe! Pretend! I know the ladies are going to feel this song," the DJ said as the song switched. It honestly felt like Elijah and I were the only ones as he held onto me.

"*Love that never ends,*" Tinashe sang softly as the girls down below had their hands up, trying dance sensually on their men.

I looked up at Elijah, who was enjoying his blunt, dreads in his face, looking so mean, so rough; yet the moment his eyes landed on me, he softened up, eyes smiling down at me in awe and appreciation. This song was setting the mood for us as he leaned in to kiss me again. You know how, like, in the movies, where the eyes close and everything begins to move in slow-mo? Noise was tuned out, and the only thing that mattered was that single kiss from Elijah given to me.

"Jodie!" some girl called out as he pulled back, looking me in the face before kissing me again. "I know you hear me!"

I tuned her out as I listened to the song, pulling away from his mouth as I looked up at him.

"*I pretend it's you,*" Tinashe sang. "*A love that never ends.*"

"Why are you looking like that?" I giggled as he kissed me, lips pressed against mine. He tightened his grip on my body like he didn't want to let me go.

"I think I'm in love with you, shawty," he slurred against my mouth. "In love with you."

"Jodie!" one of his brothers called out as I deepened the kiss.

"I'm in love with you too," I replied before realizing what I'd just said.

Hell, no.

Definitely had to be this alcohol, because the moment we realized what we'd said to each other, we burst out into laughter. Wouldn't be the first time we got drunk together.

"I can't keep fucking with yo' ass, man," he let out, smoothing my hair down.

"I know it," I agreed as I pushed him back gently, seeing all eyes were on us. "I'm going down below to mingle. I know you have some girl you taking home tonight."

"Yeah." He smiled slowly as he looked back at the girl who was eyeing me hard, arms crossed over her chest. She looked like everything about her body was fake. Only thing real might have been the anger she was displaying toward us. "Don't drink nothing from nobody, not even the bar," he warned me with a serious tone. "You want something to drink, get that shit from me only. Mothafuckas out here slipping shit into drinks left and right, baby."

I just nodded as the girl made a puffing noise, like she was irritated with me standing there.

"I'll let you two go," I said as I walked off with his cup.

"Aye," he called out.

I looked back at him, watching him hold onto the girl.

"Call my name out if a nigga get stupid on you, a'ight?"

I nodded as I continued to walk, no doubt eyes watching me. I even spotted my roommate, Jade, who looked at me with her mouth dropped, eyes wide. I just kept moving with a simple wave. Tonight, I wanted to enjoy myself, and down below I already could see that was where the fun was at.

So, the moment I stepped out onto the dance floor, my eyes locked with another girl as she coaxed me to come to her. I definitely planned on having some fun that night. I deserved it.

That entire night felt like one big, amazing time. I saw a few people from school who gasped at the sight of me. Even Leon, the tall, lanky boy who liked to pick on me, attempted to pull me aside to apologize for the last three years of our college lives, and tried to stay by my side the entire night. I did listen to Elijah about the drinking, so on the main floor, I didn't have any drinks. So many people offered to buy me one, but I politely turned it down.

When the Carter Boys came to the main stage, I made sure I was front and center to see Elijah do his thing, watching the crowd go crazy. It was something for the guys, and something for the girls to jam to. Still not my type of music, but I respected it for sure.

"Aye!" Leon called out as he leaned in close to me, hand circling around my waist. "You need a ride back to the yard?"

I shook my head no, not even looking at him as I watched the performance. Girls were going wild around me, dancing, as I scanned slowly through the crowd, letting a few girls catch my eye. Leon being next to me the entire time was starting to become annoying, but I didn't have the guts to tell him so.

"You sure, Jordyn?" he yelled out over the music as he leaned in close to my ear again, hand tightening up around my body. "I can't get over how the fuck you looking right now. Like, damn! Had I known, I would have *been* tried to get at you!"

"I bet," I mumbled, eyeing one light-skinned girl in particular who locked eyes with me.

"Aye! Leon! What's good, bruh?" a guy greeted as a couple of them walked over, slapping hands with Leon. "This you right here, nigga? Damn, she bad as fuck!"

"Nah, she was with Jodie Carter up there," another said as I politely pulled away from Leon's disgusting grip. "Shit, you do look good as fuck, though. He stay having bad bitches with him."

"Nah, she's my girl now. Fuck Jodie Carter," Leon retorted with a laugh as he slapped hands with another guy. "Nigga don't even know her like I know her, bruh."

I looked at Leon like he had lost his damn mind, before walking off with a flip of the hand. I didn't even care to entertain it.

"Give it up for them Carter Boys!" the DJ yelled out as the crowd went crazy.

"And make sure y'all download our newest single on iTunes!" Elijah said into the mic as he hopped down from the stage into the crowd. Girls, like moths to a flame, bombarded him and his brothers as the music changed.

I was trying to make my way to the walls to find some space when I felt someone grab my hand. I looked back, seeing it was Leon again.

"Aye, where you going, baby?" he asked with a laugh. "I told you I wasn't letting you out of my sight."

"So, you think all these years of making fun of me suddenly disappear the moment you see me in a dress?" I snapped, and he dropped his head in shame, smiling.

"I mean, I fucked up, Jordyn, but you—"

"I don't care, Leon. I don't have anything to say to you." I cut him off as I watched Elijah attempt to make his way toward me. Girl after girl was trying to dance on him, and he definitely wasn't trying to stop it, either. Leon was starting to make me uncomfortable, and I just needed Elijah hurry the hell up.

"Aye! I apologize," Leon let out, trying to move closer to me, grabbing on my body with his bony hands. I smacked his hands away, but he thought it was a joke, thought it was funny. I didn't know if it was the alcohol or he was serious, but he kept pressing himself up against me despite my protest.

"Stop touching me! I'm serious! We have nothing else to say—"

"So, you not fucking with me because I don't sing like no bitch nigga?" Leon snapped, grabbing my wrist aggressively.

"Aye, man, you need to chill," a guy standing by said, trying to back Leon up as I struggled to get out of his tight grip on my wrist. "She said she's not interested, so—"

"Nah, nigga, fuck you! Don't even know who the fuck you are with yo' big ass. This is between her and me," Leon spat as he jerked me closer to his body. It was the definitely the alcohol. I could tell he wasn't in his right mind now.

"Let go!" I cried out as he tried to kiss me, sticking his tongue out like it was funny. I didn't realize the guy who stepped in was part of Elijah's team until he called him out.

"E! Come get yo' girl, nigga!" he let out as I snatched my arm away from a laughing Leon.

"Jordyn, you know you want it!" Leon yelled out just as Elijah came over, weaving in and out of crowds only to stand in front of me.

"What's the problem, nigga?" Elijah snapped, hands pulling up his jeans on both legs like he was ready to fight. "You fucking with my girl?"

"You got all the girls in Atlanta. Why you trying to fuck with the one I been wanting for years?" Leon spat with a drunk laugh. They were eye level, height for height, but Elijah held his alcohol well.

"Not my problem, bruh. You fuck with her, you fucking with me," Elijah stated as the crowd started to circle around him.

I grabbed Elijah's arm, attempting to pull him back.

"Man, whatever. Nobody got time to deal with yo' wannabe thug ass, nigga. You not about that life. Jordyn, let's go," Leon let out, attempting to reach around Elijah to grab me. That might have been the biggest mistake I could have seen anyone make that night.

Elijah gripped Leon's neck, forcing him back into the crowd as he pulled out a gun he kept tucked behind him in his jeans. The whole crowd literally shifted as Elijah pressed up against him, with the gun no doubt against Leon's stomach.

"Nigga, I dare you to mothafucking try me!" Elijah screamed as I backed up frantically, not sure what was happening. I'd never seen this side of him before.

Leon's eyes were in full-blown panic, hands in the air as if he were surrendering.

"I don't have no problem going back! Nigga, you not about that life with yo' college-boy ass. I was born into that shit, so fuck with me, bruh."

"Aye, hold up! What's the problem?" one of his brothers asked as all six of his brothers came up, looking to jump in.

"I'm good. I don't want no trouble, man!" Leon let out, voice shaking as Elijah backed up, eyes never leaving Leon. "I don't want no issue."

One of his brothers grabbed Elijah, whispering something hard in his ear before backing him up completely.

"Ayo! Let that music play! Everybody go back to partying!" another brother yelled out with a laugh. "False alarm. We thought a nigga was ready to get popped tonight. Turns out he was just a bitch."

"Y'all trying to turn up for real. Shit!" the DJ let out in the mic as the music cut back on, lights going black once more. "Don't get that shit confused. Carter Boys are still very much on that street shit, the black family mafia of Atlanta."

Like it was nothing, the party continued. I could see some girls were still stunned, some people decided to leave, while others thought it was cool to see some action in the club. I looked around, seeing his brother was giving Elijah a pep talk in the corner of the club, trying to calm him down.

I walked over hesitantly, not sure how to approach him. He stood against the wall, eyes wild with rage, as his brother kept his hand on his head, looking him directly in the eye, talking hard to him.

"I told you about that stupid shit! Every time someone come at you, don't mean you gotta react on that!"

Elijah said nothing, just stared, expression blank like he was out of it.

"You listening?" his brother snapped. "You shouldn't be about this so-called life anymore. You got out! Why the fuck you keep trying to go back to it? Huh?"

I flinched, seeing his brother slap him upside the head in frustration, but Elijah kept a stone face. He bit his lower lip to hold back, but the amount of respect he had for his brother showed by the way he didn't react to the hit. I slowly walked over, feeling like all of this was my fault to begin with.

"You understand, Elijah? You hearing me, nigga?"

"I hear you, Shy," he mumbled.

It was like looking at twins. His brother just looked like an older, light-skinned version of him. Both had those low-set eyes, and tattoos on their faces.

"Fuck nigga was drunk anyway. He wasn't about to do shit to yo' girl that she couldn't handle herself. Calm down. You on a good path in yo' life. Don't fuck it up by doing some stupid shit," his brother continued before grabbing his head to bring him in close before letting go.

When he turned to look at me, I felt just as guilty, almost like I needed a pep talk my damn self.

"Take care of him, shawty," was all he said before walking off.

I stood in front of Elijah, who just stared at me. I didn't know what to say, and neither did he. Yet, I knew one thing we both enjoyed and that could probably cheer him up and take the stress of the night away. So, I stepped closer, locking his fingers with mine as I looked at him.

"You want to go?" I asked softly, barely loud enough to be heard above the music.

"Yeah."

I met up with Rita to give her the keys to my car, and left with Elijah in silence. Neither one of us spoke in that truck. It was dead silent the entire ride. I glanced over at him occasionally, seeing his jaw flinch in hard thought as he leaned to the side, driving with one hand on the wheel. Slow jams were playing throughout the car. I had already took my contacts out and replaced them with my glasses, and heels were already off as I tucked my feet in the car seat. Looking at him again, I felt like he was a different person. Dreads pulled back, tank top on, with his jeans low as he drove in tense silence.

Tuning into the radio, I could hear Lloyd's "Southside" with Ashanti coming on, and I turned it up. I had to be one of the few people that actually liked this song. Humming along with the chorus, I watched the cars go by on the highway. Me singing out loud was only something I did in the privacy of my own space, but this song usually brought it out of me, having me think I could hit the high notes.

When Elijah chimed in, singing Lloyd's part, my eyes lit up at how smooth he made it sound. I looked at him, smiling. I loved his voice. He didn't have to make it sound whiney like most singers these days. He actually had an old-school R&B sound, with a hint of Harlem jazz.

"ATL, Georgia, what do we do for ya," we sang together as the song started to fade into the next.

We eventually pulled up to a nice neighborhood somewhere on the east side of Atlanta, and he pulled into a garage. He lived in a three-story townhouse, and I could already hear his dogs barking in the house as he cut the car off.

"I don't have much to eat," he said as we got out.

I looked around the neatly organized garage, seeing he had everything from boxes, tools, old furniture, and shelves full of random stuff. I followed behind him, heels in hand.

"Whoa, whoa! Chill out!" he greeted his two white pits as he popped the kitchen light on.

I looked around, seeing it was spotless: marble countertop, hardwood floors, with a tray of fruit on the island counter in the middle of the huge kitchen. I didn't really know what to expect coming to his place of rest, but this wasn't it. His two dogs came at me, smelling, licking, and barking all at once.

"Go outside for Daddy," he said to them, smacking his teeth in a rapid fashion as he opened the back door so they could roam the yard. He turned to look at me, grinning.

"Daddy?" I repeated.

"Those are my main bitches, man," he cheesed. "Lala and Bam-bam."

"Oh my God, Elijah." I laughed, thinking how cute the names were.

After he gave me a short tour of his place, including the basement where it looked like no woman had ever stepped foot, I took a quick shower, washing my hair, getting the smoke smell out of it, and brushing my teeth with his spare brush. I didn't know if it was because it was his place, or me seeing a different side of him, but something was different. Something was completely different about this night. I stepped out of the bathroom fully naked, no towel. He sat on the edge of his king-size bed in his boxer briefs, looking at me.

"Come here," he commanded as he stood up, eyes working over my body.

Pushing my glasses up, I walked over to him.

"I apologize for tonight," he said, wrapping his arms around my waist as he kissed my wet shoulder.

I attempted to pull his briefs down, but he stopped me.

"Nah-uh, you not running it tonight. My place, my rules, baby," Elijah stated as my eyes grew wide. He had never spoken truer words.

For the first time, I wasn't ready for what he gave me. Our eyes never moved away from each other as he laid me back on the bed, body coming onto mine as he gripped my stomach on both sides. He lifted me up gently while his mouth came down onto my stomach, just in that lower corner above my hip where I was known to be sensitive. His heated mouth began to caress me, tongue lapping and teeth pulling at the thin skin as I hissed in response, arching for him with my feet gripping the edge of the bed.

Suddenly, he pulled away, wiping around his mouth as he walked around the room, placing soft music on, lighting up two candles to give the room an orange glow before sliding out of his boxer briefs. Coming back to bed, he brought the warmth that was deeply missed.

I smiled up at him, my head on the pillow, hair sprawled about, with Elijah coming down to me. He took my hand to kiss the knuckles lightly before placing it around his neck, dark eyes never leaving mine as he hovered over my face. I smiled slowly while my hands cupped his neck.

"Jordyn with a Y," he said softly, eyes traveling over my features in lust. "Done showed a nigga something new."

"I did not," I teased gently with a laugh. My hands were running through his locs on both sides before he came down to kiss me. He was beginning the motions of something I never felt before when it came to sex. Every inch of my body was attended to—my hands, wrists, ears, neck, and shoulders. Strong hands slid down, with his mouth surely following, finding my nipples to pluck and pull, suck and tease before continuing the trail past my hips. He lifted my leg up, gently popping a bite of a kiss on the side of my cheek before slapping it playfully. He went past my thighs, kissing the back of my knees, with one hand already on my foot, massaging it like a pro as my body went through the motions.

I didn't have the luxury to play over-the-top freak with him this time. No, this was something I wasn't used to; something completely different than just sex. Elijah knew it. I knew it. The way we locked eyes, never leaving each other's gaze as he probed gently into me, caused me to release a sigh of relief, a breath of pleasure.

I was holding onto his shoulders as he began that slow, deep stroke against the walls. My body pushed up, holding against the headboard, before he brought me down on his own accord. He was slow and deliberate, against my desire to go fast and aggressive.

"Baaae," I breathed, head going back as I arched. "Elijah, please . . ."

"Shit," he let out, kissing my chest as he pushed deeper.

My mouth dropped as I looked at him, locking eyes with him as he worked his hips to the music.

I gripped his back as we kissed again. I didn't know how to take it.

"Damn, Jordyn, you got me going crazy over yo' ass," he let out, pulling out before dipping back in. We moved as one, breathing in unison as his body stiffened up, pressing hard inside as he came, with me following close behind.

We didn't need any more rounds after that. I was done. We lay back on the bed together, with me resting on his chest, wondering, *Did something just change between us?* Looking up at his face, seeing his eyes closed in deep thought, I took the time to reflect on everything that had happened between us. These were newfound feelings I was discovering that I had for him. I really was starting to fall in love. I never thought I would say it, but I was in love with Elijah Carter. It was the one thing I was so against, so anti-romantic, yet my heart fluttered at the thought of him, whether I was near him or not.

Feeling a single tear come down my cheek, I wiped my face quickly. A rush of emotions were hitting me at once. I wasn't ready for this at all, yet I knew I had to tell him eventually. I just didn't know how he was going to react; whether he would love me back. . . .

To Be Continued in

The Return of the Carter Boys

Coming May 2018

Noelle

"This is my jam!" my coworker Layla called out, raising her cup in the air as we moved through the packed crowd at the Gold Lounge.

It was so much going on this weekend with the Classic and after parties that I'd had enough for one day. We'd been there for over an hour, and so far I'd been hit on by the creepiest men or the sheistiest-looking guys, who probably approached every girl. It had been a rough week for me, my first week in Atlanta, so I thought a little night out would help me get over that. Now that I was there, smoke filled the air, drinks spilled on the floor, with girls wearing God knows what and men feeling the need to touch up on you, I'd had about enough.

Finding a decent spot to hang back at, we stood to ourselves as we enjoyed the music. I looked down at my two-piece ensemble: royal blue skirt with the matching cropped long-sleeve top, hair with a slight curl and wave to it, with my side bang on point.

"We gotta do this again next weekend," Layla called out.

I rolled my eyes with a smile. "This might be my last," I responded over the music just as a dark-skinned guy with a box cut walked over to me, looking like he stepped out of an Eighties music video. He looked me up and down in a dramatic fashion with a hand on his chin, smiling.

"Aye! You look even better up close with yo' sexy, dark-skin ass!" he let out, chomping on gum. "What's yo' name, shawty?"

"Nigga, take yo' whack ass somewhere else." Layla laughed, with her head thrown back. "I can't believe you even approached her with that line."

"Wasn't nobody talking to yo' short, dumpling-looking ass!" he snapped.

My eyes grew wide, looking from him to Layla.

"My name is Ronny. What's yours, chocolate?"

"Apologize to her and maybe you'll find out," was all I said before moving farther down in disgust. I couldn't believe the nerve of some of these men here. I continued to move to the beat of the music, seeing Ronny and Layla going at it, with her finger all in his face as she rolled her neck.

"Damn, you sexy as fuck, girl. What's yo' name?" a guy said, coming up behind me as he eyed my backside. He had gold tooth in the front, braids going back. Need I say more? "You look like one of them model bitches. You a model?"

"Girl!" Layla let out as she moved passt the man, hand soaked. "I had to throw my drink in that nigga's face. He is too crazy."

"Are you serious?" I laughed, seeing the guy who tried to talk to me walk off. Layla was pure craziness, and I was sure he wanted no part of it.

She moved her weave back off her shoulder as she continued to bounce to the music, occasionally twerking on me, trying to make me laugh. "It's too many fine niggas in here to be getting hit on by the rejects," she let out, sipping through her straw. "Speaking of fine," she said, eyes zooming in on someone in particular. "This nigga has been staring you down the entire time."

"Who?" I asked, feeling my body tense as I looked around.

She grabbed my arm. "Don't look, bitch. Just let me describe him before you freak him out." She laughed. "Tall, light skin, with some sexy-ass lips. Nigga looks like he could kill someone just by glancing at him. Definitely a trill nigga," she said, and my mind immediately went to Shiloh.

I casually turned my head in her direction, and sure enough, it was him, standing with a group of guys and a few girls, eyes on me. We locked eyes for a brief second as he tilted his head up toward me. I just smiled and did a small wave before looking back down at Layla, who was cheesing.

"Who is that?"

"That's my neighbor, the one I was telling you about," I said as I glanced back at him, seeing he hadn't taken his eyes off me. I hadn't spoken to him since the night I stayed at his house, but I was forever grateful. I was still hesitant around him, but nonetheless grateful.

"Girl, he is fine as hell," she let out with a smack of her teeth. "And the niggas he's with look good too. Shit, tell him to come here."

"I'm not going to—"

"Fuck it," she said, waving them over as my mouth dropped. I felt myself trying to hide within the people around us as she continued to frantically wave him and his friends over.

"Oh my God, Layla, what is wrong with you?" I laughed, turning around so that my back was turned.

"You already slept in this nigga's bed. Why are you so shy all of a sudden?" She laughed.

"Because we—"

"Shit! He's coming, too!" She laughed as I dropped my head in embarrassment.

"What am I supposed to say? He doesn't talk to me when I'm home; barely talks at all. What am—"

"Heeey!" Layla greeted, and I turned, seeing Shiloh and another guy walk over with his eyes on Layla. Shiloh said something to the guy before slapping hands with him.

"What up, li'l sexy?" the guy said to Layla, putting his arm around her neck as he walked her off. Shiloh had deliberately told this man to occupy my friend while he stood next to me, acting shy and on mute.

Looking him over in a brief second, I kept my smile hidden. Shiloh cleaned up well and smelled really good. He wore a red long-sleeve shirt, diamond stud in each ear, dark blue jeans, with the matching black high-top Gucci sneakers, fancy all-black watch, with his curly hair low and neat. His low-lid eyes had a red tint to them as he licked his lips. The red was amazing against his light complexion, and he smelled really good considering we were in a club.

"Hi," I greeted, sticking my hand out for him to shake.

He just stared down at me, licking his lips, expression stone cold mean.

Clearing my throat, I thought of a way to break the awkward ice. "You enjoying yourself?"

"It's straight," Shiloh said in a deep voice as his eyes scanned the crowd like he was the protector of the club. "I just came through to support my brothers."

"That's nice." I smiled, looking at the group of guys he left behind. "Are those your brothers?"

"Nah," he said, looking back before pointing to the stage where a group was performing. The Carter Boys. I liked a few of their . . . *Hold up.*

"You're related to them?" I asked, shocked, remembering his last name was Carter. He nodded. "So, why you not up there singing and rapping?"

"Nah, not for me," he said with a small smile.

I could have seen pigs fly at that moment. I couldn't believe this man just smiled at me. I tuned back into the song, bobbing my head, just as Shiloh leaned in close to me, mouth against my ear.

"You probably the most beautiful girl I have ever seen."

My mouth dropped as he leaned back to see my expression, slow smile creeping on my face. I mouthed a *thank you* just as he leaned back in, a gentle hand on my lower back.

"Do you mind if I stay by your side for the rest of the night?"

My heart started to thump as I shook my head no. I knew it took all of him just to get those two sentences out, but for some reason, they meant the world to me. To hear him say it was completely different than to hear some random guy tell it to me.

"You got a ride to the crib?" he asked as he stood close next to me, sipping on his drink.

"My friend is my ride. I left the car at home," I said, looking at him as he nodded. I watched his eyes watch everyone else. Girls had their eye focused hard on Shiloh, who barely seemed to notice. Occasionally, they stepped up to him with the intention of talking, but he showed no interest.

There was one brave soul that decided to try his luck as he walked up to me with his friends laughing behind him. I could see Shiloh out of the corner of my eye, going completely still in mid drink as he eyed the man approaching over the rim of his cup. The man was tall, brown-skinned, with a little weight to him, wearing Lord knows what. It was borderline women's clothes, with his jeans cut off and folded at the knees. I didn't realize I had moved closer to Shiloh until I felt his body lightly bump mine. He kept his eyes hard on the guy, almost like he dared him to overstep.

About the Author

Contact Desiree
https://www.facebook.com/desiree.granger.1
Grangerdesiree@yahoo.com

Okay, so, it's always pretty weird talking about myself, but whatever. Here it goes. I'm currently twenty-six years old, obsessed with traveling. Flew for the first time to Puerto Rico by myself for my birthday, and it was amazing! Definitely think I'm going to write a book about that one day—about all my travels, really. Writing urban fiction is just something I do to pass time, but there are soooo many other styles I would love to tap into.

I'm an on-again, off-again college student with a major in foreign language. Team Aries all day, every day. I'm a fashion merchandiser maybe one or two days out of the week, couple times out of the month. I love to eat and hang out, socialize. Anything to do with nature, I'm there.

I've been writing since seventh grade. Used to start out as plays. Didn't turn into book or story format until high school. I would write stories for my friends, pass it around to the point where teachers would find me, and I would get in trouble because their students were reading my works. On top of that, I would write fan fiction online after school, with over 1,000 followers reading new chapters that I would write every day.

Probably not the best resume to say I'm a writer, but sometimes you don't need a degree to do something that feels natural to you. You know?